ALSO BY AMIE KAUFMAN AND RYAN GRAUDIN
The World Between Blinks

ALSO BY AMIE KAUFMAN
The Elementals series
Ice Wolves
Scorch Dragons
Battle Born

THE WORLD BETWEEN BLINKS
REBELLION OF THE LOST

AMIE KAUFMAN
AND RYAN GRAUDIN

Quill Tree Books
An Imprint of HarperCollinsPublishers

Library of Congress Control Number: 2021945753
ISBN 978-0-06-288227-1

Typography by Catherine San Juan
21 22 23 24 25 PC/LSCH   10 9 8 7 6 5 4 3 2 1
❖
First Edition

For Pip and Sabriel—
we're so lucky we found you.

INCIDENT REPORT
COMPILED BY CURATOR PARK MIN-JUN
(RATING: 9.98/10)

After going back through records and interviewing several witnesses, I, Curator Park Min-jun, have compiled the following report. It is an abridged account of what is now known to Curators as "The Creaturo Incident," since its antagonist was the Agent of Chaos himself, one Christopher Creaturo.

Christopher Jacob Creaturo entered the World Between Blinks on July 4, 1949. He got himself lost in order to find his one true love, Hazel Susan Clive, who arrived here on January 12, 1945. His mission? To restore Hazel's faded memories and find a way to return them both safely home. This was, of course, against the Administrator's rules. But Christopher did not care. He spent more than seventy years searching for a way to save Ms. Clive.

Then, finally, he found the Beruna cousins.

Jake Beruna and Marisol Contreras Beruna crossed into the World Between Blinks through the Morris Island Light—a lighthouse currently crumbling off the coast of Folly Beach, South Carolina, in the United States of America in the old world. They were discovered by the crew of the Patriot and dropped off in the care of a Curator. Or so they thought. Unbeknownst to everyone, this man was actually Christopher Creaturo in disguise.

After that, the records get ... fuzzy. There was a break-in at our Crystal Palace records repository, and ledger 341,069.512 went missing. Once Jake and Marisol were caught by the Aral Sea, they admitted that Christopher had asked them to steal the book. What they did not admit, yet was glaringly obvious through our monocles, was that Mr. Creaturo had used the ledger to send the Loch Ness Monster back home, creating a crack in the Unknown fabric between the worlds. My colleagues and I were distraught, and we urged the children to fix their mistake. Find Christopher Creaturo and return the ledger, we told them. Only then can we send you home.

The Beruna cousins chased Christopher Creaturo far and wide! Amelia Earhart reports she met the children at the Frost Fair, where they befriended Oz the Tasmanian tiger. The SS Baychimo's passenger log records them sailing to the underwater cities shortly after. Witnesses place them at Queen Nefertiti's court in the ever-stretching desert. They even parachuted from an airplane into the Amazon rainforest, according to explorer Colonel Percy Fawcett! Many of these locations correspond with new tears in the Unknown, created by Christopher as he sent items from the stolen ledger back to the old world. I surmise he was testing a method he might use to transport himself and Ms. Clive back as well.

Jake and Marisol eventually caught Christopher Creaturo, but instead of turning him over to the authorities, they decided to help him save Hazel Clive. Could this be because they found out Christopher was, in fact, their beloved Nana's brother? Which would make him their great-uncle! Perhaps. I have no way to confirm this theory.

Whatever the case, the Beruna cousins became involved in not one, but two more robberies. The ledger containing Mr. Creaturo's entry went missing from the Crystal Palace. Four hourglasses disappeared from the Great Library of Alexandria and were used to restore the lost memories of Ms. Clive, Mr. Creaturo, and the Beruna cousins. Their names were crossed out of their respective ledgers by an unknown person, and they were sent home.

Most of my colleagues consider this outcome disastrous.

I myself am not so sure. It felt much more like a happy ending to me. . . .

On a related note: I have received several verbal complaints from citizens about the current memory repository system. They do not believe it is fair. I am beginning to agree and propose that we bring up the subject for review at the next committee meeting.

1

MARISOL

IT WAS A PERFECT DAY TO GET LOST.

Marisol Contreras Beruna leaned over the ferry's railing, letting alpine air thread through her hair as she peered into the waters below. Lake Titicaca was much clearer than the waves off Folly Beach—so clear that she could see the reflection of the sky on its surface and the killifish weaving through the green weeds just beneath. As the boat pulled away from the dock, Marisol stared even harder, trying to see traces of a lost city below.

Wanaku.

When she and her cousin Jake had been stuck inside the World Between Blinks, nearly six whole months ago, they'd wandered through the lost parts of this underwater city, breathing with the aid of the enchanted bubbler charms strung on their necklaces. Fish swam around the cousins' heads and llamas strolled past, their fur swish-ing with the currents. The brightly woven fabrics floating around Wanaku's other inhabitants had made Marisol feel at home.

Now it was the opposite: Marisol *was* home. Well, she was on vacation with her family at Copacabana, but she was still in Bolivia, still on Earth, for that matter. Marisol was home, and she wanted to see something that made her feel like she was back in the World Between Blinks.

She was itching for another adventure. Life had gone back to normal after her summer at Nana's house. She'd flown home to La Paz, where the calendar filled up with school and Saturdays spent rock climbing with Dad and FaceTime calls with Jake.

These things were fine, but they didn't make her heart race or her fingers tingle.

They didn't make her feel *magical.*

The boat began picking up speed, and soon the water was too deep to see any hints of a lost civilization.

"Don't fall in, Reina! It's a long swim to Isla del Sol!" Her mother had made the family wear life jackets, even though most of the other tourists didn't bother and Victor wasn't anywhere *near* the water. Her older brother sat in the center of the boat, slouched so his life jacket reached his ears and his feet sprawled for miles. He was so busy tapping on his phone that Marisol wasn't even sure he knew they'd left the dock.

"I'll be careful," Marisol promised as she played with her necklace. The bubbler that helped her breathe underwater didn't work on this side of the Unknown. The charm's magic had stayed in the World Between Blinks, so now it was just a fish scale, hanging on the chain beside her other charms.

There was a small scroll, a monocle, and an hourglass too.

She kept them tucked under her shirt, mostly because of Victor, who'd snorted when he noticed her strange jewelry. *Why would you want to wear a bunch of junk? You look like one of Nana's display cabinets!*

This was supposed to be an insult, but thinking about their grandmother's sprawling collections of seashells and stamps and sugar spoons made Marisol's heart swell. *I love Nana's cabinets!* she'd replied.

Her older brother wore a bewildered look. *You're lucky our new distant cousin Christopher does too. I still can't believe he wants to keep Nana's beach house the way it is after paying so much money for it. . . .*

Marisol knew this wasn't luck. Not really, but she couldn't exactly tell Victor the truth about Christopher—that he was Nana's long-lost brother, and his wife, Hazel, had been their grandmother's best friend, and they'd been lost in a different world for almost seventy years. Buying

Nana's beach house was Christopher's way of finally coming home. He'd saved the place for the rest of his family too. Otherwise, they would've had to sell it to a stranger.

"Mari!" Her dad waved her out of these memories. There was a guidebook in his hands and a gleam in his eyes. "Want to read about the sites we're going to see today?"

Victor glanced up from his phone. "Isn't that what we're paying a tour guide for?"

"There are over eighty ruins on the island," their father explained. "We won't be able to visit them all, but we can do our research. It's important to learn about history and the people who came before us."

"¡Sí!" Marisol agreed. Granted, reading about history wasn't as thrilling as seeing it with her own two eyes, but there was nothing else to do on the hour-and-a-half boat ride.

Dad smiled, then picked up the book. "Isla del Sol is named the 'Island of the Sun' in honor of the Incan sun god. Many of the settlements here date back to the fifteenth century—"

"Does it say anything about a city called Wanaku?" Marisol couldn't help asking.

"Hmm . . ." Her dad started scanning the pages. "Let's see."

"No," Victor grunted.

8

"How would you know?" she challenged her brother.

"I just looked it up." He said, still immersed in the screen. "Wanaku is from much earlier, before the Incans. The city belonged to the Tiwanaku people and was considered a legend until its temple was discovered underneath the lake. There have been over two hundred dives done to document the ruins."

Marisol laughed. Victor almost sounded like a Curator, reading a file entry through a monocle. There was no way to explain why she thought this was funny, though, and her brother's eyes narrowed.

"How would *you* know about Wanaku, hermana?"

The real answer? *I was summoned to a world full of lost things with our cousin Jake, where we walked through Wanaku's underwater streets with a very excited Tasmanian tiger named Oz. I saw the legendary city of Kitezh too. And the Lost City of Z. Oh, and I flew with Amelia Earhart. She helped us parachute into the Amazon rainforest to chase down our great-uncle Christopher Creaturo and a magical ledger of lost things he tricked us into stealing.*

For a brief moment Marisol wanted say all of this, if only to see the look on Victor's face.

"We learned about it in school," she answered instead.

Their father looked thrilled. "Knowledge is power, no matter how you find it!"

He went back to reading.

Marisol listened to the story of the Incan sun god's birth, while the more literal sun beat overhead. It was as bright as an unshaded light bulb, glaring off distant white-capped mountains, turning the lake into something sparkling. It looked a lot like the Great Mogul Diamond she'd found in the World Between Blinks. Queen Nefertiti had given the giant jewel to Marisol as a gift, but it was too much to carry in the end. She chose to throw the diamond away so she could save Hazel from the Curators.

Marisol's chest ached, remembering this. It wasn't because she regretted the decision—love, she'd learned, was worth far more than diamonds—but because she wanted to go back. Back to ancient Egyptian royalty and valiant explorers, to buried treasures and adventure on every horizon. Her hands fidgeted with her life jacket, finding their way to the necklace beneath. She never took it off, even when she went to sleep, just in case the Unknown decided to call her again.

Was it?

Calling?

Her magnet fingers felt glittery now, but that could've been because Marisol was squeezing her charms so hard. Or because something on this boat had been lost.

There had been many moments like this over the past six months, when Marisol's gift for finding lost things flared, and she hurried to follow it, hoping to turn a corner and bump into Amelia Earhart. But these hunts always ended with trinkets. Mom's keys. (Again. Always.) A knight piece from Victor's untouched chess set. Dad's climbing shoes. Once, she'd found a fifty bolivianos banknote on the sidewalk.

It was a lot of money.

And she'd still been disappointed.

As Isla del Sol came into view—with so many hills and stones and twisty eucalyptus trees—Marisol felt the pull in her fingers getting stronger. Her heart began pounding with excitement. If she hadn't been wearing such a puffy life jacket, she was sure everyone would be able to hear it.

"Do y'all all have your water bottles? Snacks?" Mom asked as their boat docked. "Sunscreen?"

"Sí. Sí. Sí." Victor gave an exaggerated groan and hoisted the backpack. "I think we have enough food to last a week."

The road out of the port was rocky and, according to their guide, old. It had been built by the Incans, who seemed to enjoy climbing hills. Marisol's heart thrummed faster and faster as they hiked to the north end of the island—partly because of the exercise, but mostly because her magnet fingers were still buzzing. She kept waiting for something around her to change. But Lake Titicaca remained Lake Titicaca, and all the rocks stayed where they were. Including the square stone slab of the Mesa

11

Ceramónica and Titikala—a sacred cliff that looked like a puma.

"The next set of ruins is called Chincana!" Their guide's English was clear but thinned out by the fierce lake wind. "In Quechua this translates into labyrinth! Or, more literally, 'the place where one gets lost.'"

Marisol stopped short.

This had to be a thin space . . . right?

She knew there were windows into the World Between Blinks all over this world. Nana had traveled to a lot of these spots, and she had been careful to mark them on her many maps—using Xs that weren't Xs at all, but an inverted version of Christopher Creaturo's initials. ꜾꜾ. Marisol had memorized every single drawing that hung on the walls of her grandmother's beach house. Nana's adventures had taken her everywhere: Cairo's pyramids, base camp at Mount Everest, a complex of ancient temples in the Cambodian jungle, a crumbling castle on a cliff top in Ireland, and on and on. There were no maps of Lake Titicaca in the collection, but that didn't mean there wasn't a door here.

It just meant one hadn't been discovered yet.

"OOF!" Victor stumbled into Marisol, the phone flying out of his hands and onto the road. "Watch where you're going, Mari!"

"I wasn't moving." She picked up the iPhone. Or

eye-phone, as Amelia Earhart had called it. A better name, maybe, since Victor's were always so glued to the screen. Right now it was displaying a chess game.

"Watch where you're stopping, then!" Her brother scowled.

She handed back the phone and ran to catch up with the rest of the group.

Chincana—*the place where one gets lost*—looked nothing like the last thin space Marisol had slipped through. The Morris Island Light was tall, for one thing. These ruins were short. Made with sand-toned stones that had been sculpted by hundreds of years of wind and rain. Plants grew from the cracks, and windows framed bright blue views of the lake.

But there were darker corners too.

Ones that made her fingers hum.

Ones that promised to turn into a different world entirely.

"We believe Incan priests used to train here. . . ."

The guide's voice faded, lost to the winds again, as Marisol crept closer to the ruins. She wasn't entirely sure what to expect. Another shiny key? A window that looked out onto the ever-stretching desert? Sir Percy Fawcett—the explorer—sitting on a quagga?

She stepped into the maze of stones and pulled out her necklace, studying its hourglass hopefully. In the World

Between Blinks, the charm was used to keep track of a person's memories. Marisol and Jake had spent the final fading gold days of summer—their last days together after their adventures—testing these timepieces in Nana's attic. Jake's theory was that if the sand stuck to the top, that might mean that the other World was close. . . .

Marisol held her breath and turned the hourglass around, watching the grains inside. To her disappointment, they fell, obeying gravity instead of the magic of the Unknown.

"Hey!" She jumped at the sound of Victor's voice. Her brother stood in a doorway, blinking off his last digital chess move. Looking . . . disoriented. He must've followed her here without realizing that she'd snuck away from the tour on purpose. He was probably just staring at her feet while he played, lost in his game. "Where's the rest of the group?"

"They're back on the path." Marisol sighed. Her fingers had stopped buzzing: another dead end. "Atrás de ti."

Victor looked over his shoulder. "No, they're not."

"What?" Marisol froze. Was she imagining things, or did the walls suddenly look taller? There didn't seem to be as many plants in them either. It was as if all of Chincana's missing stones had filled in. As if the ruins and its lost masonry were overlapping. . . .

She ran to the nearest window.

The water looked different. It was blue still, but rough with waves, and Marisol spotted a dorsal fin that was *much* too big to belong to a killifish. Her fingers shook with excitement as she pressed the monocle to her eye. If its magic was back, the charm would show her the entries that Curators wrote for every single person, place, and thing that turned up in the World.

Sure enough, words began to scroll through the eyepiece's glass: *Megalodon, swam Earth's oceans 3.6 million years ago. KEEP OUT OF RESIDENTIAL ZONES AT ALL COSTS!*

She never thought she'd be so happy to see a megalodon again. "We made it, Jake! We're back!"

"Did you just call me Jake? You're acting really weird, hermana."

Oh . . . Marisol dropped the monocle and turned back to her brother. *Oh no.*

The overlap was already disappearing, most of Chincana's stones fading back to the Bolivian side of the Unknown. The ones that were left—the ones that had migrated to the World Between Blinks—looked as if they were floating around Victor's head. He was too busy frowning at his screen to notice.

"Victor—"

"My phone is acting weird too."

"Victor," she tried again.

It was no use. Her brother hardly ever paid attention to her, and most of the time Marisol was fine with this. They didn't have much in common now that Victor was a teenager, and he'd never been young enough to believe Nana's stories. The ones Marisol lived and breathed and laughed by. The ones that had eventually led her here.

"I know this island gets service." He held his iPhone toward the sky, waving it wildly. "It was working fine just a second ago!"

"Victor Contreras Beruna!"

"¿Qué?" he asked, slightly irritated.

"¡Mira!" Marisol waved at the scene around them. "Look!"

Her brother turned, his eyes widening when he realized that the labyrinth's walls were no longer there. Mostly. "Um . . . why are those rocks floating?"

"Tranquilo," Marisol said quickly. "Don't freak out."

But Victor kept turning. The drawstrings of his red hoodie whipped around and around. His questions sounded dizzy. "Where are Mom and Dad? Where are *we*?"

"Mom and Dad are on Isla del Sol. We're . . ." It was Marisol's turn to look around. *Sí*, they were in the World Between Blinks, but it was a big place, filled with jungles and submerged cities and desert kingdoms. She and Victor were standing on a hill—both sides sloping down into the ocean. There were no trees in sight. "We're on a different island."

It was the easiest answer she could offer. Victor didn't look like he could handle anything else. After a few more spins he sat, his backpack landing on the ground with a *WHUMPH.*

"I'll call the navy." His voice sounded wobbly. "They'll send a boat for us." Marisol watched her brother swipe his screen, then frown. "Well, I would, but I don't have any signal."

"That's because we just passed through the Unknown," she told him.

"The what?"

"The Unknown."

"What's the unknown?"

"The Unknown. With a capital *U*," Marisol emphasized. "It's a veil of magic that separates our world and this one."

"This one?" repeated Victor.

"Remember how Mom used to read us stories where children discover a magical land through a wardrobe?" Victor had never believed those tales either, but it was the easiest example Marisol could think of. "It's kind of like that. Except this world is filled with stuff that's been lost back home—keys, socks, dogs, submarines. You can get most of those at the market at Ostia Antica. What you *can't* get is cell service, though. We had to use a walkie-talkie to call Amelia Earhart last time. . . ."

Victor clutched his phone to his chest, staring at Marisol as if she'd suddenly sprouted an extra head.

"Este es loco," he whispered.

"It's not crazy." She couldn't help but smile. "It's the World Between Blinks."

Victor was not an ideal sidekick.

One hour into being stranded and he'd already eaten most of their snacks. Candy wrappers stuck out of his pockets, and the ground around him was littered with salteña crumbs. Marisol had to stash some of the savory pastries in her pocket, in case she and Victor weren't rescued before dinner. This was starting to look like a very real possibility. She kept scanning the horizon with her monocle, but there was no sign of the *Patriot*, which had rescued her and Jake last time, or any other ship. She didn't see any submarines either.

Victor lay on his back, digesting a dozen chicken salteñas along with the story she'd shared. "So you're telling me that you and Jake were stranded here for days on end last summer because Christopher Creaturo—who isn't our second cousin at all, but Nana's long-lost brother—wrote your names on a piece of paper?"

"It was a ledger page," Marisol clarified.

"Oh, that makes so much more sense."

She didn't have to look away from the vast blue waves to know that Victor was rolling his eyes.

"The Curators use ledgers to record who gets lost here. Great-Uncle Christopher discovered he could call me and Jake to the World Between Blinks by writing down our names. He needed us to help rescue Hazel, his one true love."

"And all four of you found your way back home?" Victor asked.

"Yep."

Her brother fell into a thoughtful silence. It didn't last long. "So, if Christopher and Hazel are at home right now, who wrote our names in the ledger this time?"

"Oh!" Marisol frowned. "I don't know."

She'd been so excited about the idea of returning to the World Between Blinks that she hadn't stopped to wonder why the Unknown had let her through. Was it because she'd *wanted* to get lost in another adventure so badly? Or because someone in the World needed her?

And why, oh why, was Victor here too?

Brothers are treasures, Nana used to say, with a wink and a warm wrinkled smile. Marisol had more trouble believing this than any of her grandmother's fanciful stories. It had only made sense once she found out about Great-Uncle Christopher and the ⊃⊂ marks on all of her

19

grandmother's treasure maps.

She could tell Victor was skeptical as well. He hadn't interrupted Marisol's story about the lighthouse and everything she and Jake had discovered afterward—but his lips stayed knotted in an *I'm-older-and-I-know-better* frown. Figures.

Stones would float before Victor took her seriously. . . .

"HEY!" Marisol's brother nearly bashed his head on a hovering piece of Chincana's wall when he shot to his feet. "OVER HERE! ¡POR AQUÍ!"

He was yelling at the sky. She soon saw why. There, hanging between clouds like an overripe fruit, was a hot-air balloon. Lemon yellow. Drifting. Two tiny figures rode in its basket. They were so far away, it was impossible for Marisol to tell if she recognized them.

Well, almost impossible.

She peered through her monocle, hoping to see a familiar name.

Patrol Balloon #37—Phantom Island Sector

Marisol's stomach tightened as she read. *Patrol? Sector?* That sounded suspiciously organized. . . .

"WE'RE DOWN HERE!" Victor had taken off his hoodie and was waving it over his head like a flag. The figures in the basket waved back. "YES! HERE!

20

¡AQUÍ!" Wrappers fluttered around her brother's boots as he started dancing. "They're coming down, Mari! We're saved!"

"I'm not so sure about that." As the balloon drifted closer Marisol could see that its passengers were dressed in white. One of them was holding a clipboard. "Those are Curators."

"They're going to fix this?" Victor sounded so hopeful.

"They'd like to think so. . . ." Marisol's stomach kept churning. She and Jake had had several run-ins with the Curators during their last trip here. Several *break-ins* too. She didn't feel bad about stealing the ledgers, but she doubted the Curators in the balloon shared her sentiments.

The aircraft drew closer.

The ropes the Curators tossed out of the basket must have been woven with Unknown magic—no hands were needed to knot them around some floating stones. As soon as the balloon was anchored, a ladder dropped.

Victor ran toward it.

Marisol wanted to run in the other direction, but there was only sea there, and even though she had her bubbler charm for breathing underwater, it wouldn't protect her from the megalodon.

"Hi! Hello! ¡Hola! Can you help us? Can you fly us

back to Copacabana? We're staying there with my parents." Her brother was waving at the Curators—a man and a woman, who were both scribbling furiously onto some forms.

"Copacabana, you say?" The woman frowned. "What sector is that in?"

"Um . . . Bolivia?" Victor was met with a grim silence. He tried again. "South America? Earth?"

Both of the Curators lifted their monocles in unison.

"Identify yourselves!" the man commanded.

"What are your designations?" asked the woman.

"My name is Victor Contreras Beruna and this is my sister—"

Clearly no introduction was needed. When the woman official saw Marisol, she gasped with such drama that her monocle fell out. "The Crystal Palace Cat Burglar! The agent of the Agent of Chaos! Number four on the Administrator's Top Ten Most Wanted Rebels List!"

"What?" Now Victor was looking at his sister as if she'd sprouted *three* heads. "Mari?"

"Oh yes! She is wanted in all two hundred and fifty sectors! And counting!" The woman turned to her partner excitedly. "This will be sure to get us a promotion!"

"It will! If I can find the warrant." The other Curator flipped through the blizzard that was his clipboard— white paper flurries. "Ah, here it is!" He held up the form

22

for everyone to see. Sure enough, Marisol's name was at the top in black and white. An angry-looking signature weighed down the bottom. "By orders of the Administrator, you, Marisol Contreras Beruna, are under arrest!"

2

JAKE

JAKE STOOD FACE-TO-FACE WITH A DINOSAUR. He gazed up at the beast's jagged, yellowing teeth as it towered above him, head tilted thoughtfully, as if trying to decide whether he was food or not.

"You don't have a stomach," he told it.

When Hazel whispered in his ear, he jumped. "I hope you've got your T-rex repellent with you."

With a laugh, Jake turned away from the huge skeleton. There were several more like it, looming in this hall of the Melbourne Museum. Jake could even see a pterosaur strung up from the air-conditioned rafters. It looked strange without the skin that made up its wings.

"Mari and I never managed to buy any T-rex repellent when we were in the World Between Blinks," he told his great-aunt. "We spent most of our money on charms and ship passages so we could chase Christopher. I don't think we'll need any peppermint spray on the *DINOSAUR WALK*, though."

He nodded at the display description behind them. The gray letters went on: *science and imagination bring prehistoric animals to life.* Hazel smiled as she read. Her grin was bright—easy to see with that signature red lipstick. It made Hazel look like a person from the 1940s, which, of course, she was. She'd also spent the past seventy years living in a world where dinosaurs were *more* than bones.

"It's a good thing this sign is exaggerating! I, for one, prefer my prehistoric animals fossilized." Hazel put her hands on her hips. She was wearing a slim-waisted yellow dress that looked like it came from a vintage boutique or another museum display. "Speaking of chasing Christopher, where in this world has my husband ended up? Honestly, you'd think he hadn't met a real dinosaur, the way he behaves around these displays."

She wandered off in search of Christopher, and Jake pulled out his phone, angling it up to snap a picture of the T-rex's empty eye sockets. He texted it to Aunt Cara's number with a screaming emoji—Marisol didn't have her own phone, but Aunt Cara would know who the message was for. Then he went back to wandering along the long avenue of bones.

He'd been amused when Hazel and Christopher had

25

wanted to visit the Melbourne Museum—after all, they'd practically lived in a museum during their last several decades in the World Between Blinks—but he had to admit the displays were kind of awesome.

He and his mom were just on a short posting to the United States Consulate here in Melbourne, Australia, which meant living in an apartment filled with other people's furniture. Everything felt upside down.

It was summer here, even though it was winter back in South Carolina. School was out, so it was hard to meet anyone his age, and the hot weather always made him feel like he should be with all of his cousins at Nana's house on Folly Beach. He liked the beaches here too, and he liked the gelato and the singing cicadas and the barbecues on long evenings, but his loneliness always got a little bit worse after the sun set.

So when his great-uncle Christopher—or his second cousin twice removed, as the rest of the family thought—and his new bride, Hazel, decided they wanted to honeymoon Down Under, Jake had been thrilled.

As he approached the end of the dinosaur walk, he looked up at the sign above the archway to the next exhibit. *WILD*, it read. He passed through and found himself in a large, bright, white room, with tiered steps on either side going all the way up to the ceiling. These held every kind of animal Jake could imagine, a tall red kangaroo on his right and a grumpy-looking badger on his left. Each one had been carefully preserved—lovingly, even—by someone who wanted to show what the animals had been like when they were alive.

But they weren't alive. A small shiver of lostness traveled through Jake, from the nape of his neck to the tips of his fingers, as he gazed at them.

When he saw the next animal, tucked away in a case to his right, he stopped short.

It was a Tasmanian tiger, staring curiously through the glass, one paw forward, as if waiting to see if Jake would wave back. The eyes were glass too, of course. And the limbs were stuffed, but his heart tugged him to it, beating a little bit faster as he crouched in front of the display case.

"Now there's a memory." Christopher's reflection appeared beside his, overlapping with the thylacine's fawn-colored fur. "He could be our Oz's twin, don't you think?"

"Yeah." Even their stripes were the same: dark-brown marks laddering up the animal's back all the way to its stiff tail. Oz's would have been quivering. Jake felt a swell of sadness when he stared at it. "I wonder what he's doing now."

"Probably hounding someone for a treat." Christopher grinned and pushed to his feet, offering Jake a hand. "You know he's all right, don't you?"

"I know," Jake said, taking his great-uncle's hand and hauling himself up. "He was fine for a long time before he came on an adventure with us, and he'll be fine now."

They were both silent for a moment. Jake couldn't exactly say he *missed* the World Between Blinks. After all, they'd seen some incredible sights—okay, a *lot* of incredible sights—but he'd spent most of his time there worried about getting back home.

And yet . . .

"Are *you* all right, Jake?" Christopher was staring at him, concerned. "You've got that look in your eye."

Jake blinked. "What look?"

"The *faraway* look. The one that says you want to be somewhere else. Whenever I saw your nana staring off like that I knew she was fixing to take a trip—even if it was just to camp out in the sand dunes for a night or stow away on a shrimp boat." His great-uncle gave a wry smile. "My sister wore that expression a lot."

"She did, didn't she?" Jake knew exactly what Christopher was talking about. Nana loved laughing with her grandkids—sprinkling extra sugar into their already-sweet tea and playing card games on her screened porch. But there were times when Jake would see her staring out past his shoulder at the ocean. "She took a lot of trips! I think maybe she spent more time on an airplane than Amelia!"

His great-uncle laughed, but the sound was short, and then it was Christopher who had that *faraway* look. Jake could suddenly see his age—not just the thirty years he appeared to be—but all that time he'd been lost in the World Between Blinks too. His blue eyes looked dusty. Then watery.

"I miss Lucy." He said Nana's name softly. "My sister was always there for me—even when I left her to go looking for Hazel. She searched all over this world for thin spots in the Unknown. Even when she got married. Even when she had children, then grandchildren. Even when she was sick. I just wish she'd lived long enough to see that we came home."

Jake swallowed.

There was a time, not *too* long ago, where he might have stumbled away from this conversation, using some excuse about needing to use the restroom. But his adventures in the World Between Blinks had taught him that it was okay to have a lump in your throat. It was okay to cry when you had to say goodbye, because that was what happened when you loved someone.

"I'm sorry." Christopher cleared his throat and pulled out a cloth handkerchief to dab his eyes.

"Don't be sorry!" Jake didn't have a fancy handkerchief, so he used his shirtsleeve instead. "Nana would want you to cry. I mean—she'd want you to miss her.

She'd want you to laugh too. She'd be happy that you and Hazel live in her house now. I know *I'm* happy about that," he added. "I can't wait to go back for Christmas."

Fine lines etched Christopher's eyes when he smiled. "You're welcome anytime." He put a hand on Jake's shoulder and squeezed. "Hazel and I will always be there for you, Jake. Even if we're half a world away."

"Thanks."

This word came out as a croak, and it didn't feel like nearly enough, but Jake couldn't say any more. He had to wipe his face with his other sleeve because the first one was too wet. Oz's cousin looked like a tan-and-brown blur.

"Now," Christopher said after a moment, "let's see what other mysteries from history we can find. Hazel's probably looking for us."

By silent agreement, they went hunting for a room that was completely different from the *WILD* display. They made their way back out past the dinosaurs and through a beautiful enclosed forest that stretched up over two stories tall. In the end, they chose the Melbourne Gallery, a display about the city itself.

Jake wasn't sure if it was the feeling of just having seen Oz, or reminiscing about Nana, or just the loneliness that had been chasing after him the last few weeks, but as he stood at the entrance of the gallery, he felt lostness shimmer from his neck to his fingertips again. It tickled his nose, and for a moment he thought he smelled salt water. Huh.

The sensation faded as he turned to wander toward the row of glass cabinets, light glinting off them, each item inside laid out with a neat label explaining how and where it had been found and what part it had played in history. This section of the exhibit was about a sleek red racehorse called Phar Lap—his shoes and saddle were on display, and so was Phar Lap himself. Just like the animals in the *WILD* display, he'd been caught in a pose that made it seem as if he might take a step forward at any moment.

Jake couldn't help touching the chain around his neck, and the little monocle strung alongside the other charms. He always wore it—it reminded him of Amelia Earhart, of his friends the explorers, of Queen Nefertiti's court, and of the underwater cities. Looking through it had been a much more interesting way to learn about history. He . . .

Huh.

It looked like the museum had a second Tasmanian tiger. But what was it doing up here, away from all the other animals? It was kind of out of place, standing between a pillar and a bench, just behind Phar Lap. Maybe it was one of those things meant to tempt you to go check out other parts of the museum? But . . . where was its sign? Its display case?

A family passed between Jake and the Tasmanian tiger, a mother laughing as she herded along four children. "Jack, Raiden, Sabriel, the dinosaurs are this way! Freya, what are you doing?"

Though you weren't meant to have food in a museum, the girl lifted her hand to her mouth as if she were yawning and definitely snuck a bite of something, her jaw working to chew it. When she saw Jake looking at her, she winked.

After they passed by, Jake almost expected the Tasmanian tiger to be gone, almost expected he'd been imagining it.

But the animal was still there.

And it looked for all the world like its nostrils were flaring. Like it was sniff-sniff-sniffing after the girl's snack. But it couldn't be.

Right?

Jake eased one step closer, and this time there was no mistaking it—the creature's tail quivered, just the tiniest of movements, a greeting that escaped despite its best efforts to play at being a statue. Jake gasped.

"Jake?" Christopher and Hazel were already turning toward him.

"It's, it's . . ." He couldn't finish the sentence, but he lifted one hand and pointed, then remembered other people were around and tried to turn it into a head scratch.

"Hot dog," Jake's great-uncle murmured. "That looks just like . . ."

The tail trembled again. Now Christopher and Hazel gasped too, frozen in place.

Hazel was the first to recover her senses, snapping into action. She grabbed Christopher's arm, pulling him forward as she power walked over to Jake and the creature that was absolutely, unmistakably their friend Oz. She herded Jake before her too, and the three of them crowded around the Tasmanian tiger, shielding him from view. With the bench and the pillar behind him, and his three friends crowded around in front, Oz was quickly hidden from sight.

Jake dropped to a crouch, wrapping his arms around the thylacine, pressing his cheek to the creature's fur. "What are you doing here?" he whispered. "Did we summon you somehow?"

Oz just whuffled at him, snorting softly into his ear.

"I've never heard of that happening." Christopher ran a hand through his sunshiny hair. His blue eyes flooded with wonder. "Someone must have *sent* him. But why? And *how?*"

Oz twisted around and took the edge of Jake's T-shirt in his teeth, tugging gently.

Jake blinked, then blinked again.

Between those two blinks, he caught a sudden flash

of sunlight, a glimpse of blue sky, a jolt of salt in his nostrils, and then it was gone.

"Jake," Christopher whispered. "I know that look. What did you see?"

"The World," Jake whispered back, barely believing it.

Christopher looked around wildly, head swinging, as if he were going to find a museum attendant who knew how to deal with this. One hand curled around Jake's upper arm, holding tight and keeping him close.

Hazel was all business. "Jake, do you have your charms?"

Always. Jake had worn the necklace they were strung on for six months straight and now he pulled it out of his shirt with his free hand—the monocle was there, alongside an hourglass, a bubbler, and a small scroll, which helped him understand any language spoken in the World Between Blinks.

"My love," said Hazel quietly, "he's flickering."

"No!" Fear flooded Christopher's blue eyes—it was the same expression he wore all those years ago when Hazel faded from his sight in the field hospital. He'd fought for decades to bring her home, and now his grip tightened around Jake, not just squeezing but trying to anchor the boy. "No, hold on to him!"

"Christopher Creaturo, that's not going to work," she replied firmly. "What can we do to help him? Hurry!"

Christopher dug through his pockets and pulled out an object that looked like a flashlight. Jake knew it was far more special than that—the Illuminator's light could shine through the sand of an hourglass, bringing all sorts of memories to life. Even forgotten ones.

"Take my Illuminator," his great-uncle said, pressing the silver instrument into Jake's hand. "You might not need to see memories, but this has a lot of value in the World. Maybe you can trade—no, another flicker!"

"We'll tell your mother something," Hazel promised. "Find a way back, Jake. Stick with Oz."

Their advice was coming thick and fast, but he couldn't help blinking, and he couldn't hear them over the scream of seabirds.

Blink.

Oz's cold nose pressed into his arm.

Blink.

The glare of sunlight off water.

Blink.

The fluorescent lights of the museum.

Blink.

A bright rainbow of color.

Blink.

"Find the cove," Christopher said urgently. "I'll be there for you! Just like Lucy was! I'll write!"

"Wha-augghhhhhbbbbbppffft!"

Jake opened his mouth to ask what in the worlds Christopher meant about a cove, and writing to him—how was that possible?—and suddenly he was swallowing seawater. The stuff was all around, above his head, cold and salty. He kicked his legs automatically, and a heartbeat later, before his bubbler charm even had time to help, he burst to the surface. Oz was beside him, and gave a delighted whuff as Jake shook wet hair out of his eyes and coughed.

Once his breath was steady, he doggy-paddled in a slow circle (so did Oz, or perhaps it was a tiger paddle) to get a look at his surroundings.

He was in a U-shaped harbor with a jumble of buildings packed into every available space around the edge of it, crowded together as if they wanted a good view of the water. He was back in the ancient Roman city of Portus, where he'd stopped with Marisol on their way to Queen Nefertiti's court.

But it wasn't nearly as busy as he remembered. There was a neat line of vessels making their way in and out of the harbor, one behind the other, as if they were following invisible traffic lanes. From submarines to catamarans, kayaks to schooners, sails flapped crisply and paddles flashed efficiently, and the sloppy waves from their wakes jostled Jake where he was treading water. Each of them seemed to have a large number prominently on display, black numbers painted on a white background and pinned somewhere in clear view. He didn't remember that from his last visit either.

He grabbed an inflatable unicorn inner tube that didn't seem to be a part of the neat queues, slinging one arm over the float and wrapping the other around Oz. "Don't you try to climb on," he warned his friend. "Your claws will go right through it."

There was a tag tied to the unicorn's rainbow horn, and someone had labeled it in a neat hand: *Unicorn Inner Tube, orig. unknown, Zone 43, Permit No. 42956/3b.*

"What does that all mean?" Jake asked Oz.

Oz whined.

"Jake, Jake! Great Scott, it worked!"

As Jake twisted around to see who was calling to him, Oz broke free, paddling enthusiastically toward an approaching dinghy. A lean man with his face hidden under a broad-brimmed hat leaned down to scoop him up, and with a great scrabble of claws, the pair landed in the bottom of the boat.

But there was another figure still sitting on the cross bench, rowing toward Jake and the inflatable unicorn. "Oz, you weren't meant to go through the door to get him," she scolded. "How did you even manage that? Jake, are you all right?"

It was Amelia Earhart! And appearing over the

gunwale, dripping from Oz's welcome, was the explorer Raleigh Rimell. They were both Jake and Marisol's friends, and though he was glad to see them here, his head was swimming with questions.

Two pairs of hands reached down and helped Jake scramble up into the boat.

"Welcome back!" Raleigh began wringing out his shirt. He had a ready smile and a neat, dark moustache, his fair skin turned pink by a hint of sunburn.

Amelia shipped her oars and reached out with one hand to steady Oz, who was turning rapidly in circles as he tried to investigate his own wet tail, making the whole boat rock. Her auburn curls were still trying to escape from under her flying cap, though she wasn't wearing her leather jacket—and like Raleigh, her pale skin had seen a lot of sun lately, her freckles more numerous than ever.

"Amelia, Raleigh!" Jake coughed up a little water, and they thumped him helpfully on the back. "You're a long way from the Lost City of Z and a long way from . . . well, from an airplane! What are you doing at Portus?"

In answer, Amelia pulled a piece of paper from her pocket. The ink was bold. And *familiar.* Jake's and Marisol's names had been crossed out at the top of the torn-out ledger page—it was how they'd been sent back home last time—only now they were written *again* at the bottom.

Jake realized he had another question. "Wait, what am *I* doing at Portus?"

His rescuers exchanged a grim glance. "A lot's happened since you left," Raleigh replied. "That's why we needed the two of you. Now, where's Marisol and her magnet fingers?"

"Marisol?" Jake looked back down at the water, as if he might find his cousin bobbing there. "Did she come too?"

"We assumed she would." Amelia glanced down at the page. "We wrote both of your names. We thought the two of you would pop out right here, where we wrote the note."

"Why did you write the note in the middle of the harbor?" Jake asked, more bewildered than ever.

Amelia grimaced. "It's hard to find a crack in the World that someone's not keeping an eye on right now, and Queen Nefertiti wasn't about to risk her Amber Room disappearing again, so this harbor was one of the only places where we could call you two back. But . . . where *is* Marisol? Didn't she follow Oz through as well?" She looked across at Raleigh. "You said it would bring both of the Beruna cousins!"

"It will have brought both of them," Raleigh replied slowly. "I'm absolutely positive. I don't know why Marisol isn't here."

"She wasn't with me," Jake said slowly. "She was in Bolivia. I was in Australia."

"But . . ." Raleigh and Amelia exchanged a look that was even grimmer than the last. "But we called her," Amelia said.

A cold shock went through Jake, as if he'd been plunged back into the water, where the unicorn float was now spinning off into the harbor. Its rainbow horn swept over empty stretches of water—around and around.

He felt dizzy watching it.

He felt sick.

If Marisol had been pulled into the World Between Blinks from Bolivia but she hadn't landed here . . . then she could have landed anywhere in this endless, ever-changing world.

How would they even begin to find his cousin?

And what might happen to her before they did?

3

MARISOL

THE CURATORS HAD CLEARLY NEVER ARRESTED anyone before.

It took several minutes for the two officials to sort through their paperwork, and neither of them seemed to know what to actually *do* with Marisol. Or Victor, for that matter. The siblings stood beside each other in awkward harmony while pens scratched on clipboards and notes were compared.

The man's eyes screwed tight to read some fine print. "It says in this subsection that we must secure the prisoner!"

"But if we tie up her hands, she won't be able to climb into the balloon," the woman pointed out.

"We could let her dangle. . . ."

"Or," Marisol suggested, "I could climb the ladder

and *then* you could tie up my hands."

"Or you could let us go." Victor was looking very strained, his eyebrows trying to escape his face. *Does he believe me now?* Marisol wondered. *Or does he still think we can fly back to Copacabana?* "I'm sure this is a mistake. . . . My little sister is less rebellious than a pair of khaki pants. She won't even steal money that's lying on a sidewalk! A few weeks ago I watched her walk right past fifty bolivianos!"

Both Curators frowned, examining her brother through their monocles.

"Oh no! We can't leave you here!" the woman insisted. "You don't have permission to be in the Phantom Island Sector. In fact, you don't have permission to be *anywhere.* You are unsettlingly unlabeled."

Permission? This didn't sound like the World Between Blinks Marisol knew. Sure, there'd been customs checkpoints, but they hadn't needed anyone's permission to float through Wanaku or trek across the sand-swept hills of the ever-stretching desert.

"Even if your sister wasn't a wanted criminal, we'd still have to take you in to be zoned," explained the other Curator. "It's the law!"

Victor set his jaw to the side. "*Whose* law?"

"The Administrator's, of course," the man replied. "After that awful rogue Christopher Creaturo created those cracks, our boss had to keep the World from crumbling into even more chaos! If we let people wander wherever they please, anything could happen. Now, up you go, foundlings!"

Marisol was the first to run to the ladder, climbing into the hot-air balloon and scanning it for something— anything—that might get her and Victor out of this mess. She hadn't met the Administrator the last time she was in the World, and, from everything Jake had told her about the man, Marisol wanted to keep it that way.

The basket floor was covered with maps, which were, in turn, covered with eraser marks. (Phantom islands had a habit of appearing and disappearing wherever in the World they pleased, which made them hard to label.) The mess was also crowded with mason jars, which looked empty but had been labeled with words like: N—LIGHT AIR. SW—GENTLE BREEZE. NE—MODERATE GALE.

It was wind, Marisol realized. Different directions. Different speeds. They must have been bottled to help the Curators steer this balloon. . . .

The ladder shuddered, and Victor's wild black hair appeared over the edge of the basket. There were salteña crumbs on his upper lip—the closest thing he could hope for a moustache.

"Here!" Swift as lightning, she snatched a jar that said EVERYWHERE—STORM, and shoved it into Victor's backpack. "We might need this later."

Her brother's jaw dropped. "You ARE a cat burglar, aren't you? First a magic world, now this?"

"Shh!"

Marisol zipped up Victor's bag and fought off a smile. Sure, she was getting arrested, but her older brother didn't think she was just some silly kid wearing junk for jewelry anymore. That had to count for something.

The Curators tossed their clipboards over, but thankfully neither of them noticed the missing jar. They were too busy drawing up the ladder and using one of the enchanted ropes to secure Marisol's wrists.

Victor stood in the corner, gripping his backpack's straps. "Where are you taking us?"

"Good question." The man riffled through his papers. "It says here all detainees on the Level 7 or above list are to be taken to the Lost Dutchman gold mine. Far, far away from any ledgers or hourglass repositories . . ."

"The Lost Dutchman gold mine? That's in the Desert Sector. We'll need an eastern breeze to get there."

The other Curator began sorting through mason jars. For a heart-splitting second, Marisol thought her crime was uncovered, but the woman grabbed a lid that said E—FRESH BREEZE. Papers whirled when the top was unscrewed. Wind whipped Marisol's curls into her face, and the balloon began drifting over the ever-blue ocean.

"Our parents will be looking for us, you know!" Victor fought to be heard over the breeze. "They've probably already called the Bolivian Navy!"

That might be true, Marisol thought, but it didn't help them much. No military could come to their rescue inside the World Between Blinks. Ooh, unless it was the Lost Army of Cambyses or the Ninth Roman Legion, both of whom were under the command of this land's most fearsome queen.

"Queen Nefertiti will save us," she began. "We're friends of hers."

"We are?" Victor asked.

The Curators seemed less surprised. And even less threatened. "Of course you are," the woman said. "Queen Nefertiti has long shown signs of defying the Administrator. If she tries to help you, that will only prove his suspicions. He'll add her name to the Top Ten Most Wanted Rebels list."

"Wouldn't that make it a Top Eleven Rebels list?" her companion pointed out. "We'd have to change the posters."

Marisol's heart fell as the balloon kept rising higher and higher into the clouds. The island with Chincana's ruins became one speck among many. She scanned the skies for pterodactyls or the quicksilver wings of Amelia Earhart's plane, but the horizon seemed quiet. Too quiet.

So did the ocean below. There should have been ships crisscrossing the water with white wakes, carrying passengers all over the World Between Blinks.

What had happened since she and Jake last left six months ago?

She wasn't exactly sure, but she had the sinking feeling that they had something to do with it.

Victor slumped to the floor, phone in hand. He kept tapping the screen out of habit. Marisol watched wistfully. If they'd had service, she wouldn't have called the navy, or even their parents. The person she wanted to talk to the most was Jake. If her cousin were here, he would have been peering over the basket's edge with her, hatching a plan.

Instead Marisol stood alone, watching the world unfold.

A feeling of relief washed through her when she spotted a city on the coast. "That's Portus!" She recognized the U-shape of the harbor. It was crammed *full* of ships, bobbing like rubber ducks in a bath. Why weren't they sailing? And why were there numbers painted on their hulls? "It's the port where all the ships trade goods and passengers," she explained when Victor finally decided to look. "And over there in the sand is the thin spot where Jake and I met a scavenger with a colander on her head. She gathers lost items that slip through the Unknown and sells them."

"I wonder if she made any money off the retainer I lost in fourth grade. . . ."

"Ew." Marisol made a face. "Who'd want to buy that?"

"They're expensive!" her brother protested. "I should know. Mom and Dad made me pay for a new one!" Victor paused. His lower lip started to tremble, but he bit it, chewing for a while before he went on, "Mari, do—do you think we'll ever see them again?"

Marisol realized, with a start, that her brother was afraid. Of course he was afraid . . . she remembered her own first few hours here, when she sat on the lost steps to the Morris Island Light and cried because there was no door leading them back home. Jake had opened a map beside her, promising they'd find a way.

Again, she wished her cousin were here.

"We'll see our parents again," Marisol said. "Jake and I were only here for a few days last time."

"Sure, but you said Christopher was stuck in the World Between Blinks for seven whole decades! I don't want to go home and find out that everyone I know has grown old! Or turned into futuristic robots or something! That would be awful!" Victor shuddered. His voice was starting to pitch, and he was gripping the balloon's basket so hard that Marisol could see his knuckle bones. "What if we get locked up in the Lost Dutchman gold mine forever?"

"That won't happen," she said.

"How do you know?"

Marisol paused, trying not to let her own lip tremble. The truth was, she *didn't* know what would happen next. This welcome into the World had been so different from the last. The World *itself* was so different. The port of Portus was too calm, and when they flew over the thin spot in the dunes, the scavenger was nowhere to be seen. Piles of junk covered the surrounding hillsides: kitchen appliances and broken surfboards and hubcaps. Someone had stitched over the area with bright yellow lines of CAUTION tape.

"I'm scared too, Victor." Her brother puffed up a little when she said this—a halfhearted argument that squared his shoulders but didn't quite reach his lips. "I felt that way the last time I was here, but then I remembered what Dad always says when we're facing a hard climbing route: tranquilo con la ruta."

"Be calm with the route," Victor repeated the phrase in English and peered over the edge of the basket. "Okay, okay. I'll try. Where are we anyway?"

Marisol knew her brother was trying to put on a brave face. She was too as she looked out over the vast expanse of orange sand. "This is the ever-stretching desert. Queen Nefertiti's court is on the other side of those dunes! It's filled with lost royals and pieces of crumbling castles. They have really excellent desserts. The deforested trees of the Amazon rainforest are over there. . . ."

She started to nod at the horizon, but the distant green line of trees was nowhere to be seen. Even when she fumbled to find it through her monocle.

"Maybe it got deforested again?" Victor suggested when she expressed her frustration.

Marisol shook her head. "This is a world where lost things are found. . . ."

But despite everything she felt more lost than ever.

Tears crept into her eyes. Fear gnawed the edges of her belly. How could she be calm with the route when the route itself was gone?

What had happened to the Amazon and everything inside it?

Where was the Titanoboa? The Lost City of Z?

Where were her explorer friends?

Where would she and Victor find themselves at the end of all this?

Their balloon landed smack-dab in the middle of the desert.

It made sense to have a prison here. There was nowhere to run . . . a giant dune held the entrance to the mine, and others undulated away into the distance, but there was no way anyone could scramble to the top without being seen. The Curators who operated the place were flying in and out: an entire rainbow's worth of balloons was tethered around the tunnel. Ready for liftoff.

For a brief moment, Marisol considered running toward one, but Victor was still climbing out of the basket and the Curators had a firm hold on the rope they'd tied around her wrists in midflight. So instead, the four of them marched toward the mine entrance. Three timbers braced the doorframe, opening up to deep shadows and a set of minecart tracks.

Despite the oil lanterns that hung from hooks on the walls, Marisol struggled to adjust her sight. It didn't help that the Curator who greeted them wore a miner's helmet, the bright lamp on their forehead blinding anyone they looked at.

Their stare burned straight into Marisol.

"Hello, Miss Beruna." That voice . . . it was as sharp as a needle.

As tight as a pickle-jar lid.

Marisol knew exactly who it belonged to. "Red Bun!"

There was an exasperated sigh as the woman tilted her helmet's lamp out of Marisol's face. Yes. She could see now. It was the strictest of the Curators—the woman with fiery hair who'd tasked the Beruna cousins with catching Christopher and returning the ledger. "My name is Karen, actually."

Victor laughed.

The Curator's smile was neither happy nor warm when she looked at the teenager. "Who is this?"

"My brother. Victor," Marisol answered quickly. "He came here by accident—"

"And you didn't?" Red Bun's—Karen's—eyebrows rose. "What is your purpose in the World Between Blinks, Marisol Contreras Beruna?"

Purpose? Again, Marisol thought of Victor's earlier question. Had someone written her name in a ledger? Had she been called here? "I—I don't know."

Karen's smile vanished. "Do not lie to me, Miss Beruna. I know there's some plot afoot! You and your friends are determined to turn this World into a place of mayhem and bedlam and hullabaloo!"

"I haven't seen any of those friends in half a year!" Marisol protested. "I haven't plotted anything!"

"She definitely hasn't stolen anything else either!" Victor squirmed beneath his backpack. "You should let us go before Queen Nefertiti comes to our aid!"

The expression on Karen's sharp face turned even sharper. "So you're conspiring with the 'Most Powerful Queen in the Land of the Lost'?" Marisol could practically hear the air quotes. How could anyone doubt Nefertiti's power?

"No!" she shouted. "We're not conspiring with anyone!"

"We're friends with her!" Victor said at the exact same time.

51

ARGH! "My brother doesn't know what he's talking about—"

"A few days in a cell should fix that." Karen grabbed Marisol's rope and began tugging her along the tracks.

She had no choice but to follow. They descended deeper into the mine—more and more gold threaded through its rocky walls. The air grew cooler. The tunnels grew bigger, until they entered a cave filled with pans and rusty pickaxes and minecarts and . . .

Prison cells.

The bars were made out of gold. So were the locks. So was the key that Karen unclipped from her necklace. She opened the nearest door and waved Marisol in. When Victor tried to step in after his sister, the Curator blocked him.

"You're not a prisoner," she said matter-of-factly. "There's no warrant for you."

"I'm not leaving my sister!"

"Until you have your zoning assignment you can stay here," Karen informed him. "Just not in the cage."

The door *clanged* shut, and the rope unraveled itself from Marisol's wrists, slithering back through the bright bars like some magical snake.

Victor watched from the other side, bewildered. "No tiene sentido."

"Rules are rules," Karen said as she tucked the key

back beneath her collar. "We'd be lost without them!"

Her miner's helmet was the only source of light in the cave. When the Curator left, so did the visibility. It was pitch black, which made the surrounding sounds echo that much louder. Karen's footsteps faded. Victor rattled the door to Marisol's cell to no avail. When he spoke, she could hear the scowl in his voice.

"Why are these Curators in charge? Their logic makes no sense—"

"PSSSSSST!"

Victor paused. His voice lowered. "Mari, was that you?"

"No."

"PSSSSST!" The noise was coming from the other side of the cave. "Marisol! It's us!"

"Us *who*?" she asked.

A white light seared out of nowhere, lighting up the bars of the other cages and tracing the silhouettes of the prisoners inside. One was wearing a broad-brimmed hat.

"By Jove that's bright! Care to spare an old man's eyes?"

"¡Lo siento!" Victor fumbled with his phone. "Sorry! At least my flashlight still works!"

"I should say it does, good sir!"

Marisol knew that voice too. It was British—as proper as cucumber sandwiches with the crusts cut off. "Sir

Percy Fawcett!" He wasn't the only prisoner she recognized. As Victor readjusted the light, Marisol saw that the cells to Percy's left and right were occupied by three more friends. "Uemura Naomi! Herr Leichhardt! And Jack, hello!"

Naomi waved through the bars, the sleeve of his red flannel shirt torn and flapping. The Japanese mountain climber looked a little worse for wear but pleased to see her. His grin was wide and beaming. "Hello, Marisol Contreras Beruna! It is good to see you again."

"That it is!" Percy's son Jack chimed in. "Current circumstances aside, of course! Jail is no place for free spirits such as us."

The iPhone's light rippled over the bars, back and forth, as Victor studied the other prisoners. "You know these guys, Mari?"

Oh, right. "These are the explorers I told you about—we met them in the Amazon. They made us tea and caught Christopher in a giant net and helped Jake steal some hourglasses from the Great Library of Alexandria. Everyone, this is my brother, Victor."

This prompted another round of greetings from Percy, Jack, and Naomi. Herr Leichhardt, she noticed, stayed silent. The explorer was standing next to a rock wall, clenching a smaller rock in his fist. He'd been using it to hack vertical lines into the stone. There were dozens of them.

"Is that how many days you've been here?" Marisol asked.

"No. It's his initial. Or . . . what's left of it." Jack sighed, and Marisol realized what it was she was seeing. An L without the lower line. Herr Leichhardt had a habit of carving that letter. He'd been hacking it into the trees of the Amazon when they first met.

Percy grimaced. "Ludwig was leagues better after you and Jake went home, telling us all sorts of tales about his adventures in the Outback and his childhood in Prussia. And then, all of a sudden, his memory got so much worse. I've never seen a person's hourglass shift so fast. . . ."

"Everything else has turned upside down too," Naomi said sadly.

Marisol thought of the silent skies and stifled sea. "The World seems different."

"It's terrible!" Percy pounded his fist into his palm. "After you left, the Administrator grew ten times stricter. The Curators roped off all the thin spots so they could fix the cracks Christopher Creaturo caused by sending things back home. But they never opened the areas up again. Every day there are new rules. No one is allowed to leave their sector. Ships have been anchored. Planes have been grounded. The Amazon has been untangled and replanted like a formal garden, stripped of all its wildness. The Curators say things are safer this way, with it all laid out in lines for one of the queen's garden parties.

They call it order, but . . . it's wrong."

"So why hasn't anyone done anything?" Victor asked.

"Plenty of someones are doing somethings," Percy Fawcett retorted. "But the Administrator has been rearranging this World for a very long time, and he is incredibly organized. So far everyone who's tried to stand up to him has been forced to run or . . ." He filled his silence with a sweeping hand.

Marisol looked back at Herr Leichhardt's cell, where the explorer kept carving line after line. The sight made her sad and mad and determined. "There has to be some way to stop the Administrator!"

Naomi, Percy, and Jack exchanged a glance. Three ways and filled with purpose.

"There is," the Japanese explorer said.

"We think." Percy cleared his throat. "We've heard rumors from a reputable source that there's a secret weapon lost in the World. Something the Administrator has been searching after for years and years! It's called 'the Rocket.' We'd only just heard of it when we were captured—our excitement got the better of us, and I'm afraid we lowered our guard."

"If we can track down this weapon before the Administrator does, we can use it to defeat him," Naomi explained.

"Our plan was to call you and Jake back to help with

the search. Since you're so good at finding items . . ." Jack glanced at Victor, then back to their jail cells. "Obviously a few things went wrong."

"Do you think you can find the Rocket?" A hint of hope lit Naomi's question.

"Sí." Marisol nodded, her fists tightening around the bars. There was a buzzing feeling in them already—mostly adrenaline. "But first, we need to get out of here."

4

JAKE

"YOU WANT TO FIND A WHAT?" JAKE SQUEAKED. "A *rocket*? Like, a go-to-the-moon rocket or . . ." His voice dropped to a whisper. "A weapon? Like, a *missile*?"

Their dinghy bobbed up and down in Portus's restless harbor. Amelia and Raleigh exchanged a wavy glance.

"We don't *think* it's a space rocket," admitted the pilot. "I don't know what he'd want that for, there's not much up there except for ancient stars and the occasional glimpse of Pluto. Apparently it's still annoyed about being demoted from full planet status, so sometimes it decides to be lost."

"Nobody wants to use a weapon," Raleigh said. "Percy fought in a war, he knows as well as anyone what it's like. And that's never how it's been in the World Between Blinks. But . . ."

Amelia began rowing with quick, cutting strokes as they caught Jake up on what he'd missed. They had to be fast—for even though most of the harbor's boats were anchored, the Curators were watching the fleet. Always watching. The number the duo had hastily painted on their dinghy wouldn't match up with the official lists. Neither would Amelia or Raleigh, for that matter. Both the explorer and the aviatrix were outside of their assigned zones.

"We're on thin ice, our final warning. If we get caught in Portus without the proper permits, they'll send us to the big house!" Amelia glanced over both shoulders as she steered toward a rickety pier. She looked a little shaky herself.

"The big house?" Jake thought through all the residences he'd seen on his last visit. Viking longhouses and London townhomes and buildings with grass growing out of sod-covered roofs. None of them had been particularly big. "Which one is that?"

"She means prison," Raleigh explained. "Well, she means the Lost Dutchman gold mine. That's where Percy, Jack, Naomi, and Herr Leichhardt are being held by the Curators. They were arrested a week ago."

"What for?" Jake asked, a chill going through him that had nothing to do with his soaking-wet clothes.

Amelia and Raleigh exchanged another uneasy look. Oz whimpered.

Their boat lurched to a halt in the gravel underneath the pier.

Jake's stomach heaved too. "It was for helping me and Marisol, wasn't it? The Administrator knew. . . ."

"He has a list," Raleigh said. "Top Ten Most Wanted Rebels, he calls us. I believe you're ranked number three—"

Amelia cleared her throat—a sound meant to silence the explorer. "There's no use worrying about the past. We helped you then, Jake, and we'll help you again! Sure as the sky's blue. And with any luck, you'll help us too!" She tucked the dinghy's oars away as Oz hopped out into the shallows. "We'll find Marisol, but first we have to get out of Portus. This place is crawling with Curators!"

Jake glanced up at the overhead dock boards. He couldn't see the sky through them—only bright lines of sunlight and foot-shaped shadows. Did they belong to Curators?

"Why are there so many of them here?" he whispered.

"There's a big crack just outside town they're trying to repair," Raleigh explained. "And Portus has always annoyed them. They'd much rather it was next to Ostia Antica, where it was in the old world."

Jake's mind went immediately to the market he and Marisol had explored—Romans had sold their goods alongside Brits on the frozen Thames, everyone and everything full of life. Were they all separated now, sent to proper zones, like entries in an encyclopedia instead of living, breathing people?

And where, amid all of that, would someone file Marisol?

Was *she* on the Top Ten Most Wanted Rebels list too? They had to find her before something terrible happened.

"So, what's the plan?" he asked, trying to wring more water out of his clothes. His phone had been in his pocket, he realized—he couldn't even muster up a pang of sadness that it was soaked through. All of his worry belonged to his cousin.

Amelia yanked off her cap. Auburn curls sprang everywhere, as flying and free as aerobatic maneuvers. They bounced as the pilot pulled a suitcase out from the bottom of their boat. "The plan is that some friends— members of the resistance—will pick us up on the edge of town," she said. "Oz, will you go ahead, so they know we're coming?"

Oz gave a soft whuff, butted his head against Jake's legs once, as if to say *don't worry*, and then scrambled out from under the pier, his sandy fur blending in to the dusty streets. There *were* plenty of Curators—with clipboards in hand, taking notes on cargo that clearly hadn't moved in months.

Jake watched them watch the thylacine. "Won't he get caught?"

"The rules don't seem to apply to Oz. He goes where he pleases. Always has. Always will. Us, on the other hand . . ." Amelia opened the suitcase, revealing several piles of folded white suits. "We'll need disguises."

"We're going to dress up as Curators," Raleigh explained. "Then we'll sail to the Lost Dutchman gold mine and rescue the other explorers. That way we'll have three more people to help us search for Marisol and the Rocket!"

"Don't you mean four?" Jake asked.

"No." A shadowy expression passed beneath Raleigh's wide-brimmed hat. "Herr Leichhardt won't be much help . . . something's gone wrong, I'm afraid."

"But I gave him his memories back!" Jake protested. "I tipped his hourglass over to pour them back into the top half!"

"And it worked," the explorer agreed. "Then one day they were just gone again, and more besides. Ludwig didn't even want to explore the Amazon anymore. He just sat on a stump all day. . . ."

A sick, sinking feeling sucked at the edges of Jake's chest. Was it his fault, somehow? He'd only guessed what would happen when he flipped Ludwig's hourglass. Maybe total amnesia was a side effect. But . . . if that was the case, then why hadn't Hazel lost all of her memories again too?

A flash of white caught Jake in midthought. Not a Curator—but one of their uniforms. Tossed straight toward him.

Amelia threw another set of clothes at Raleigh. "Let's suit up!"

Five minutes later, Jake was wishing his phone was still working, so he could snap a picture of the three of them. He knew this was a serious situation, but if Nana had taught him one thing, it was that there was usually time for a giggle while you were solving a problem.

He and his two companions were clad in boxy white Curators' suits, with square shoulders and creases ironed in down the front of the legs. Their regular clothes were hidden in the large briefcase Amelia carried, and Raleigh was trying to teach Jake how to walk.

"No, no," he said. "Your back has to be *straight*— straight enough to run a ruler up and down. As if someone's tied a piece of string to your spine and they're tugging you upright."

"Like a puppet?" Jake tried to imagine himself as a marionette, his bones turning ten times lighter.

"That's the ticket!" Raleigh beamed his approval. "Now, your steps shouldn't quite be a march, but they should be perfectly efficient. And eyes ahead, on your goal, at all times."

"Anyone who looks at us for too long is going to realize

you're wearing sneakers," Amelia added. "So we'll have to overwhelm them with posture."

"I mean, I can *try* the white shoes," Jake said dubiously. "But they're huge. I'm going to look like a clown. How big did you think my feet were?"

"We only had one wardrobe to select from," Raleigh admitted. "Besides, there aren't many Curators your size. We'd best get on with it. We've got to get across town."

Jake glanced back at the dingy. Its hull number was already starting to peel. "I thought you said we were sailing?"

"We are." Amelia nodded. "Just . . . not in this boat."

"Here goes nothing!" With one last inspection, Raleigh turned to march off, and Amelia and Jake fell into step behind him, chins up, backs straight, the very picture of efficiency.

Jake did his best to keep his eyes ahead, thinking as he did of his old motto—*eyes ahead, don't look back*. He'd always said that to himself, using the words to help him leave friends and homes behind as he and his mom moved cities again and again. Last time he'd been here, though, he'd learned that sometimes it *was* good to look ahead . . . but sometimes it was good to look back and remember as well.

So instead he tried Marisol's motto, whispering it as they made their way down the docks. *Be calm with the route.*

It *was* calm. Too calm. Jake felt sick again, remembering the bustling port this place had once been, buildings from different times and places crammed in side by side, citizens of the World Between Blinks hurrying along on errands, stopping and chatting on corners. Now, everyone was in Roman tunics, and those few who weren't had passes pinned prominently on their clothes, showing they were permitted to be out of their zone. Shops had been shuttered and there were gaps between buildings. There was no fried dough smell sizzling the air. No merchant hawking single socks from their stall . . .

The life had been sucked out of Portus.

Its spirit gutted.

There were plenty of Curators, though. Most were busy with official duties—stopping people to double-check their passes or using surveying equipment to see if they could move the streets' stubborn stones. Thankfully they were too caught up taking measurements to notice Jake's footwear.

He walked quickly, following Raleigh and Amelia. They took a right turn and then a left, weaving toward the edge of town, and Jake couldn't help noticing the way the people around them stepped carefully out of their path, as if they didn't want the Curators to notice them. Nobody had ever been afraid of him before. This was *awful*.

Then a voice rang out behind them. "Ahoy! Excuse me! Yoo-hoo!"

"Keep going," Raleigh muttered, barely turning his head. "Pretend you can't hear."

"Helloooo! Attention, Curators!"

As they turned another corner, Jake caught a glimpse of white, and his stomach tried to climb straight up his throat. A pair of Curators was hurrying after them! "Raleigh, they're catching up," he whispered urgently.

"Hold your nerve, buddy," Amelia whispered back. "If we run, they'll chase us."

"If we don't run, they'll see my shoes!" One by one, Jake felt his marionette strings snapping. "And if they see my shoes . . ."

Raleigh tried a nearby door. It rattled. Locked shut.

Jake's heart ballooned inside his eardrums. *BUM-BUM. BUM-BUM.* He looked from one end of the street to the other. They were so close to the edge of town. So close to escaping! The desert ahead was just as Jake remembered it, stretching away long and flat, eventually giving way to rippling dunes. Sand and sand and sand . . .

"I have an idea!" Dust spilled from his heels as he started to sprint. "Hurry!"

"What?" Amelia gasped. "Jake! No!"

He dashed past the last of Portus's buildings, until the sand became silky and slippery and impossible to run through. He stopped to catch his breath, turning to see four white suits. Raleigh was almost as pale as his disguise. Amelia's curls flew everywhere, but the pilot's steps stayed steady, away, away from the Curators who kept trying to flag them down.

"Excuse me! Helloooo!"

Jake scuffed his feet into the warm sand. Ankle deep. Grains slipped through his shoelaces, but no one could see what they were covering. He might look a little weird with his shoes completely hidden, but he'd look even more out of place if they were on show. He forced a smile onto his face and waved back at their pursuers. "Hello!"

"What in the worlds are you doing, old chap?" Raleigh looked wilted without his hat.

"Trust me," Jake whispered.

Amelia made a grim face as she joined them. "We'll have to now."

The real Curators were closing in, cheeks flushed and brows furrowed. Both were men and both were panting.

"Excuse us, but we were wondering if you could spare an extra pen! Greg's has run out of ink and if we don't complete this census before nightfall we'll be de-monocled—" The official paused. His eyes fell, not to Jake's feet but onto the boy's empty hands. "That's strange. All three of you seem to have misplaced your clipboards."

Amelia's knuckles tightened around the briefcase handle.

Raleigh seemed close to fainting.

Jake dug into his pocket. Even though his phone was dead, he'd placed it there out of habit, and thank goodness he had. He flashed its black screen like a badge. "That's because we're on a special task force," he said, mind scrambling. "The Administrator wants us to experiment with digitizing information."

"Digitizing?" Greg frowned at the word.

Amelia's hand grew whiter, as if she were trying not to frown too.

"That's right!" Jake slipped the phone back into his pocket before the Curators could get a closer look. "Because papers can be stolen too easily. We're compiling a database."

"But . . ." Greg glanced at his companion. "Our pens are already charmed to transcribe our notes to our monocles."

Drat! More sand kept sinking into Jake's shoes, warning him not to run again. If he got arrested now, he wouldn't be able to find Marisol. But what should he say?

Fortunately, Amelia jumped in to the rescue. "True," she said, "but that doesn't do much good if your pen runs out of ink, now does it? This new system will fix all that. No more stolen ledgers. No more papercuts."

"The Administrator wants it finished as soon as possible." Jake used the same tone his mom did on very important business calls. "He'd be very upset to find out that you two have been delaying us." His voice dropped

68

another, graver notch. "He might even have you de-monocled."

At this, the real Curators took a synchronized step back. Apologies stumbled from their lips. Then farewells. And after that, another apology. The pair turned and trot-ted back toward town.

When they were almost out of sight, Raleigh let out a breath, his moustache twitching with relief. "I'll say, Jake, that was some spectacular acting! I thought we'd get caught for sure!"

"Agreed." Amelia nodded. "But we're not out of the woods—er, desert—yet."

Jake shook his sneakers loose and glanced around. The ever-stretching desert looked less deserted than it had the last time he and Marisol were here. There was . . . stuff in the sand. A rocking horse. A lone snow ski. A ger-bil. Things that scavengers would have collected in their hand carts had instead been left to pile up in the dunes. Probably because the area had been roped off with CAU-TION tape.

The only people he could see past the yellow strips were Curators. Some scuttled around with more survey-ing equipment. All of them wore hard hats. They must've been trying to repair the crack Christopher's experiments had left. The construction site stretched all the way to the horizon.

But . . . what was that?

"Aha! Our ride has arrived! See it?" Amelia leaned in close, so when she pointed, Jake could squint along the line of her arm.

He stared, the distance rippling with the desert's heat. A dark shape danced for a moment, then vanished. The next second he was sure he could see something traveling toward them, growing larger so rapidly that it must be moving really fast.

And then he realized what it was—though surely it had to be a mirage. The most magnificent ship was speeding in their direction . . . straight across the desert sands!

It was an enormous Spanish galleon, three masts towering above its dark wooden hull, white sails billowing in the breeze, a spider's web of ropes slung back and forth between the rigging.

So *that's* what Raleigh had meant by sailing!

"Amelia, Raleigh, how . . . ?" Jake gaped, stammering in his surprise.

"The *Lost Ship of the Desert*," Amelia replied with a gap-toothed grin. "Nearly as good as a plane! There are all kinds of stories about folks seeing her in the American desert, nobody ever knowing why she was there, or why she wasn't when they came back. She was here, of course!"

"But we're on *land*," Jake managed, still staring.

"Oh, right! Take a look down beneath her there. We

made a few modifications based off some of Leonardo da Vinci's lost notes."

Now the ship was closer, and Jake suddenly saw that where its hull swelled to a wide and heavy wooden bottom, what looked like giant skis had been fixed underneath.

"She's on runners," Raleigh said. "Like a sled. Look at Oz up there!"

The Tasmanian tiger was posed proudly at the ship's prow, like a living figurehead, as the ship roared toward them.

"Um . . . it knows how to stop, right?" Jake fought the urge to take a step backward.

"Sure!" Amelia grinned. "Our helmsman's got a few tricks up his sleeve that'd make any pilot proud. Any minute now, it'll . . . uh, maybe we should give them some room."

"Take cover!" Raleigh shouted, and the three of them sprinted back for the mouth of the nearest alleyway, ducking inside it just as the ship pulled in and swung around side-on, sending up a wall of sand in their direction.

"Everyone okay?" Amelia spit out a gritty mouthful and gave her head a shake, shedding sand like a dog shaking off water.

"I'm okay," Jake decided, trying to brush the sand from his clothes and failing.

"All present and accounted for," Raleigh agreed.

"Let's get aboard and join the crew."

As they made their way back across the sand, the crew lined up far above them to wave a cheerful greeting. Jake's spirits lifted as he waved back—he was worried about how they were going to find Marisol, still feeling hollow after the emptiness of Portus, and had no idea how they were going to break the explorers out of prison, but he had friends on his side as well. He mustn't forget that. Perhaps there'd even be people he knew aboard!

"I say, they're cheerful," Raleigh observed, lifting one hand to wave back.

"They're about ready to throw a party," Amelia agreed.

"Are they . . ." Doubt began to creep into Jake's mind, as the waves of the crew grew yet more energetic. Almost frantic. "Are they waving? Or are they . . . warning?"

As one, the three of them stopped and looked around.

Greg and his partner had rounded back at the sight of the Spanish galleon. Some Curators from the construction site were hurrying toward them as well, clipboards flashing furiously in the sun. "Time we were leaving," Amelia shouted. "Quick, let's blow!"

The trio took off across the sand, Jake's legs aching as they slipped and slid beneath his feet, sand weighing down his sneakers and flying into his face. The crew of the *Lost Ship* had thrown three rope ladders over the side, and they were cheering and shouting, urging them onward.

As soon as Jake got to his ladder, he reached up to grab it with both hands, immediately getting his feet tangled in the rope. This was like some kind of gym-class nightmare! Beside him, Amelia was having a hard time of it with the briefcase in one hand, but Raleigh was scampering up like a monkey.

"Keep your hands and feet to the edges," he called over his shoulder, and as Jake pushed his feet out into the corners made by the rope and the rungs, the ladder stopped twisting like it was trying to shake him off.

He could hear shouts from up above. "Free the lines! Haul in! Look alive!" Beneath him, the ship was beginning to shift and move, Jake and his friends still scrambling up their ladders even as it got underway. He was nearly at the top now, and hands were reaching down to take hold of him, to pull him in. With a wriggle and a sudden tumble he was flat on his back on the wooden deck, staring up at the sky. Cheers went up all around.

The crew were the mix he was used to seeing in the World Between Blinks—a woman with a headscarf and a small pterosaur perched on her shoulder helped Amelia to her feet, while another woman with blue stripes painted onto her face was shaking Raleigh's hand in congratulations.

A Korean man in a green sweater and a pair of jeans pulled Jake upright with a smile. "Welcome aboard!" he said. "It's good to see you again, Jake! Come and say hello to the captain, and then we'll get you out of my old clothes."

Jake looked down at his disguise—now more orange than white, from all the sand—and then did a double take at his rescuer. "Min-jun?"

The man laughed. The sound was warm and familiar, as snug as his sweater. "I look that different now, do I?"

He did. The last time Jake had seen Min-jun, he'd been the friendliest of the Curators—in fact, the only friendly Curator. He had been the one who had helped the children with money and charms—even slipping them monocles that were supposed to be for Curators only. His greatest gift had come at the end of their first trip to the World. He'd let them go home, in the end, when he could have stopped them.

"You aren't a Curator anymore. . . ." Jake swallowed, almost scared to ask. "Did they throw you out? Because of us?"

"I was de-monocled," Min-jun replied. "But I was going to quit anyway, after everything I learned while writing my incident report." He smiled. "Can't say I'm sorry to leave them behind."

Jake followed his friend's gaze and saw a row of

Curators lined up in the sand, shaking their fists in unison. White suits turned into white dots. The *Lost Ship* kept sailing into the desert.

He turned back to Min-jun. "Well, if it helps, you should know that Christopher and Hazel have been very happy since you allowed them to go home. They got married!"

"Good for them!" The ex-Curator smiled. "And what about Marisol?"

"She's not married."

"Obviously!" Min-jun laughed. "I meant how is she?"

Oh. "Fine. The last time we FaceTimed she was talking about this special hot chocolate she was going to order at a restaurant near Lake Titicaca. . . ." Jake drifted off, listening to the *shush-shush* of sand under the *Lost Ship*'s runners. "That's where she was when Amelia and Raleigh wrote her name in the ledger. She didn't appear in the same thin spot as I did, so maybe she's not fine."

Had the Curators caught her yet? Jake wondered. It seemed likely, judging by the close call he'd just had back in Portus.

"Marisol is a very special girl," Min-jun said. "I have a feeling she'll find her way to us, and then she'll help track down the Rocket."

"To fight the Administrator . . ."

"Yes." Min-jun glanced back at the horizon. There

were no more white suits there, but Jake somehow knew that the ex-Curator was looking for them. "He means well, I think. Or, at least I think *he* thinks he means well. He was the very first Curator, you know. The Administrator invented all the filing systems himself. He recruited me personally, when I first arrived in this World. He told me that without Curators, this place would fall apart. No one would be able to find anything. Maybe that was true, once—maybe it's still partly true—but the way things are now . . ."

He was interrupted when a familiar voice rang out in a rich Austrian accent. "Jake, my friend!"

Standing at the back of the ship was Giovanni Nepomuceno Maria Annunziata Giuseppe Giovanni Batista Ferdinando Baldassare Luigi Gonzaga Pietro Alessandrino Zanobi Antonino. Or as Jake knew him . . .

"Johann!"

"Welcome aboard," the archduke said cheerfully. "We have much to discuss and a prison break to plan—our friends are depending on us!"

5

MARISOL

"ARE YOU SURE WE CAN TRUST YOUR BROTHER?"

Marisol wasn't sure which explorer whispered this question. The mine shaft was pitch-black again, a dark so deep that she couldn't even see her hands on the bars. Victor had taken his iPhone with him on his quest to get Red Bun's—Karen's—key.

No. Victor wasn't the most reliable person. He tended to be . . . self-absorbed. Once he'd spent both of their bus fares on candy, and only shared two tiny pieces with Marisol on the twenty-minute walk home, so asking her brother to steal a charm straight off a Curator's neck and return to unlock their cells felt like a stretch. As the minutes ticked by, it seemed more and more impossible.

But there was no other way to break out of these

cages. They'd tried everything else—banging the golden bars with rocks, picking at the locks with pickaxes. Only the key would work.

And only Karen had it.

"We have to trust Victor," Marisol answered instead.

"I don't mean to be uncharitable"—Jack's voice echoed through the cavern—"but he doesn't strike me as the subtle type. Your brother is no cat burglar. If Karen catches him . . ."

He drifted off.

The only sound was the soft *chip-chip* of Herr Leichhardt's I carvings.

Darkness started leaking into Marisol's imagination— twisting into all sorts of terrible visions. Victor caught and imprisoned. Mom and Dad standing on the cliffs of Isla del Sol, waiting for children who would never come back. The World Between Blinks torn apart tree by tree and brick by brick, turned into a museum instead of a home.

"Have some faith," Naomi said gently. "Victor may possess his own hidden strengths."

Marisol wished this were true. She also wished—not for the first time—that Jake was the one by her side. Then again, according to what Percy and Jack and Naomi had told her, Marisol's primo had also been called to the World. *And* he was number three on the Administrator's

Top Ten Most Wanted Rebels list. If Jake had been next to her, he'd have been locked away too.

A scuttling sound interrupted her thoughts.

Then . . . a light. Not the blaze of an iPhone but the flicker of an oil lantern. Victor held the flame as far away from his body as he could, and it made his shadow stretch larger than life on the gold-threaded walls. His hair curled like kraken tentacles.

"Oh good! This is the right cave. This mine needs a map! I feel like I've been walking in circles—"

"¿Funcionó?" Marisol gripped the bars tighter. "Did you get the key?"

Her brother responded by tugging a necklace out of his hoodie. It held all of Karen's charms—including the shiny skeleton key. It winked extra bright in the lantern light.

"Bravo, young man!" With the way Percy was cheering, you never would've known his doubt. "How'd you manage it?"

A mischievous smile stole across Victor's face. It made him look five years younger. "I taught Karen how to take selfies, but then I realized it would give her a better view of me stealing her necklace, so I introduced her to Candy Crush instead."

"Candy . . . Crush?" Percy repeated faintly. "Crushing . . . candy?"

"Correcto." Victor nodded. "You don't need data to play it. She'll be distracted for hours!"

"You gave her your phone?" Marisol was surprised. She hadn't seen Victor without his phone since he'd gotten it for his fourteenth birthday a few months ago. He carried the device everywhere, and for all of his fear of futuristic robots, the machine almost seemed like a part of Victor. It was hard to imagine him handing it over to Karen. Let alone willingly.

"Yeah," her brother sighed. "And judging by what happened with my old retainer, Mom and Dad will probably make me pay for a new one, so this better be worth it."

"Trying times call for noble sacrifices," Percy said with a solemn note. "We should hurry to ensure yours is not in vain. Karen will realize her language charm is missing when the other Curators try talking to her."

Victor glanced down at the necklace. "Language charm? Which one is that?"

Percy was right, Marisol realized. They needed to get out of here. Now! "¡Apúrate!" She wanted to grab her brother's hoodie strings and pull, but he was too far away. "Hurry up, Victor!"

"¡Tranquilo con la ruta, hermana!"

"I will be calmer with the route when I can actually *go* somewhere," she said.

It was true. When Victor unlocked her cell door, Marisol felt herself relax. She saw the same thing happen with Naomi, Jack, and Percy—their shoulders turned less statue-like. Their smiles came more easily.

Herr Leichhardt, however . . .

He didn't even turn when they opened his door. The rock stayed clenched in his fist. Some of his knuckles had been scraped raw against the wall, but he didn't seem to care. He kept carving.

"This could be tricky," Jack whispered. "The whole reason we got arrested in the first place was because Ludwig wouldn't leave the Amazon when the Curators started rezoning it. We made Raleigh run for it with the ledger page—it was too precious to give up—but no matter what we tried to do, Ludwig just sat on his stump."

Victor held his oil lamp even higher, showing just how deep Herr Leichhardt's lines went. "Should we leave him?" he asked.

"No!" Marisol shouted.

"I thought you wanted to hurry."

She did, but the thought of leaving Herr Leichhardt alone in the dark was almost worse than the prospect of getting caught again. Marisol stepped into the explorer's cell.

"Herr Leichhardt? It's me—Marisol."

He gave her a foggy sort of stare. She searched his eyes for a glint, even a hint of recognition, but the only bright thing was the gold in the wall, where he kept hacking away. Each hit rattled the hourglass around his neck. Marisol watched the charm, feeling the heaviness of the sand at its bottom.

"Ludwig?" she tried again. "We have to go."

Percy cleared his throat. "Perhaps we *should* leave Herr Leichhardt this time. If the Curators catch us, we'll be no help to him or anyone else in this World."

"We have to find the Rocket!" Jack reminded her. "If we don't defeat the Administrator . . . all is lost."

Marisol bit her lip. The others were probably right, but she didn't want to admit it. Not just yet. During her last adventure in the World Between Blinks she'd had to learn how to let go of some things—most notably, the Great Mogul Diamond—but friends weren't things. They shouldn't be tossed away easily.

So she bent down and picked up a rock of her own.

Herr Leichhardt paused when Marisol reached out to his newest carving and began adding to it. Her line was horizontal. The bottom half to his L.

"There," she said. "All finished. We can go now."

Herr Leichhardt studied the letter for several seconds. It was hard to tell with the wild brambles of his beard—months overgrown—but Marisol could've sworn the man was smiling. He dropped his rock and walked straight out of the cell.

He didn't stop there.

He moved past the other explorers toward the exit tunnel.

Percy's hat fell off his head as he scrambled after the German, catching his friend by the sleeve. "Ludwig! Wait! We can't just walk out of here! We need to follow the plan! We need to—er, what is the plan again? Exactly?"

Everyone turned to look at Marisol.

"Well . . ." she thought aloud. "The desert is too big to run across on foot. I think we should fly. We can borrow one of the Curators' hot-air balloons next to the mine entrance—"

"But that's where Karen is sitting," Victor cut in.

"Isn't she busy crushing candy and self-reflecting?" Jack asked.

"Sí, but she'll definitely notice if six people file past," her brother said. "Percy has a point. We can't just walk out of here."

Marisol frowned. "Is there any other way out of this place?"

Naomi shook his head. "I don't think so. We would have seen another exit on the flight in, and you're right. There's nothing around for miles."

"We could try digging." Jack made a valiant gesture toward the pails and pickaxes.

"That would take too long, Son," Percy said.

But Marisol kept staring at the tools—so sharp in the amber light—and the large box on wheels behind them. The minecart was much bigger than the library cart she'd used to sneak past Karen—who had then simply been Red Bun—when she stole the ledger with Great-Uncle Christopher's name from the Crystal Palace.

Maybe, just maybe, the same trick could work twice. . . .

"What if we rolled past Karen instead?" Marisol walked up to the cart. There was a whole bunch of dust inside. Some of it was flaked with gold. "I'm sure she sees minecarts every day. If she's busy playing the game on Victor's phone, she might not notice."

The explorers all wore varying expressions of doubt.

Percy summed it up in a sentence. "Surely sweet smashing isn't *that* engrossing!"

"Actually, Mari's plan isn't half bad," Victor told them. "It could even work!"

Her brother wasn't quite as enthusiastic when he discovered he would have to do the pushing, since everyone else in their party was supposed to be behind bars. They walked as far as they dared toward the surface, pushing the cart as a team. It turned five times heavier when Marisol, Percy, Naomi, Jack, and Herr Leichhardt climbed inside for the final stretch.

Marisol's brother had his work cut out for him.

The minecart's wheels sang a rusty song as he pushed. Marisol found it hard to breathe, not because of the tarp draped overhead, but because she was suddenly sure it would get peeled away. Victor grunted and groaned and it was a miracle that Karen didn't look up from the screen. Marisol could see the Curator through a small crack in the cart. Her face was bathed in bluish light, and her red hair looked purple at the edges. Her tongue poked out the side of her mouth—utter concentration.

The sounds of the game grew louder as they rolled closer. Lasers. Chimes. Bubbles. No wonder Karen couldn't hear them.

Percy went stock-still when he heard an explosion. "Is there a battle happening outside?"

"It's the game," Marisol whispered.

"Doesn't sound very fun," the explorer muttered. "Sounds like war, and we can't fight yet. Not without the Rocket."

"We'll find it," she promised, trying not to wonder how. Her "magnet fingers"—the uncanny ability to find lost things that she'd inherited from Nana—worked differently in the World Between Blinks. Everything was lost here, so she needed to envision what she was looking for to help her fingers hone in on a direction. Last time, she'd known she was chasing Christopher Creaturo. She'd pictured his grinning face, and her fingers had flared. "Do you know what it looks like?" she asked Percy.

"A rocket, I expect."

"That doesn't really help," Marisol whispered.

"We'll hunt down more details," the explorer grunted, "but first we need to get out of here."

The others were getting restless too. Jack kept readjusting his hat. Naomi picked at his shirtsleeve. Herr Leichhardt had found another rock at the bottom of the minecart and was trying to resume his carving. *TAP-TAP! TAP-TAP!* Marisol grabbed his wrist, but it was too late.

The cart had stopped.

They hadn't reached the exit. A peek through the crack showed that the hot-air balloons were several meters away. Karen's desk was closer. She'd finally looked up from the phone, her eyes as glazed as a Mayflower Donut. They stared at Victor a few seconds before registering him.

"Oh. You're back." The Curator's bun looked looser somehow—coming undone—as she nodded down at the phone in her hand. "This game . . . it's . . . it's magical! I haven't had this much fun in years!"

Marisol's brother stepped between the minecart and her line of sight. "What level have you reached?"

"I—I'm not sure," Karen answered. "It has jellies."

"Can I see?"

Victor leaned in toward the screen. One hand snuck Karen's necklace out of his hoodie pocket so he could return the charms without her noticing, while the other gave a secret wave toward the cart. Marisol knew the gesture. It was sibling sign language for: *MOVE*.

She tightened her grip on Herr Leichhardt's wrist and passed on Victor's wave to the others. They peeled the tarp back carefully—wincing a little at the rich evening light. Everything outside the mine had turned sunset gold. The anchored balloons looked like teardrop jewels. Ruby. Sapphire. Emerald. All they had to do was reach the closest one and untie its ropes.

Jack and Naomi climbed out of the cart first, helping Herr Leichhardt and Marisol next. The German explorer crouched down—not to hide, but to start drawing lines in the sand. Percy crept like a soldier out of a World War I movie, ushering the rest of them forward.

More explosions sounded from the mine behind them. Then more happy chimes.

Then there were no noises at all.

Marisol glanced over her shoulder. The blue light had disappeared from Karen's face, and wisps of hair kept falling from her bun as she tap, tap, tapped at the dark screen.

It stayed black.

Victor's phone battery had died.

"WHAT? NO! WHERE DID IT GO? I HAD A HIGH SCORE—" Karen looked up. Her fury paused, then doubled, at the sight of Marisol and the rest of the explorers. "HOW DID YOU GET OUT?"

Victor dropped the necklace he'd been trying to tie back around the Curator's neck. Charms spilled all over the sand as he started to run.

"VICTOR!" Marisol screamed. "LOOK OUT!"

Karen lunged, grabbing her brother by the strap of his backpack and yanking. Hard. Victor stumbled back. Granola bars and water bottles spilled to the ground as the Curator and the teenager scuffled.

Karen caught him by the hoodie strings, cinching them so he couldn't wriggle out of the sweatshirt. "Victor Contreras Beruna, you are under arrest for aiding and abetting five of the Administrator's Top Ten Most Wanted Rebels!"

"You can't do that!" Victor fought back. "You don't have a warrant!"

For a second, it seemed like his argument might work. Karen paused. Her fist pulled on his hoodie strings. Her expression looked just as tight, but her red hair was everywhere.

"C'mon, Karen!" The more Victor tried to run, the

smaller his sweatshirt cinched. "Loosen up! Let me go!"

"But . . . ," she faltered, "I can't!"

"Sure you can! Just lift your fingers one at a time! Like this!" Victor wiggled his hands. "Without a warrant, you've got no reason to hold on to me!"

Karen considered this. Then she plucked a pen and paper from her desk, scratching out one name and writing Victor's above it.

She held the document up to his face, triumphant. "I do now!"

Marisol was torn. She couldn't leave her brother—but she wasn't big enough to free him from Karen, and the Curator's shouts had summoned a small army from the depths of the mine. They swarmed up like white-suited ants.

If she and the explorers didn't get into a balloon now, they'd be locked right back into the cages. Victor too.

Something rolled away from her brother's foot as he struggled. Not a water bottle but a mason jar.

The one with the storm winds inside.

Marisol picked up the container and twisted open the lid without a second thought. Papers flew everywhere. Including the makeshift arrest warrant. Karen shrieked as the files whipped around her head—her red bun frizzing. Of course, she tried to catch them and of course *that* meant she let go of Victor's hoodie strings.

Her brother was free!

"¡Vamos, Victor!" Sand flew into Marisol's mouth as she shouted.

The mason-jar storm quickly grew worse. By the time Victor ran from the mine it felt like one of the hurricanes that swept past Nana's beach house every few years— winds that bent palmetto trees and lifted shingles and beat at the windows their grandmother had boarded up herself. Sometimes these gales were even strong enough to lift boats straight out of the ocean.

The hot-air balloons didn't stand a chance.

Sand swirled up, up, into a furious, twisting dust devil, carrying all the balloons with it. When Percy tried to grab a rope, it lifted the explorer ten whole feet in the air. Marisol felt her heart drop back to the ground with him.

How could they escape now?

Victor, Naomi, and Jack scrambled to help Percy to his feet. Herr Leichhardt plowed on into the desert, undaunted. Sand sucked at Marisol's shins when she tried running after him. The dust devil swirled away much faster, taking the last of her hope with it.

"That's it! *Pah!* No more games! *Pah!*" A dust-covered Karen emerged from the mine entrance, spitting out sand between each sentence. Reinforcements spilled down the hill after her. "Arrest them all!"

Marisol was so busy counting the Curators—so many, too many to fight—that she stumbled straight into Herr Leichhardt. The explorer had halted. Sunset gleamed in his blue eyes as he pointed toward the horizon.

"Sí." Marisol took in the colors: coral, fire, and dew-covered plum. "It's pretty, but—"

The rest got caught in her throat, because Herr Leichhardt wasn't just admiring the sky. He was showing her something. . . .

A ship?

Marisol blinked—wondering if this was some glimpse of home she was seeing—but no. There was a Spanish galleon sailing out of the sun. Its sails seared orange at the edges, and there was a silhouette at the prow that looked very much like a Tasmanian tiger. Her heart flipped.

"Oz?" she croaked.

"Raleigh?" Jack cried out.

Percy joined in with a loud, "Hurrah!"

"Does this mean we're saved?" A sloppy smile grew on Victor's face.

It vanished as a Curator lunged forward, seizing him with a triumphant cry. More officials in white uniforms surrounded the explorers, while Karen marched straight up to Marisol. She grabbed the girl's arm and scowled.

"It means we're going to need more arrest warrants!"

Marisol's heart sank as Karen began giving orders to the other Curators. "Get the prisoners inside and prepare for more processing paperwork!" She glanced back at the oncoming ship. "This may get messy. . . ."

6

JAKE

"PRISONERS, AHOY!"

The cry came from near the *Lost Ship*'s bow, where a cluster of sailors were all keeping watch, each with a telescope held up to one eye. Some followed the twisty path of the dust devil, which swirled into dusk, scattering hot-air balloons among faintly painted stars. The rest of the lookouts stared dead ahead. Without an eyepiece of his own, Jake could only see a flurry of white suits gathered around a single dune. Or the Lost Dutchman gold mine. That's where Raleigh said the Administrator's Most Wanted Rebels were kept.

He hadn't mentioned there'd be so many Curators guarding the place.

Jake's heart sank as their vessel sailed closer.

How in the worlds were they going to free their friends?

"We'll be okay, kid." A voice sounded from behind Jake, and when he turned, he found it belonged to a slender man in a well-cut suit, with a silk handkerchief poking out of his top pocket. He looked like he'd just stepped out of a fancy restaurant—the only sign he belonged outdoors at all was his deep suntan—the sort that took years to turn white skin slowly bronze. "I've been in worse pickles before and come through in one piece," the man promised.

Beside him, Jake felt sweaty and bedraggled—they'd hung his own clothes off the back of the ship until they'd dried, but they now crunched with salt whenever he moved. It was worth it to be out of his Curator disguise but still pretty gross.

Oz's fur felt crystallized too—all spikes as he trotted over to press against Jake's bare leg. It was almost as if the Tasmanian tiger sensed Jake's fear and had decided to help him brace against it.

Amelia seemed to be on the same wavelength. "Don't worry, Jake, Richard knows what he's talking about," the pilot said as she squeezed Jake's shoulder. "He's seen a thing or two. This is Richard Halliburton, who once swam the length of the Panama Canal! He and a buddy flew all the way around the world in the *Flying Carpet*!"

"A flying carpet?" Jake gaped at Richard in astonishment. "You mean *this* world, right? The old one doesn't have . . ." He paused, remembering the stories Nana used to tell about her own adventures across the seven continents. Winning an enchanted knife in a card game in Casablanca. Meeting a wolf in Siberia who spoke perfect Russian during every full moon. For the longest time Jake thought the magic in these tales was make-believe. But he *was* standing next to an extinct animal on board a ship that was sailing over a desert, so the idea of flying rugs wasn't *that* absurd. "Or does it?"

Richard laughed. "The *Flying Carpet* was the name of our plane. And don't you listen to Amelia—nobody outdoes her in the air."

"HOLD ON TIGHT!" Johann bellowed from the stern, and sailors dashed all over the *Lost Ship*, hauling on ropes and bracing themselves in position.

"Remember," Raleigh called from beside Johann, "no hesitation! We grab them, we're gone!"

"We're all over this," promised Amelia, wrapping an arm around Jake to help hold him in place, grabbing the gunwale on either side of him. "We grab them, we're gone!"

"We grab them, we're gone," Jake echoed, eyes locked on the cluster of white-clad figures swirling around the gold mine entrance. He could see glimpses of others behind them, a hand flung up in what might be a wave— was that one of the explorers? Did he dare to hope it was Marisol?

Oz wove between his legs, steadying himself as much as Jake. They both needed to be anchored. The Spanish galleon was moving with such speed that Jake was beginning to wonder if the ship *could* stop in time. Clearly the Curators were thinking the same thing. As the *Lost Ship* soared closer, closer, closer, hurtling toward the crowd— Jake saw the exact moment the officials realized the vessel might cut a course straight through them, a blizzard of white suits springing into action as they rushed this way and that.

"Steady!" Johann raised his voice over the flapping of the sails, the thud and hiss of the sand underneath the hull. "Steady . . ."

"Hold on!" Richard shouted, and he, Amelia, and Jake clung to the rail as the ship swung into the same wild move Jake had seen from the ground only hours before— the sailors abruptly let the wind out of the sails as Johann jammed the helm across, and the *Lost Ship* screeched to a halt side-on to the gold mine entrance, sending up a huge wave of red dune sand over the Curators.

"Over we go!" Amelia shouted, climbing up onto the side and jumping, with Richard a moment behind her— they sent up clouds of sand where they landed and rolled straight down the dune toward the gold mine.

Jake scrambled to follow as Raleigh jumped, and Minjun too, the ex-Curator landing neatly and setting off for the battle at a run. There were dozens of rebels leaping from the ship now, and the wood was rough beneath Jake's hands as he grabbed it, then planted one foot and . . .

. . . launched!

The world was right way up, then upside down, then right way up, then upside down, the dark blue of the sky and the red of the sand flashing past as he rolled down the dune. He came to rest on his back, staring up at the endless desert sky, then scrambled up to join the fray.

The Curators were valiantly trying to bring order to the situation, flourishing clipboards and shouting directions, the wave of rebels crashing over them like a chaotic sea. He could hear the shouts and cries on both sides as he hurtled down the dune, feet sinking into the sand with each step. Their voices mingled together like a flock of seagulls all screaming for snacks.

"—can't possibly have filled out the proper application to—"

"—freedom for all!"

"—restricted area and—"

Then he was in the midst of them, pushing his way past white-clad bodies and adults wrestling in the sand, ducking under a frying pan turned into a weapon, while a monocle whipped overhead like some cowboy's lasso.

"JAKE!"

Jake froze. A clipboard that would've caught him

straight in the face whistled past his ear instead.

Could it be? Was he hearing things?

The voice that called out his name sounded like backyard summer barbecues at Nana's house and jokes over FaceTime and sweet tea brewed with lemons the color of sunshine.

It sounded like Marisol.

Her shout—if it was indeed hers—came from the back of the fight, near the entrance to the mine! Jake wove through the combatants, leaping when they lunged, diving when they dodged. There were more rebels than Curators, but the Curators were far more organized, and it seemed some of their pens really were mightier than swords.

Then Raleigh ran past him in pursuit of a tall, thin Curator, and Jake grabbed for the explorer's coat, nearly getting yanked off his feet before Raleigh skidded to a stop.

"This way!" Jake shouted. "Near the mine entrance!"

"Right you are!" Raleigh bellowed back, and the two of them fought their way through together, tearing free of grabbing hands and suddenly bursting out the back of the main scrimmage to where the explorers stood, holding out their hands as Min-jun hurried along the row, unknotting a long and strangely sentient piece of rope that bound all of the prisoners together.

At the end stood Marisol!

Jake hadn't realized how much he'd hoped to find his cousin here until he did. She broke out into a crescent moon smile, her brown eyes beaming. Sand swirled around his heels as he rushed over and helped free her wrists from the rope.

"Mari! You're here!"

"¡Buenas noches, Primo!" Marisol squealed and threw herself at Jake, her arms wrapped around his neck. "Oh, Jake, I was so worried about you!"

"About *me*?" he protested. "But we're rescuing *you*!"

"About time," said another voice—a familiar voice. But it wasn't possible . . . was it? Jake looked over Marisol's shoulder, and there stood his cousin Victor, arms folded across his chest.

Jake's jaw dropped. Several grains of sand slipped into his mouth. "Victor?"

"That *is* my name."

And this was definitely his other cousin. No one else could perfect the *I'm-a-year-and-a-half-older-than-you* tone during the heat of a clipboard battle. Victor watched the surrounding fight with grim amusement. As if it were one of the video games he owned but never let Jake play.

"But . . ." Now, suddenly, *Jake* was the one feeling possessive. The World Between Blinks had been a secret for so long—just between him and Hazel and Christopher and Marisol. "What are you doing here?"

"I was teaching a Curator how to level-up in Candy Crush, and it all went downhill from there. Oh, you mean what am I doing here in the World? Yeah, I have no idea—"

"He got lost in his phone," Marisol added in a low voice. "I think that's what happened, anyway. He was walking behind me and followed me through the Unknown without knowing it."

Percy shook his wrists as Min-jun unraveled the last of the rope and sized up the fight raging around them. "What say we conclude the explanations later, chaps?" he said. "Good to see you, Jake, Raleigh, Min-jun. Shall we beat the hastiest of retreats and regroup, as it were?"

"Not so fast, Colonel Fawcett." The voice was a whip-crack, and in the middle of the desert it still sent a sliver of ice straight down Jake's spine. He broke away from Marisol to swing around, and there she stood, clipboard at the ready, her white uniform spattered with sand that matched her brilliant, frazzled hair.

Red Bun.

Victor rolled his eyes. "Seriously, Karen, not now. We're leaving."

"*Karen?*" Jake choked. It didn't seem possible that the formidable Red Bun actually had a name.

"And you, Min-jun," she said coldly, turning her gaze

100

on their ally. "You are a traitor. You were never worthy of your monocle."

Min-jun drew himself up straighter, and quiet Naomi rested a hand on his shoulder, as if to say *you're not alone*. "I find," said Min-jun with great dignity, "that I see more clearly without my monocle than I ever did with it."

"You have nowhere to go," Red Bun—uh, Karen, apparently—said, glaring at them. "There is nowhere you can hide. You will be found, and you will be cataloged."

Jake knew they were probably supposed to make a big speech in reply, tell her they were going to stand up for everyone's freedom, that the World Between Blinks was beautiful when it was disorganized, and he could see Percy drawing himself up with a breath, readying to do exactly that.

But Jake had a much better idea. He grabbed Marisol's hand and pointed at the ship, which was anchored in the fires of the swiftly setting sun. "RUN!"

As one, the explorers, the visitors, and Min-jun broke for freedom, and all around them the shout was taken up.

"Rebels, retreat!"

"To the *Lost Ship*!"

"The rescue is all wrapped up!"

The Curators suddenly found themselves with nobody left to fight, as the rebels turned for the dune and the *Lost Ship*, where Johann and his sailors were already hauling in the sails.

A long voice rang out behind them. "Thank-you-for-interacting-today-with-members-of-our-Curator-staff! We-appreciate-your-time! Please-rate-your-customer-satisfaction-on-a-scale-of-one-to-OOF!"

"Shut up, Erik!" Karen snapped.

By then the rebels were scrambling up nets slung over the side of the *Lost Ship*, and with a creak of timbers she was underway—Jake landed in a heap on the deck, all tangled up with Richard Halliburton, Amelia, Marisol, and Victor.

"Jake, why do you smell like fish?" Victor asked. "Es asqueroso. And is this boat on skis? Where is it taking us?"

"Because I arrived in the sea and we didn't have time to do laundry on the way to rescue you." Jake spoke slowly, trying to be patient with his older cousin's onslaught of questions. It was hard. Especially when he imagined how Victor might answer if their roles were reversed. "And yes, this boat is on skis, and . . . I have no idea where it's taking us."

"Halliburton, good to see you," Jack Fawcett said cheerfully as Raleigh pulled him to his feet. "Glad to see you've joined the cause."

"Of course!" Richard replied while readjusting a pocket square that had been turned into more of a trapezoid during battle. "When did I ever let anybody fence me in? You know, I once—"

"And I'll bet it was amazing," said Amelia, cutting off what was clearly going to be a long-winded story. "We've set course for Queen Nefertiti's court. She'll give us safe haven. Victor, did you say your name was? Any friend of Marisol's and Jake's is a friend of mine. I'm Amelia Earhart."

Victor gaped—his mouth open and speechless.

Jake wished his phone was still working, so he could take a picture and make this moment his wallpaper. He'd never seen his older cousin look so shocked before.

"Just wait until Victor sees a dinosaur," Marisol whispered to Jake.

At that exact moment, Oz came skidding across the deck. Not quite a dinosaur, but not nearly a dog either. The way the Tasmanian tiger bounded toward Marisol— his entire striped back half trembling—reminded Jake of a kangaroo.

"OZ!" Marisol threw her arms over the thylacine's neck, laughing as he licked every available inch of her face.

It was good to be back.

They sailed into the night, until the sky was black and the dunes were only shapes where stars were not. The

Lost Ship plowed forward, as if these sandy hills were nothing more than waves. It felt strange, traveling on a ship but not on the ocean. What should have been a nice lullaby of water was a razor-*hiss* of sand, and Jake kept missing the smell of salt as he joined Marisol and Oz near the prow.

The three of them made a funny figurehead as they sat exchanging tales of their return. Marisol giggled when Jake described Oz in the Melbourne Museum, gasped when he told her about Curator Greg asking for an extra pen. Her own run-ins with the World's official organizers made all his hairs stand on end.

"The World is so different from last time," his cousin said as she looked out at the ever-stretching desert, "and I think—I think maybe we're to blame. We broke so many of the Curators' rules trying to help Christopher and Hazel return to the old world."

More than rules . . . Jake bit his lip, remembering the shelves of shattered hourglasses after his encounter with the Administrator. The head Curator hadn't just been angry. He was the very definition of fury—trembling fists and blotchy neck and rage in every word.

"I think you're right," he told Marisol.

"The rules were silly before, but now they're suffocating. Did you hear what happened to the Amazon rainforest? Percy said it's been torn apart and replanted.

All in rows, like a vegetable garden."

"That's horrible." Even though there was a very hot wind gusting past, Jake shivered. "Portus was awful too," he recalled. "It wasn't *moving* like it was last time—so many shops were closed down and all the ships were just sitting there."

"I saw that from the hot-air balloon." Marisol nodded.

They sat in an island of lantern light, and there were other similar spots behind them, where Jake could see their friends huddled on deck, playing a board game that had been cobbled together by all sorts of lost pieces. It looked like some sort of mash-up of Candy Land and Mouse Trap and Scrabble. Amelia was consoling Victor, who appeared to be losing—sorely. Herr Leichhardt was slipping all of the *L* Scrabble pieces into his pocket.

"Mari, we can't leave them like this."

"No." His cousin glanced at Ludwig. "We can't."

"Do you think you can help find the Rocket with your magnet fingers?" Jake asked.

"I can try." She didn't sound convinced. "It—it might be hard since I don't even know what this secret weapon *is*. It helps if I can envision what I'm looking for. Maybe someone at Nefertiti's court knows what it looks like. . . ." She drifted off, watching the crew laugh over their game. "It's nice to be back, isn't it? I mean, apart from the whole rebellion against the Administrator thing."

"I know," Jake agreed. "I just can't believe *Victor* is here."

"It hasn't been that bad," Marisol admitted. "It's been kind of good, actually. He hasn't teased me about anything since we came through the Unknown. Well, he *did* compare me to khaki pants, but that's because he was trying to protect me from the Curators."

"He said I smelled like fish."

"You *do*," Marisol pointed out.

On the other side of the deck, the Mouse Trap cage slammed down on Amelia's stack of vowels. More laughter erupted, lighting up Jake's insides like a lantern flame. Again he wished his phone was working—so he could record the sound and replay it during darker, lonelier nights.

"Lights ahoy!" Someone called out behind them, and for a moment Jake was afraid that the Curators had found a way to chase them, but no, the twinkling was coming from the horizon ahead. "We're five minutes out from Amarna!" Johann announced to his crew. "Prepare to dock!"

Amarna: an ancient Egyptian city swallowed by the Sahara. Sand swamped its buildings in the World Between Blinks too, so that the *Lost Ship* was able to glide right between a pair of columns covered in bright hieroglyphics. A sphinx statue gave Jake and Marisol a solemn stare as they disembarked with the rest of the crew. Like

Portus, this place had a hollowed out, abandoned feeling, but it wasn't because of the Curators. In fact, it had more to do with the clipboards that had been hung from pillars with CAUTION tape. There were dozens of them, clattering together like strange wind chimes. Bold handwriting defaced their documents:

PAPERWORK WILL BE PUNISHED
FILE AND FAIL
ALPHABETIZE AT YOUR OWN RISK

"Her Majesty certainly knows how to inspire fear, I'll give her that!" Amelia landed with both boots in the sand. "Queen Nefertiti banished the Curators from the premises when they tried taking over her Amber Room to repair the crack in the Unknown. They've been too terrified to come back."

Jake could imagine. He'd been scared too, the first time he'd met the queen. Nefertiti was the type of person who didn't have to yell to be loud, who seemed taller than she really was, who made every head turn and every knee bend. If anyone was a match for the Administrator, it was her.

Victor appeared next to them with a dramatic huff. "Wait, so Queen Nefertiti *is* actually helping the resistance?"

A frown flickered over Marisol's face—there and gone. Jake didn't miss it.

"Helping?" Amelia guffawed, her auburn curls bouncing. "She's our leader! Her court is the heart of the resistance. We'll be safe here!"

Jake hoped she was right.

7

MARISOL

MARISOL DID NOT SLEEP WELL THAT NIGHT.

It wasn't for lack of comfort. The bedchamber was just as luxurious as she remembered: silk sheets, rugs so thick your toes disappeared when you walked on them, and incense that smelled like moonlight shining on blooming jasmine. She'd scrubbed off all the prison grime using water from the big, beaten-bronze bowl, and her belly was filled with silphium-seasoned meat and juicy Taliaferro apples from a platter one of the servants had brought up.

Usually after a good meal, her head hit the pillow and her dreams came easy. But now she tossed and turned, trying to forget Karen's warning: *If Queen Nefertiti tries to help you, the Administrator will add her name to the Top Ten Most Wanted Rebels list.*

Had she and Victor accidentally betrayed the resistance?

By claiming the queen's friendship, would they lead

Red Bun and the other Curators straight here?

These thoughts twisted Marisol up in the silky sheets, so she kicked them off and crept to the window instead. It showed the desert: all darkness before dawn. She searched for any flickers, any sign her fears might be right, but there was nothing.

It was the same the next hour.

And the next.

And the next.

Until a silver-lavender light began creeping across the horizon and the courtyard below stirred with morning chores. Servants carried boxes of Mayflower Donuts. A plucky rooster crowed louder than any iPhone alarm. Amelia strolled to Amarna's outskirts to check on her plane—the *Flying Laboratory*. There were other aircraft parked by the landing strip too. It made sense that so many pilots would join the resistance after having their skies stolen from them.

Marisol scanned the distance one more time. There was still no sign of the Curators, and she tried to let out her breath. Relax. *Be calm on the route. Eyes ahead, don't look back.* Instead of worrying about being followed, she needed to start thinking about what they should chase.

"The Rocket."

What was this weapon? Where had it come from? How could it defeat the Administrator?

Marisol started asking these questions over breakfast, moving from table to table in the large dining hall. The place was the most crowded she'd ever seen, both with old friends and new acquaintances. Australian prime minister Harold Holt and Alexander Helios, son of Cleopatra, were in their old seats, while the garum vendor from Ostia Antica sat next to them, drizzling the pungent fish sauce all over his donuts. Oz sat attentively at the man's feet.

Bessie Hyde—the woman they'd met on the *Baychimo* on their way to the underwater cities—sat across the table with her husband, Glen. Both gave Marisol a friendly *cheers* motion with their coffee cups.

None of them had the answers Marisol wanted.

"The Rocket?" Alexander Helios repeated. "Hmm. No. Sorry. I've never heard of it. It belonged to the Administrator, you say?"

"I'm not sure," Marisol replied. "Possibly."

"Well, if it did, it would have arrived here in the last century or so," he said. "That's how long the Administrator's been here."

Marisol paused and blinked. She'd never considered where the Administrator had come from or when. "What was it like before that?"

"Chaos," said the garum vendor cheerfully. "Everything everywhere. Remember the Great String Entanglement of five hundred years ago?"

"Who could forget?" Alexander Helios nodded, then added, "Things were very confusing. It didn't help that there were no monocles . . . or language charms, for that matter! The Administrator was the first person who figured out how to use the Unknown's magic so we could communicate with each other." The boy tapped at the necklace he was wearing. "He united us with these tiny scrolls."

"The Administrator invented the language charm?" Marisol glanced down at her own small scroll. It was hard to imagine what the World would be like without these charms. There were so many people from so many different places and time periods. . . . Why, right now, Alexander Helios was probably speaking Greek!

The boy went on. "The Administrator did a lot of great things. He opened up the underwater cities with bubbler charms. He established residential zones and found ways to keep predators out. Suddenly we could sleep much better at night, knowing a saber-toothed tiger wouldn't curl up in bed next to us! That actually happened to me once."

"Me too!" The garum vendor interjected. "Except it wasn't a bed, it was a lake. And it wasn't a saber-toothed tiger. It was a thirty-nine-foot crocodile."

"You stopped to measure it?" Marisol shuddered, thinking of the smaller crocodiles she'd seen on the banks of the Amazon back home. No way would she pause to get out a measuring tape. "Sounds like something a Curator would do!"

"None of us really minded the Curators before now," Alexander Helios said. "In fact, we were so pleased about how the Administrator had changed this World that we asked him to be king a few decades back. . . . Nefertiti has always been sore about that."

"It's a good thing he said no!" Bessie Hyde said over her coffee.

"He did?" Marisol asked.

"He said he was too busy administrating," Alexander Helios explained. "And he *has* been busy."

"But these days," said Bessie Hyde, "the Administrator has gone from keeping people happy, healthy, and safe to putting everyone in their place and on their shelf like a museum exhibit."

"Which is why we need the Rocket," Marisol replied. "It's the one thing that might stop him."

"Maybe it's the Tybee Island bomb," suggested Harold Holt. "Did you know the US Air Force simply *lost* one of its nuclear weapons off the coast of Georgia? You'd think they'd be more careful."

"You'd think!" Bessie agreed.

"I never found any bombs in my stash." This from the scavenger with the colander on her head. She was still wearing the perforated bowl, and donut crumbs covered her fingerless gloves while she ate. "Found plenty of broken toy rockets, though. Kids shoot them off into the Unknown all the time. Maybe you're looking for one of those!"

Marisol doubted this. How could they beat the Administrator with a toy? She hoped the Rocket wasn't a nuclear bomb either. While the Curators had made the World joyless, using a weapon like that would certainly make everything worse.

"¡Buenos días!" Jake's lemon-bright hair was still mussed from his pillow when he appeared. "What did I miss?" If he had waited for Marisol to answer, he might've learned that the donut he grabbed was covered in fish sauce. He took a big bite of the pastry instead. "Ack! That is NOT caramel—"

"No!" interjected the Ostia Antica vendor. "It's better! The best fish sauce your discontinued currency can buy."

Jake's face twisted. Clearly her primo didn't want to offend the merchant, so he swallowed and tucked the rest of the donut behind his back. "It's . . . something."

"It's an acquired taste." Alexander Helios pushed a box of non-fishy donuts toward Jake.

"I was asking around about the Rocket," Marisol started to explain, "but so far no one seems to know anything—"

"Ooh, breakfast! What are we eating, Primo?" Victor appeared, plucking the garum donut from Jake's hands and taking a giant, oldest-cousin, first-dibs bite.

Marisol smiled as her brother spluttered.

Oz did too, for a different reason. The thylacine did a happy dance as the rest of the pastry rained to the floor, his striped fur turning into a blur.

"Glad someone's enjoying it." Victor brushed off his hands. "I can see why these donuts went extinct."

Marisol glanced at the garum vendor—afraid that the man's feelings might be hurt—but the stall keeper shrugged and went back to eating his own stash.

Harold Holt poured Victor a steaming cup of coffee. "This'll help with the taste." Then the prime minister turned toward Marisol. "As for your predicament, if anyone knows more about this rocket you're searching for it's Queen Nefertiti. She's been in this World longer than most. She has ways of knowing its secrets."

The last time Marisol and Jake had feasted here, the queen had sat at the head of the center table. The golden snake on her crown had slithered beneath the torchlight, while her blue wig rippled. She'd looked fearsome. And legendary.

Now the seat was empty.

"Where is she?" Marisol asked.

"I believe I saw her up on one of the Hadrian's Wall turrets," Glen Hyde offered. "Tower 37A maybe? Or was it 62B? Anyway, she's getting ready to give a speech to rally the resistance. A big *rah-rah* pep talk. We're supposed to gather in the Old Summer Palace gardens in five minutes to listen."

"Which means we should get going!" Bessie stood. "You kids can come with us and talk to Queen Nefertiti afterward!"

Chairs began scraping all around the high-pillared hall. Donuts got tucked into pockets. Final swigs of coffee were taken. Resistance members swept toward the exit. Marisol's heart started to swell as she got caught up in the crowd—there were so *many* rebels! Roman centurions marched next to Vikings. Knights in shining armor walked beside ladies in ball gowns. There was a woman in a headscarf, who Marisol recognized from the *Lost Ship*, only now she had several cat-sized dinosaurs following her. Behind them trailed a man playing a trumpet. Behind him, a team of sled dogs howled along to the notes.

How could the Curators compete with such wonderful chaos?

Losing this World to the Administrator suddenly felt much less likely, when Marisol joined the rest of the resistance in the garden. They stood around lotus-covered ponds, craning their necks for a look at Queen Nefertiti.

Jake paused next to her. "This could be an army, couldn't it?"

"I think some of it already is!" Marisol recognized scouts from the Lost Army of Cambyses.

"Did you see that woolly mammoth over there? And those redcoats?" Jake said excitedly. "The Curators don't stand a chance!"

She hoped he was right. Maybe they wouldn't even *need* the Rocket to win, which would be fantastic, considering that the weapon remained so mysterious. Marisol hadn't tried using her magnet fingers yet, but she doubted that a rumor was enough to search with. Maybe Queen Nefertiti would know more. . . .

"Welcome, friends and former foes, to the last free zone in the World Between Blinks!" Her Majesty's voice boomed across the gardens, followed by a reverent hush. Nefertiti stood at the top of a nearby turret. If she hadn't been moving, the queen could've been one of the statues that decorated the royal complex. Sphinx-like. A deity unto herself. "I am Neferuaten Nefertiti, Great of Praises, Lady of Grace, Sweet of Love, Most Powerful Queen in the Land of the Lost."

Victor leaned over, close enough for his hoodie strings to tap Marisol's face. "Did she just say she was Nefertiti?"

"SHH!" she hissed, annoyed.

The queen's speech began in earnest. "I see a World standing before me. I see men and women and children and animals. I see living, breathing history. But the

117

Curators . . . when the Curators look at you, they see a museum. They see dates and designations and Dewey decimal labels."

Marisol's brother kept whispering in her ear. "Do you actually understand what she's saying? Or are you just pretending?"

Oh! She glanced at Victor's neck. There was no scroll there. No necklace at all. He'd never managed to get a language charm of his own. His Unknown magic must be wearing off, which meant he was hearing Nefertiti speak in . . . whatever language she spoke. Ancient Egyptian, maybe?

Again, it struck her, how much the Administrator *had* helped this World.

"You need a language charm to interpret for you." Marisol pulled out her scroll to show him. The chain was long enough to fit over two heads. "You can share mine. Por ahora."

He bent down and slipped his head through.

"If the Curators had their way, they would encase this place in glass!" Nefertiti swept an arm over the grounds. "They'd take our homes and turn them into archives! They'd keep us trapped, imprisoned inside their first impressions, kept forever exactly as we were, like paintings, caught in a single moment! We would not be free to become the people we want to be!"

"Whoa!" Victor had very bad coffee breath, laced

with hints of garum. "THIS IS SO MUCH BETTER THAN GOOGLE TRANSLATE!"

"I am an ancient Egyptian and I am a queen, but I am also a citizen of the World Between Blinks, and I will not stand by as this Administrator and his Curator cronies strangle it with red tape. We will drive them from the ever-stretching desert, as we did from Amarna. We shall take Portus, and reseize the seas! We will turn the Amazon into a rainforest again!"

"Huzzah!" Percy Fawcett shouted, waving his hat in the air.

Raleigh and Jack joined him.

The cheers only made Nefertiti's voice more brazen. Each one of her words was an ember—bright and searing. "We will not stop until their zones are unraveled and their ledgers are turned to ash!"

Marisol frowned. Burning books was never a good thing. Besides, hadn't Christopher's experiments proved how important the ledgers were? The Curators' pages somehow tapped into Unknown magic—they could control who entered and left the World. Destroying them would be a big mistake. It would trap her and Jake and Victor here too. . . .

She glanced over at her cousin. He also had a frown on his face. "But if Queen Nefertiti gets rid of the residential zones, what happens with the T-rexes?" he reasoned. "Aren't the Curators the only thing keeping the dangerous animals away from people?"

Jake had a point . . . but the rest of the rebels didn't seem to be thinking about beasts or books. They roared their approval. More hats flew into the air. Everyone scattered when a Viking's helmet sailed upward, hurtling back to the ground horns first.

And then something else shifted too. The voices at the edges of the crowd grew louder, swelling to a chorus of . . . of screams?

Marisol swung toward them, rising up on her toes to gaze anxiously out toward the ever-stretching desert, heart pounding as the crowd shifted and moved like a powerful sea, starting to push toward her.

What she saw across the dunes turned her blood into ice.

A sandstorm rolled over the horizon. Its amber clouds were thick, beating the sun into gray.

But Nefertiti stared at the oncoming storm with such ferocity that no one seemed shocked when it stopped. The crowd stilled around Marisol, and the winds died just outside of Amarna's borders, dropping sand back into the desert. The sky reappeared.

And so did a single hot-air balloon.

Its fabric was a bright, glowing green, and as it drew closer and closer, the man inside the basket somehow managed to remind Marisol of both a wizard and a turtle.

Maybe it was his sharp chin? Or his doughy cheeks? His eyebrows certainly looked cursed—unable to stop growing.

"Mari!" Jake grabbed her arm as the balloon drifted to a halt just overhead. "That's the Administrator!"

Marisol's stomach dropped so fast, it felt like she'd swallowed a bowling ball. What was the Curators' boss doing here alone? Why wasn't he afraid to fly over an army who shouted for his demise? The balloon floated just out of the woolly mammoth's reach, hovering a few meters from Queen Nefertiti's tower.

The Administrator lifted a megaphone. The machine screeched with feedback, causing almost everyone in the garden to wince. "A permit has not been granted for this gathering, nor will I issue one! Disperse at once! Return to your designated zones and you will be spared citation."

"So that's the big baddie?" Victor asked. "I'm pretty sure Nefertiti could beat him at arm wrestling."

The queen also looked like she could pop his balloon with a glance. "You have no power here!"

"On the contrary," the Administrator replied. "I've spent my time in the World Between Blinks learning how to control the Unknown. My Curators harness its magic every day. As do I. We understand this place far better than anyone else—under my leadership, the Curators have made a home where before there was only chaos!"

"You think a filing system and some charms can make you a king?" Nefertiti asked.

"A king?" The man shook his head. "No. I never wanted to be a king. I'm an Administrator. I keep things in order so they will never, ever get lost again."

"I am not some curiosity to be shelved! I am a queen, and this world has been my home for over three thousand years. I will not be cowed by a man who has lived a fraction of that time." Nefertiti drew herself tall. "Leave my land or you shall face my wrath!"

Marisol certainly would've been scurrying, had the command been aimed at her, but the Administrator did not move his balloon. He sighed into his megaphone instead.

"I don't want any trouble, and I'd really, truly hoped it would not come to this. I'd rather everyone just follow the rules and go back to where they belong, but you have forced my hand. . . ."

"As you have forced mine!" Nefertiti's pleated gown whirled as she turned to grab a spear from one of her guards.

The weapon was long enough to pierce the Administrator's balloon, and would have, if the man hadn't dropped his megaphone and held up a giant hourglass. The Egyptian queen froze when she read the brass plaque at its base.

"Those . . ." She faltered, confused. "Those are my memories."

Most of the sand sat at the top of the hourglass, which meant that Nefertiti remembered most of her life in the old world. As well as the long, long time she'd spent in the World Between Blinks.

"Not anymore," the Administrator said. He tapped the top of the hourglass. Sand started to fall. "I told you I have power. And I must use it to make an example out of you, Neferuaten Nefertiti. I must take away your memories to keep you from plunging this World into chaos."

The crowd below began to murmur, horrified as grains slipped through the neck of the timepiece faster and faster. Each one represented a memory of Nefertiti's— falling away.

"Oh no!" Jake gasped. "It works in reverse too."

Victor tried to stand on tiptoes for a better view, forgetting he shared Marisol's necklace. She yelped. He slumped back. "What's going on?"

"People's memories start to fade when they stay in the World Between Blinks," she explained. "The hourglasses help keep track of how many memories they've lost. The sand falls at different speeds for different people, no one knows why." Or, at least, they *hadn't*. "Last time Jake restored all of Herr Leichhardt's memories by turning his timepiece upside-down . . . and Christopher did the same for Aunt Hazel."

But when their great-uncle had flipped Hazel's hour-glass, Marisol had felt like she was watching someone's soul get poured back into their body. Light had flooded the nurse's eyes. Her smile grew roots while her memories flowered.

This was the exact opposite.

Nefertiti's stance changed almost at once. Her shoulders slouched. Her neck slumped, as if it suddenly found her crown too heavy. Marisol was too far away from the turret to see the queen's eyes, but the rest of her expression went empty. Over in the green balloon, the Administrator gave Nefertiti's hourglass a few extra taps, until every single grain of sand had fallen.

Until the great queen was gone.

Then the Administrator exchanged the timepiece for his megaphone. It screeched like a hungry vulture when he spoke. "Consider this my first and final warning! If you do not follow my orders and return to your assigned zones by tomorrow evening—that is, within thirty-six hours—you'll meet the same fate as Queen Nefertiti. I will confiscate each and every one of your memories. And we will be watching—one step out of line before that, and I won't hesitate to turn your hourglass early!"

"Okay," Victor relented. "That's definitely a big baddie move."

Marisol wanted to throw up. The Administrator was only here because she and Victor had told Karen that Nefertiti was their strongest ally. It was true. The queen had been. But who was going to stand up to the Curators after this?

The crowd had been stunned back to whispers:

"Did he just—"

"What happened?"

"Wait, the Curators are the ones stealing our memories?"

"Knowing them, they'd say *saving*!"

"Shh! Don't say that too loudly. You could be next!"

The Administrator picked up a mason jar and unscrewed its lid. Sand whipped throughout the garden, lifting the green balloon, stripping leaves from trees, and causing everyone to cover their face. By the time things were clear enough to see again, the leader of the Curators had disappeared.

Queen Nefertiti had too—mostly. She was still standing on the turret. Her wig had blown off with the gust and she made no move to retrieve it. There was a slight frown on her face as she stared at the rebels below. This reminded Marisol of how Herr Leichhardt had looked in the cell, carving all of those almost *L*s.

Oh . . . she realized, feeling sicker. The Administrator must have stolen all the German explorer's memories too, as punishment for helping her and Jake the first time around. This made Marisol sad, but mostly it made her angry—not with hot screaming rage but with a feeling that pumped gold through her heart. Like armor.

Like hope.

She turned to her cousin.

He was already looking at her, the same determination shining on his face.

"Are you thinking what I'm thinking?" Marisol asked.

Jake nodded.

"¿Qué?" Victor wondered. "What are you two thinking?"

"We need to defeat the Administrator once and for all." Marisol cracked her knuckles. Her *magnet fingers*. "We need to find the Rocket."

8

JAKE

IT WAS TIME FOR AN EMERGENCY MEETING.

The Amber Room provided the perfect place to regroup. Thousands of amber pieces—all puzzled together—winked at Jake when he walked through the white double doors. Marisol, Oz, and Victor followed, along with the five explorers. Richard Halliburton and Min-jun were already sitting at a long table, and as Jake went to join them, he tried not to look at the largest chair. Vacant—like Queen Nefertiti's eyes. Empty—like the ruler's smile had been when Johann had ushered her away to a safe, quiet place.

The sight made Jake feel sick.

Finding a place at the table now, he noticed there was something a little wobbly about the walls of the Amber Room too. It wasn't just because of the candles flickering in their sconces—this whole place had vanished when Christopher had sent it back to the old world with a single stroke of his pen. He'd crossed the Amber Room's entry out of the Curators' ledger, crossing the room itself out of the World Between Blinks. After Jake and Marisol had asked their great-uncle to return the room to Nefertiti's court, Christopher had called it back here, but the parquet floors and red-gold walls didn't feel as *solid* as they had before. Sometimes . . . well, they almost seemed like they shimmered, and then settled again. Was that what the Curators had been investigating before Nefertiti drove them out?

Jake didn't have much time to wonder.

As the rest of the group got themselves seated, Amelia hurried up with the Australian prime minister Harold Holt. "I thought Harold might have managed a crisis or two in his time," she said as the two of them pulled up chairs. "We need all the smarts we can get right now."

Everyone exploded into talk at once.

"We've only got a day and a half until he wipes our memories if we're not—"

"My houseplants will never forgive me if I forget to water them—"

"How are we going to run a rebellion from different zones?"

"Have you *seen* my zone?"

"Don't you understand? There *is* no rebellion. Not if the Administrator can turn us into living ghosts whenever he wants!"

"But ghosts have memories, don't they? Isn't that why they haunt things—"

It was the prime minister who raised his voice above the others. "Quiet and calm, my friends, QUIET AND CALM!"

After a long moment the chatter died away, reducing in volume like someone was turning down the radio, and then clicking off entirely.

"We must make decisions with calm heads," Harold continued. "We have a great deal of experience in this room, and between us we have weathered many crises, from the wildest of storms to conversations requiring the utmost delicacy. Let us use this to our advantage."

"You're right, of course," said Percy, turning to the children. "First things first, let's try the reason we brought you here. Marisol, is there any chance your magnet fingers can find the Rocket? It's our one chance at freedom, and it's well and truly lost, even in a world of lost things."

"Her *what* fingers?" Victor asked, his brows lifting. "¿Magnéticos? Are you actually a futuristic robot and you never told me, Mari?"

"No!" Jake was pretty sure this counted as *teasing*, and

he couldn't help but feel defensive on Marisol's behalf. "She's more like a superhero! Her power is that she can find anything lost."

"Almost anything," Marisol corrected, her brow creasing, her voice edged with uncertainty.

"Oh." Victor's expression was flatter than a Coke bottle left open overnight. "I thought you meant like, actual magnets. That would be way cooler. Mari just finds stuff because she's lucky—"

"No," Jake broke in again. Even though he'd only known about Marisol's gifts since his last trip here, he was annoyed at Victor for being so dismissive. "Nana had magnet fingers too. She used them to find windows into the World Between Blinks so she could communicate with Christopher. Like that cave in Iceland, where she met the elf folk. Or that bazaar in Tehran, where she found a hidden alleyway where the merchants sold magic lamps. Or that forest in Virginia, where she waved hello to Bigfoot!"

"But . . ." His older cousin glanced around the table, as if expecting Amelia Earhart to jump in and say that Bigfoot didn't exist. "I thought those were just stories."

"They *were* stories," Marisol said softly, "but I think a lot of what Nana told us was true. Jake's right. I inherited our grandmother's gift for finding things. I never told you about it before because I knew you wouldn't believe me."

130

Victor sat for a moment, watching Marisol. There was a gleam in his brown eyes that made it seem as if he were reading an entry through a monocle—absorbing new information, seeing his sister in a totally different light.

"So, *can* you find the Rocket with your fingers?" he asked.

"I want to. But . . ."

Marisol bit her lip and looked down at her hands. Jake was glad she did, because the rest of the room was starting to squirm. Percy's own hands were clasping each other until the knuckles whitened in tension. Amelia was holding her breath, and even Min-jun had a doubtful look on his face.

"Can anyone tell me more about this weapon?" Marisol asked the room. "It helps to know what I'm looking for, if it's far away. At home, I can tell if there's something lost really close by, even if I don't know what it is, but *everything* is lost here. I was going to ask Queen Nefertiti, but . . ."

Jake could see the memory of what had happened to Nefertiti washing over his companions. Walls kept wobbling in the corner of Jake's vision. The rest of the table sat silent. How would they cope, filed away like entries in an encyclopedia, instead of being allowed to grow and learn, to change and explore?

Then Min-jun cleared his throat. "It's a Curator

legend. Something that's whispered around the water-cooler whenever someone gets upset with upper management. I never thought much of it until I was sorting through files to compile my report on the Creaturo Incident. Most of the Administrator's personnel files are redacted—covered in these thick black lines—but there was one scrap of paper in the deepest part of the folder that had been overlooked. *Rocket is the Administrator's greatest weakness*, it said. The rest of the page had been torn off. I showed the top piece to Nefertiti when I first arrived at her court, as proof of my loyalty. She was the one who decided to hunt for the weapon."

"What?" said Victor, blinking around at everyone—it took Jake a moment to realize he didn't have a language charm, and he couldn't understand the Korean that Min-jun was speaking.

Amelia must have figured out the same thing. With a sigh, she leaned in to loop her charm necklace over Victor's head as well, and whispered a translation for the words he'd missed.

Jake, though, was looking at the former Curator with a sinking heart. "That's it? Office gossip and a scrap of paper?"

Would it be enough for Marisol's magnet fingers?

Would they get incredibly lucky?

"Okay." Marisol closed her eyes, straightening her

back and taking a deep breath. "Here goes nothing."

Everyone else *held* their breath as she lifted her hands, holding them out in front of her. Her breathing slowed, and she wiggled her fingers as if she were playing an invisible piano.

After a few scales she pushed up from her chair to stand, and Jake's heart thumped harder in his chest. Was she sensing something? He reached across to pull her chair away, and she turned in a full circle, moving slowly, hesitating several times before she continued.

When she was back where she began, she opened her eyes . . . and her shoulders slumped.

"It's here," she said. Jake could tell from the way her head dropped that she did not mean the palace. "I *know* the Rocket is here. It's like hearing an echo, but not knowing where it came from. It's somewhere in the World, but I just can't find it without knowing more details. I'm sorry."

Her voice cracked on the last word. Jake pushed her chair back in so she could thump down on it, and he could wrap an arm around her shoulders, squeezing her tight.

"None of that," said Richard. "We know now that we're not just hunting for a story some angry Curator made up. That's a start!"

"Absolutely right," Percy agreed briskly. "It's not just

a rumor, it's reality. And it's somewhere on this side of the Unknown! Most encouraging."

"Knowing it's real is more than we had before," Amelia agreed.

"Together, we'll find a way," Harold promised.

Victor didn't say anything encouraging, though he didn't say anything mean about Marisol's magnet fingers either. He kept watching his sister with a strange expression. It wasn't the *faraway* look that Christopher had described, but something much closer. Like noticing a door was made of glass just before you were going to try to walk through it.

Jake gave Marisol one more squeeze, then he spoke. "So we need to find someone who knows what the Rocket is. Or knows more about it than we do, anyway."

"Who?" His cousin let out a frustrated sob. "Karen?"

"No." Min-jun shook his head. "Not Karen. We don't just need a Curator. We need someone who knows everything *about* the Curators. Someone who spent years and years and years studying them. Someone daring enough to impersonate them . . ."

"Great-Uncle Christopher!" Jake and Marisol shouted in unison.

The ex-Curator gave a quick nod. "Who knows? He might even be the person who tore out that page about the Rocket. It wouldn't be the first time he's vandalized Curator paperwork."

As if on cue, Amelia pulled the ledger scrap out of her leather jacket. "We could write down his name and call him back here to help. . . ."

Jake pictured Christopher's face as he'd watched his great-nephew and Oz fading into the World Between Blinks. The rush of fear, the way he'd tried to stop Jake going by grabbing his arm so tight. It made sense. He hadn't just spent decades learning about Curators because he wanted a white suit. Christopher had spent all of those years trying to escape this place.

Dragging him back now—when he was at the top of the Most Wanted list—would be cruel.

"We shouldn't write Christopher's name," he said. "But . . ."

"But what?" Amelia prodded.

Oz was nudging him too, pressing his nose against Jake's arm. The Tasmanian tiger had been doing the same thing when they slipped through the Unknown together. The rest of that memory was settling in Jake now—not just the squeeze of his great-uncle's hand or the fear in his voice or the chilly silver of his Illuminator, but what he'd said. "I think there's a way to write *to* Christopher. He told me he'd be there for me, just like Lucy—our nana—was."

"What? You mean they were, like, interdimensional pen pals?" Victor asked, eyebrows lifting. "How? Is there a post office around here?"

Min-jun shook his head. "No."

"Not in the traditional sense," Richard Halliburton said. "But there is a spot down the coast where lost letters wash up. . . . It's a glorious place! There are so many messages in bottles that the ocean sounds like it's singing with every wave, and the eel-mails make everything glow."

"*Eel*-mails?" Victor's eyebrows rose even higher.

Richard nodded. "Oh, yes. They're the most marvelous things—made of light! I'm assuming that's why they got named after electric eels."

A jaunty grin broke out on Victor's face. "I think you mean—"

"This place where lost messages wash up!" Jake interrupted so his older cousin wouldn't waste time trying to explain electronic mail to a man who was born before most houses had telephones. "Is it a cove?"

"You could call it that," Richard said. "Or a bay, I suppose. It's rather large."

Find the cove! This had to be what Christopher was talking about. A bay where lost messages washed up? Maybe there was a way to write back. . . .

"I think we might be able to communicate with Christopher at this cove," he explained to the table. "Can you take us there, Richard?"

"Sure," the old explorer said, "but it's a long way from Amarna. We'll need a pilot who's willing to fly deep into Curator territory."

A pilot who was willing to get their memory erased for defying the Administrator. That's what Richard really meant. Amelia must have known this too, but she just smiled and raised her hand. "Count me and the *Flying Laboratory* in! We'll fly you kids to this cove."

"Hold on!" Harold Holt held up his own palm, a look of concern creasing his face. "I'm not sure it's safe to send you children so far from Nefertiti's palace."

"You don't think it's too late to be talking about safety?" Victor asked, raising his brows. "In case you haven't noticed, we're in another world, and my sister just got locked up in jail!"

"We've outsmarted the Administrator before," Marisol pointed out.

"And anyway, it *has* to be us," Jake said. "Me and Marisol and Victor. We're the only ones who haven't been cataloged. The Administrator said they'll be tracking everyone else."

"Cataloged?" Victor muttered, looking alarmed.

"He's right," Marisol agreed. "You need to act like you're getting ready to go to your zones, like he beat you. And if it takes longer than a day and a half, you have to *be* in your zones, or . . ."

137

She didn't have to finish. They all knew what would happen otherwise.

"What about their hourglasses?" asked Percy, frowning. "Amelia, you still have them?"

"Safely stashed in the *Flying Laboratory*," she promised. Jake had stolen his and Marisol's hourglasses from the Great Library of Alexandria last time, before they left—it seemed they'd gone to Amelia for safekeeping. "And the Administrator is pretty busy right now, so it'll take him a while to make one for Victor."

"Then we should get moving." Marisol pushed to her feet. "We only have until tomorrow night to find the Rocket. There's no time to waste!"

It didn't take long to gather up everything they needed—backpacks from a pile of lost luggage, some food, and extra clothes. Jack and Raleigh tracked down a language charm for Victor, and then far more solemnly, they handed over six feather charms to the three children, Amelia, Richard, and Oz.

"What are these for?" Victor asked as he threaded his onto his new necklace, beside a bubbler and a small scroll.

"They're in case the Administrator flips my hourglass," Amelia said quietly. "Feather charms help you float for a while. It's a lot harder to control than a plane, and you're out in the cold air, so my way of flying is always better. But the Administrator knows I'm here, and he has to know I'm a good transport option. If he sees the *Flying Laboratory* heading in the wrong direction, or he just decides not to risk it . . . well, at least we can float down."

The thought sent Jake's stomach plummeting as he knelt silently to thread Oz's feather onto his collar. "We should find another way there," he said. "We can't risk them seeing you fly in the wrong direction."

"No time," said Amelia.

"This is a risk worth taking," Richard added. "If we don't do everything we can to beat the Administrator, we'll never have another adventure again. And if we fight and lose . . . well, at least this will have been one last adventure."

"We won't lose," Marisol vowed. Jake wished he felt half as confident as she sounded.

"Indeed we won't," Richard agreed. "We'll hang onto our memories, and we won't be cooped up in zones. We've learned too much, come so far. That's the thing the Administrator doesn't understand, or doesn't *want* to understand. Put everyone back in their zones, and they'll be exactly the same forever. But everything changes. I'm not the same person I was back home. I used to think some things, say some things that—well, I've learned a lot. That's what happens when you're always exploring.

You learn new lessons."

"Or you fall out of a plane. . . ." Victor muttered under his breath.

"We did that last time," Marisol reminded him. "Jake and I had to jump out of the *Flying Laboratory* into the Amazon. It was great!"

Jake did not have similarly fond memories of that experience. While Marisol had been grinning through the air, spreading out her arms like wings, he'd worn an expression similar to Victor's: teeth gritted tight.

"Sure," his older cousin said. "But there's a difference between a parachute and a single feather." Wind from the surrounding desert bent the charm as Victor held it up, tickling the back of his hand. "Are we absolutely certain this floating magic works?"

Amelia gestured to the ladder that led up to her gleaming silver plane. "There's only one way to know for sure!"

"Um, no gracias." Victor swallowed. "I mean, I know magic is real, and I'm sure Nana would've loved to try flying with one of these, but there's no way I'm throwing myself into the sky without proof that it works first."

Jake couldn't blame him. He remembered how he felt standing on the deck of the *Baychimo* the first time he tested out his bubbler charm. The ocean's water seemed so endlessly deep and the scale around his neck looked so small—and even though everyone was telling him it would work, the fear inside Jake shouted louder.

Marisol just laughed. "Amelia means we should test the feather charm here, silly! Watch!"

His cousin clambered up to the wing and ran—as fast as she could—off the edge. It was more of a dive than a jump, and watching her made Jake's heart stick to the sides of his throat. Victor cried out. But as soon as Marisol's hiking boots left the Lockheed's silver surface, her feather charm started to float, somehow carrying the rest of her body with it. Instead of landing face-first in the sand, she drifted down, giggling when she finally came to rest on her belly.

"You should try it, hermano!"

Victor—who was never one to back down from a challenge, especially if that challenge was issued by his little sister—swallowed again and climbed a few rungs up the boarding ladder. Four, to be precise. It was barely tall enough to let the charm's magic kick in, but Victor managed to float for a few inches.

He broke out into a smile when his feet settled into the sand. "Okay, okay. That was cool!"

"Nana would be proud," Jake told him.

"I still can't believe she seriously *did* all that cool stuff she talked about." Victor's grin started to fade. "Nana was a really neat lady, wasn't she? I wish I'd gotten to know her better. . . ."

There was a moment of silence where they could only hear wind scattering grains of sand against the Lockheed's wings. Memories of Nana swept over each of the cousins too—Marisol and Victor had *faraway* expressions, and Jake's own chest ached remembering the sound of his grandmother's laugh. It used to be as shiny as the plane in front of them.

Amelia Earhart stepped up to the boarding ladder and buckled her helmet. "Well, I never met your nana, but I think it's safe to say that all three of you share her spirit of adventure."

"I wish I'd had the chance to meet her," Richard said. "We'd have swapped some stories, all right! But you three have plenty of your own to tell. Sounds like she'd have liked that."

Jake looked at Victor and Marisol.

Marisol looked at Victor and Jake.

Victor looked down at his feather, but then he grinned at his sister and younger cousin. Jake had never noticed how much the teenager's smile looked like Nana's, until now. He supposed he'd never noticed a lot of things about Victor, since Victor had never taken the trouble to notice him.

But now the three Beruna cousins were exploring a new world and learning new lessons. Even about each other.

"What do you say?" Amelia waved at the group. "Are you ready to fly?"

Oz gave an eager *ah-ah-ah* sound.

"Always!" Richard rearranged his pocket square before climbing the ladder. "Let's go teach the Administrator a thing or two!"

"Let's do it," Jake agreed. They *had* to find the Rocket in time. There was no other choice. He refused to let himself imagine Amelia's gap-toothed smile erased from her face, or the strong set of her jaw stolen. To picture Richard without the jaunty handkerchief sticking out of his top pocket, poised on the balls of his feet, ready for action. It couldn't happen. He wouldn't let it.

The flight was mercifully quick, though every time Amelia so much as turned her head, everybody tensed. Jake was pretty sure he didn't actually let out a breath until the wheels kissed a lost section of the Via Appia, a Roman road that was far too bumpy to make a very good runway.

The silver plane rumble-bumped to a stop, and out his window Jake could see a sparkling sea stretching all the way to the horizon. If he'd been at Nana's, this was the kind of morning when he'd be slathering himself in sunscreen and waiting impatiently for his cousins, so they could run down to spend the day dancing in and out of the waves.

Today, though, he wriggled into the straps of his backpack, and the six of them jumped down to the soft, warm sand.

"The cove's about five minutes back, behind that rise in the lost package sand dunes." Richard waved the group down the cobbled road. "A very accurate landing, Amelia. I flew across the Sahara once—or rather, my pilot Moye did, I was along for the ride. We had to hunt for our fuel caches, and picking out just the spot to set down is an art form. Ah, I think I see the glow of the eel-mails up ahead."

It was a glow. And it was bluish—reminding Jake of a computer screen in the middle of a dark room at midnight. Only now it was day, so the sky looked extra electric, crackling against the edge of the package dune as they climbed, clinging to tufts of grass and cardboard box flaps to help themselves along. Whatever Jake was expecting to see at the top was blasted away by the view.

The cove below was teeming with bottles of all shapes and sizes, piled together so closely that the sand itself was invisible. They were strewn on the shore and bobbing in the water, the sun glinting off the glass. There were so many that they joined together like one great, glassy raft, moving with the swell of the sea, so each wave sounded like Nana's sea glass wind chimes.

Letters were jammed in between the bottles, lying atop them, papers scattered about like leaves in fall, so many that it was impossible to imagine how they could ever, ever hope to read them all.

But it was the air overhead that had Jake blinking, staring, then blinking again.

"Are you seeing this?" Marisol murmured.

"I know we just came with Amelia Earhart from Queen Nefertiti's palace," Victor muttered, "but this place is *weird*."

Glowing letters hovered above them, all lit up in neon blues and greens. Most of them formed words, but some were roaming around on their own, and all of them were on the move. They zipped this way and that, colliding and ricocheting off in new directions, as if they were all in a hurry but didn't have any idea where to go. He could see why Richard had called it eel-mail—they were slithering around exactly like a pond full of eels.

Jake stared as two huge @ signs bounced off each other—one zoomed skyward, and the other cartwheeled past a stack of brown glass bottles.

"Behold the eel-mails," said Richard. "There used to be a nasty creature called a Mailer-Daemon that defended them, but I haven't seen it here in quite some time, so we ought to be safe."

"Are those . . ." Jake said.

"Undelivered emails?" Victor finished. "Yep."

"Wow," Marisol said.

"I guess my permission slip for the field trip last month is here somewhere," Jake mused. "This place must be lit up like day even when it's nighttime."

"Which is good," his prima added grimly. "Because that's how long it's going to take us to search through this. I'd use my magnet fingers, but I don't think remembering what Christopher's handwriting looks like is enough to go on. . . ."

"Er, what *would* be enough?" Victor was trying to be delicate, but Jake could still hear the doubt in his older cousin's voice.

"I don't know." Marisol sighed and looked out at glassy shoreline. It stretched on and on.

"We'd better divide and conquer," Amelia said. "Christopher is close to my age, so I'm guessing he doesn't know how to send eel-mail. And if he's been to this cove before, he'd know that a letter in an envelope would be too soggy to read. So we should check the bottles?"

"Let's check as many bottles as we can," Jake agreed.

Oz dove snout-first into the glassy waves, while the five humans split up, each taking a section and beginning the painstaking task of opening each message in a bottle. Jake took off his shoes and waded into the shallows, trying to keep track of which bottles he'd checked, and which he hadn't. It didn't take long to realize that they weren't going to be done with this job by tonight, even with the overhead light of the email. They weren't going to be done with this job by the end of this *year*.

Off to his left, Marisol squeaked and ducked as an email zoomed overhead, then went back to wrestling the cork out of another bottle. The sun beat down on Jake, and sweat trickled down his back. The dazzle of the light off the endless glass bottles was giving him a headache.

Christopher couldn't have wasted a year looking for letters from Nana every time, could he? How had he known which one to open?

"There has to be a special bottle." He straightened up, his voice rising too. "A container that Christopher thinks we'll notice."

Amelia wiped her brow. "Maybe something from the 1940s, the time when he arrived in the World?" she suggested. "Let me think. A Coke bottle? They were green back then, that's unusual?"

"Or an Orangina bottle?" Marisol suggested. "When Christopher and Hazel came to visit us in Bolivia a couple of months ago, she said they'd tried it in Paris. They're thin at the top and fat at the bottom, like most of the bottle slipped down."

"Doesn't it feel like he'd be taking a chance, thinking we might know about old Coke bottles, or remember

Hazel talking about the Orangina?" Jake asked.

"I'm not even sure Christopher was there for that conversation," Victor added. "Wasn't he in bed sleeping off his altitude sickness?"

"What do *you* think Christopher would expect you to look for, Jake?" asked Richard. "He didn't even know Marisol and Victor were going to be here. What would he choose that he'd be sure you'd have fresh in your mind?"

Jake ran a hand through his hair, trying to shove back the heat, the sweat, the headache. Trying to calm his mind and figure out what Christopher would expect him to remember. And what Christopher could actually buy—a weird antique would be hard to get his hands on in a hurry.

That's when it came to him.

"Melbourne Museum!" he shouted. "We were at the museum when I came here. I'll bet you anything the first thing he did was run straight to the gift shop for a bottle, then head to a thin spot to send us a message. Everyone look for something with a big M on it."

Victor found the metal drink bottle an hour later, dancing through the water with glee, waving it above his head and sending up a spray as he plowed over to where Jake and Marisol were searching close together. "Got it, got it! It says *Melbourne Museum: Home of Phar Lap*! What's a Phar Lap?"

"A famous Australian racehorse," said Jake, taking the bottle from Victor and unscrewing the top with hurried hands. It looked brand-new—this felt right.

Inside he found a slip of paper, and he nearly got his hand stuck fishing for it. Amelia and Richard came splashing over, and they all stood knee-deep in water as he unfolded the note. Its writing was old-fashioned. Almost too curly to read.

Sitrep? C&H

"Huh?" Jake glanced at the others. "C and H, that must be Christopher and Hazel. But what does *sitrep* mean?"

"They're asking for a situation report! I'll get some paper from the *Flying Laboratory*," Amelia said. "We can write on the back of one of my maps."

A few minutes later, Jake was carefully writing his own message, resting a piece of paper on Richard's back.

Christopher, Hazel, is that you? I'm here with Marisol and Victor. (And Oz, of course.)

"What now?" he wondered.

"Try throwing it in?" Amelia suggested.

He tossed it out into the floating raft of bottles, and it

sat there for a moment, then disappeared under the water with a soft slurp. They all waited, but nothing else happened.

"Seriously?" Victor scowled. "We have to start looking *all over* again? That'll take hours!"

"This is quite expedient," Richard added, rather unhelpfully. "Back in my day it took weeks to send mail overseas—sometimes months!"

But they didn't have months, or weeks, or even hours. Jake looked back over the blue, green, brown carpet of bottles, his stomach rising and falling with each wave. They'd already spent so much time here. . . .

"Christopher will send his reply in the same bottle, right?" Marisol smiled and cracked her knuckles. "That should be enough."

They all watched as she held her hands in front of her, as if she were reaching out to find a light switch in a pitch-black room. After a few seconds, Marisol turned and pointed. Sure enough, there was the Phar Lap bottle, bobbing beside a faded Sprite can.

"See?" She jabbed her finger at the container, staring directly at Victor.

"Good eye," he told her.

"It wasn't my eyes! It was my magnet fingers!"

"You've always been good at finding things at the beach," Victor said.

"Because that's where Nana trained me!" Marisol explained. "I didn't know it at the time, but whenever she took me out to find shells and shark's teeth on Folly, she was really teaching me how to use my magnet fingers. I—it's how I feel connected to her. Still."

Victor didn't argue with this. How could he? Instead, Jake's older cousin waded over to retrieve the bottle and open the note. He read it, then turned the paper upside down and tried reading it that way. In the end, Amelia had to translate the cursive for them.

Y! Wut deets?

"I think my language charm might be malfunctioning," the pilot lamented.

"It's still English!" Victor seemed more than happy to interpret. "He means 'what are the details.'"

"Is that how people talk these days?" Richard asked. "What became of the beauty of language?"

"It's not how most people talk," Marisol said. "And it's *definitely* not how Christopher talks. This could be the Administrator setting a trap."

"Let's test him," Jake said. "I'll write another note."

Are you sure that's you? Christopher doesn't speak like this. What was Nana's favorite drink?

The answer was with them a few minutes later.

Dear Jake,
Hazel here. Apologies—her favorite drink was sweet tea.
Sometimes she even sprinkled extra sugar in it. Christopher
was in a hurry and said 'text speak' would be quicker. I
thought all writing was text, but this strange world is always
teaching me new things. Let us know how you are. Are you
with friends? Please scratch Oz under the chin for me.

Christopher here. We don't know how you were called
back, but we are ready to help you return. We are a
few hours from Melbourne—we drove straight here,
to a known thin spot in a cove near Loch Ard Gorge,
which is the site of a famous shipwreck. In fact there
have been many shipwrecks along this coast, and the
local history is fascinating.

Ah—Hazel has reminded me that I am in a hurry!
We will camp surreptitiously on the beach and keep a
lookout for your return message.

With the others chipping in, Jake explained the situation as best he could, and asked if Christopher knew anything about the Rocket, while Marisol delivered Hazel's requested chin-scratches to Oz, who was happily paddling around and trying to catch a bottle in his jaws.

When Christopher wrote back, he didn't have much to offer.

The Rocket. I heard whispers. I wondered if I could use it to blackmail the Administrator, but I was never able to find it.

Jake's throat tightened as Amelia read this. Marisol clenched her fists, while behind her Victor wore a most impressive scowl.

"Hold on," the pilot assured the cousins. "There's more."

Toward the end of my time in the World Between Blinks, I did find a lead—but I was never able to pursue it.

Jake's heart soared again, and he had to make himself take a breath while Amelia kept reading.

I discovered the location of the Administrator's original cottage, where he lived when he first came to the World. If you are able to learn anything, it will be there. But the journey is perilous: you must make your way through a heavily patrolled area, crawling with Curators, and there are checkpoints set up with special charms that detect residents of the World Between Blinks. Only you uncataloged children will have any chance of making it through.

It is the wildest part of the World—go carefully! From everything I've learned, you will also need a woman called Yusra with you. If you send word she is to meet you at the wall, and ask her in my name, I think she will come. I have drawn a map below and marked the place where I suggest you cross. Good luck. We will stay in the cove in case we are needed again.

They all looked at each other, the challenge ahead sinking in. They had to head into the wildest part of a world that had *prehistoric monster sharks* in it! What could be wilder than that?

Jake wasn't sure he wanted to find out.

"I guess we have to send a message to Yusra," Marisol said softly. "Wherever and whoever she is . . ."

"Yusra is back at Nefertiti's court," Richard said. "Did any of you see the woman with a pack of small dinosaurs following her?"

Amelia dug through her pockets, pulling out a small spray bottle and handing it to Marisol. "You'll need this where you're going."

Marisol's eyes went huge. "This is T-rex repellent!"

Jake glanced from the bottle to Christopher's map. Was—was that a Tyrannosaurus sketched in the corner?

Victor summed their feelings up best: "Uh-oh."

"Richard and I will find Yusra," Amelia promised. "Let's hope Christopher's right, and she'll agree to meet you there."

9

MARISOL

"SO THIS IS THE END OF THE WORLD?"

Victor's question did not sound sarcastic for once. Marisol paused next to her brother, eyeing the basalt columns that rose from the ground. They looked like giants' teeth, crowded together to form a wall too tall for the cousins to see over. Not even when they stood on tiptoes.

What the cousins *could* see were dozens of battered stop signs posted to the dark black stone. Someone had graffitied beneath each set of four white letters: *END OF THE WORLD AHEAD.*

"It's the end of the Curators' World," Marisol guessed. "Last time we were here, Amelia told us that the World Between Blinks is always growing to fit new lost things, which means it *can't* end. Right?"

"Maybe." Victor frowned. "But I'd rather not walk off

an edge if I can help it. What does Christopher's map say, Jake?"

Their cousin grunted, turning the piece of paper around in his hand. "I *think* it says Wildlands, but the rest is just drawings. Thankfully. I don't know how Amelia could read Christopher's cursive."

Marisol glanced back up at the sky. The *Flying Laboratory* was long gone—back to Nefertiti's court to find Yusra and ask for her help. They still had one of Amelia's walkie-talkies, but Amelia and Richard had hurried them to the borderlands, and with a worried expression, the pilot had made them jump from the Lockheed Electra's rear door almost a mile before the crossing. There were too many Curator patrols to risk getting much closer, and the Administrator had been clear: *we will be watching—one step out of line, and I won't hesitate to turn your hourglass early.*

Besides—it had been a good chance to test their floating charms again.

She looked down at the feather on her necklace. Its magic felt different from parachuting. The whole experience was more like dream-flying—where your body was as light as your mind. One leap could last for minutes.

It could also clear a massive wall covered in stop signs.

"We should go," Marisol told the boys—and Oz, who was sniffing longingly at the snacks in their packs.

"Before any Curator patrols come and arrest us."

"We should figure out *where* we're going first," Victor pushed back.

"The Administrator's original cottage. It says so right there!" Or maybe a few lines down. Marisol couldn't read the penmanship she pointed at either.

"It also says *go carefully*, which is what I'm trying to do." Her brother was using his *oldest sibling* voice, the one he used whenever Mom and Dad went out for a date night and left him in charge.

But this wasn't some babysitting stint. This was a mission to help their friends—and if they kept standing here, stopped in front of hundreds of stop signs—they would fail.

"Victor might have a point." Jake said, with an apologetic glance.

"Thank you, Jake!"

"Christopher's art isn't much better than his handwriting, but I'm pretty sure this isn't a regular lizard." Their cousin showed them a drawing in the map's corner. It reminded Marisol of a scene from the Jurassic Park movies. "It's got too many teeth."

Marisol ground her own teeth, wishing they were as big as the lizard's. "Victor is just trying to take charge—"

"Yes!" her brother interrupted. "Because I don't want to get eaten by a Tyrannosaurus rex."

Another good point? Jake's eyebrows rose, but he clearly didn't dare say this.

"We have repellent! What we don't have is time!" They'd wasted too much already, so Marisol turned for a nearby boulder that sloped up on an angle, backing up and crouching, ready to make a run for it—if she flung herself off, she'd be high enough to use her charm.

Victor threw himself after her, grabbing at her arm just as she began to move.

She scowled at him. Tempted to kick. "¡Sueltame, hermano!"

"I don't want *you* to get eaten either, Mari!"

He might as well have said *te amo*, in Victor-speak. Not wanting his little sister to get devoured by dinosaurs was a strange way of saying I love you, but it was enough to make Marisol stop fighting. Victor wasn't just trying to be bossy, she realized. He was trying to protect her.

She straightened. Her scowl melted.

"This is just like rock climbing," she told him. "It's okay to be afraid, but you can't get stuck. That's when you fall. Tranquilo con la ruta."

"I just don't know if that applies to flying into a pit of dinosaurs." Victor gnawed his lip. "Maybe we should wait for this Yusra lady—"

There was a distant shout, too soon and too sharp to belong to any of the cousins' friends. Marisol jerked her head up to see a set of white suits walking along the top of the wall. A Curator patrol had spotted them. How could they not? With Marisol running around and Victor wearing a sweatshirt as loud as a fire truck siren and Jake's map waving in the breeze and Oz trotting around the entire group.

One of the white suits paused and waved. "Stop!" They had a megaphone like the Administrator's. It crackled down at the children—chiding. "Can't you see the signs? This is the end of the World! Stay where you are for your own safety!"

Marisol glanced back at her brother. "As soon as those Curators look through their monocles and find out who we are, they'll arrest us! We don't have time to wait," she told him. "It's now or never!"

"T-rexes or Karen," Jake added. His face creased as he folded up their great-uncle's map and tucked it into his pocket. "I know what I'm choosing."

"Me too!" Marisol pulled her arm free of Victor's hand. "Let's go!" He didn't follow, but he didn't stop her as she backed up a few steps, running at the slope of the boulder, her heart giving a great *THUMP* as she threw herself off the edge of it.

The charm took over, and as if tiny bubbles of helium had been injected into her limbs, she began to sail upward.

"Hurry, Victor!" called Jake, taking his own run at the

boulder. Oz was hard on his heels, and the two of them launched up like a pair of moonwalking astronauts—blond hair frayed everywhere and a tan tail whipped wildly.

"Come on, hermano! Our friends are depending on us!" Victor still stood where Marisol had left him, his mouth twisted into a thin, uncertain frown. She had to believe he would follow them.

And he did.

Together, the quartet rose over the wall. The top of its columns looked like stop signs with fewer sides—black hexagons. The Curators hopped across them wildly.

"Halt!" The one with the megaphone squawked. "You are entering a restricted area! Anything could happen!"

Marisol wasn't sure she could obey, even if she'd wanted to. The feather charm tickled her nose, and the officials on the wall grew smaller and smaller. She drifted over them to see . . .

Nothing.

Maybe it *was* the end of the World. . . .

Everything beyond the wall was covered in a thick fog. From up here, it looked like a blanket of snow. Or a view from an airplane at thirty-thousand feet. Marisol wasn't going to get that high, though. She could already feel her momentum vanishing. Her heart fluttered. Her thoughts spun.

She started to fall.

Jake, Victor, and Oz drifted down too. The fog below them began to swirl, thinning enough to show shapes. *Moving* shapes. It reminded Marisol of standing outside of Kitezh and looking out into the ocean's awesome blue, where sea monsters' shadows collided. She'd been happy for the distance then. Grateful for the signs that informed her she was still in the residential zone.

But the Curators and their signs were well behind her now. Neither official dared to chase the children into the Wildlands.

"Mari!" Jake began flapping his arms. "I think you better have that T-rex repellent ready!"

"Why?" she asked.

"There's something really, really big below us. . . ."

Mist twisted to show a hulking, clawed figure, but before Marisol could get a better look, the clouds thickened again. Panic rose as she sank into them.

"I told you soooooo!" Victor shouted, just before the fog swallowed his panicked face.

Marisol twisted off her backpack and pulled out the bottle of repellent. Where had Amelia gotten this? Or, more to the point, when? Rust circled the sides of the can, and it felt half-empty. She doubted it would do much good for a dinosaur as big as the one she was about to land on, but she twisted the top and aimed between her feet.

But then the fog swirled below her again, and for an instant she had a better view.

That wasn't a T-rex below.

It wasn't even a lizard.

Jake scooped up his monocle to examine the mountain of fur, which became clearer and clearer as they floated toward it. "Is that . . . a giant sloth?"

"Un perezoso gigante?" Victor echoed.

Marisol couldn't help but smile. In Spanish, sloths were known as lazy bears, and as she landed right next to the animal she could see why. It was, indeed, bear-sized. And it was napping. Its paws—and the long claws at the end—twitched like those of a sleeping dog.

"¡Qué lindo!" she exclaimed when she landed. "Do you think sloths run in their dreams?"

"Do you think they run in real life?" her brother asked back. "What happens if this one wakes up?"

Jake kept reading the entry through his monocle. "The *Megatherium americanum* is one of the largest land mammals that's ever existed . . . yada-yada . . . oh, good! This says it's an herbivore."

Victor sighed with relief. "It must eat some gigantic salads!"

"Did Christopher draw a giant sloth on his map?" Marisol asked Jake.

"No. . . ." Their cousin looked for landmarks, but

anything farther away than ten feet was hidden by fog. "I guess the best thing to do is to keep walking until we see something familiar."

"Shouldn't we wait for Yusra?" Victor asked. "Just because *that* wasn't a dinosaur . . . We could walkie-talkie Amelia and ask how far away she is?"

A voice echoed from the direction of the basalt wall. "Come back here! It is not only forbidden to enter restricted areas, it is also wildly ill-advised! Anything could happen! Everything is out of order!"

"I'm guessing their monocles can't penetrate the fog," Jake whispered. "But they'll be sending for backup, right? I don't think we *can* wait for Yusra. If she knows this place, hopefully she'll catch up. If she's even coming at all. She might be too scared about her hourglass getting turned over."

"I'm guessing Yusra doesn't frighten easily, if she keeps dinosaurs as pets," Victor pointed out.

"Well, we can't wait for her here." Marisol tucked the T-rex repellent under her arm. "Let's walk. I'll use my magnet fingers to find the Administrator's old cottage." Their great-uncle's sketch was probably enough to go on.

Sure enough, when she pictured the house, her fingertips started to crackle. Relief rushed through Marisol—her magnet fingers were working. If they could find any clue about the Rocket in the cabin, any clue at all, she'd probably be able to track the weapon.

"The cottage is this way!" She started walking into the mist, then paused when she didn't hear anyone following her.

Jake was tying his shoelace, and her brother was watching her strangely. The way his jaw squared made Marisol brace for another argument, but the fight never came. Instead, he just looked at the sloth one more time, then shook his head. "Lead the way, little sister!"

Smothered in fog, the Wildlands felt endless.

The cousins and Oz traveled carefully. Anything, *anything*, could be waiting in the next step. They walked through a mini-blizzard, growing icicles as long as walrus tusks. These melted off in a steamy stretch of jungle— where penguinesque birds glared from a safe place beside a large log. *Great Auks*. Marisol was pretty sure they weren't in the right climate at *all*, but the birds made no move to follow the quartet down a giant slope of pens.

Hundreds and thousands and maybe millions of lost pens—Marisol was sure if she looked hard enough, she'd find the yellow one she and her father had always done the crossword with, until it had gone missing at the end of last year. It had been a gift from Nana, and said *Hótel Djúpavík* down the side in faded letters.

"This place is wild all right!" Victor muttered as he

picked through BICs and Sharpies. Some slid, starting a small avalanche. "This feels like some weird art installation or a rich person's junkyard or—AHHH!"

He stopped abruptly, throwing his arms out to keep Jake and Marisol from sliding with the pens into a molten river. Plastic hissed and burned. An ugly smell. "Lava!"

Oz kept loping ahead, using the feather charm on his collar to clear the glowing orange stream sluggishly making its way around a bend and out of sight.

When Marisol, Jake, and Victor gathered the courage to follow, gliding through the hot air above it, they landed in another pile of debris. Guitar pics, this time. And coins. And popcorn kernels. So, so many TV remotes, and sticking out between two of them, a beat-up board book. Things that had probably slipped into the World Between Blinks through couch cushions.

Next was a mountain of mismatched socks, which they had to climb with pinched noses. Then a pool so deep that it was almost black. There was a whirlpool in the middle, and something with *tentacles*, which made the cousins grateful they could use their feather charms to cross instead of their bubblers.

"This is kind of like all those piles by the thin spot outside of Portus. Was the whole World this way, do you think?" Jake wondered as they floated to the other side. "Before the Curators took charge? It would be impossible to live like this—it's just piles of stuff *everywhere*."

"Maybe," Marisol admitted, dodging a spare tire as she landed. "Alexander Helios did say something about a Great String Entanglement in the olden days, before the Administrator. . . ."

They landed on solid ground—thank goodness—and her fingers were still humming brightly. The cottage had to be close by. Maybe it was on the other side of these rock formations?

"Or maybe the Administrator made this part of the World this way on purpose. Big baddies like having their hideouts guarded by snakes and moats and lava and stuff. At least, that's how it is in the video games." Victor seemed to be talking more to himself. "And if the Administrator *is* hiding the weapon that could ultimately defeat him out here it makes sense to have defenses—"

Every hair on Marisol's neck sprang up at once. Not because her brother was making sense, but because one of the rock formations had just . . . nodded?

Oh.

That was definitely *not* a rock.

Jake saw it too. "Um, guys? Who has the T-rex repellent again?"

Marisol squeaked when she whipped out the can, but this noise only seemed to excite the creature.

It took a ground-quaking step forward.

BOO-OO-OO-M.

Marisol's bones kept shaking even when the T-rex fell still. Christopher hadn't drawn its teeth right at all. They were much, MUCH sharper off the page. . . .

"What are you staring at its teeth for? Cavities?" Victor yelled. "Spray it, hermana!"

Her magnet fingers were still humming. This pins-and-needles feeling made her fumble the repellent bottle. The T-rex took another step closer, and even though the dinosaur was large enough to swallow Oz without even chewing, the Tasmanian tiger scrambled in front of the children and growled.

This gave Marisol enough time to pick up the can. Point and spray.

A plume of mist washed over the dinosaur's face.

It smelled like candy canes and those melty mint candies old people always carried in their pockets. As soon as the T-rex caught a whiff, its eyes widened, turning a startled yellow. It tossed back its head as if it was going to give the most horrible roar, and then . . .

It sneezed!

"Ugh," Marisol shielded her face. Whatever misted back over them did *not* smell like Christmas.

"Is this dinosaur snot?" Victor looked down at his damp red hoodie—horrified. "Am I covered in DINO-SAUR SNOT?"

They were. But this was currently the least of the

Beruna cousins' problems. Instead of retreating, the T-rex sneezed again, and the other "rock formations" in the fog started moving. One turned into a triceratops. Another looked a lot like a stegosaurus, and there were several that seemed like smaller, feathered versions of the dinosaur in front of them.

"Are those T-rex babies?" Marisol whispered. "If we've made Mom mad . . . we should run!"

"No!" Jake said quickly. "Those are velociraptors. And they're definitely faster than we are. If we run, they'll pounce."

Marisol shook the bottle in her hand. It was woefully light. "I don't have enough repellent to spray all of them!"

"We could jump," Victor suggested.

"So can they!" Jake whispered. "Ten whole feet! They'd snap us up like cheese puffs."

"If you did a project on dinosaurs," Marisol whispered back, "you could have mentioned this stuff earlier!"

"I doubt that's what we taste like anyway. . . ." Victor shook a long greenish string off his sleeve. Then paused. "Oh. Oh! Mari, give me the repellent!"

It didn't seem like the right time to fight for a *please*, so Marisol tossed her brother the bottle. He immediately turned and sprayed her.

She could see why the T-rex had sneezed. It felt like breathing frost.

"We don't need to spray the dinosaurs!" Victor grinned

as he aimed a stream of peppermint at Jake's chest. "We just have to cover ourselves! That way we taste like a Starbucks Holiday drink instead of tasty, tasty snacks!"

The idea was smart, and it seemed to be working. The velociraptors kept their distance, hissing at Oz, who stood defiantly between them and the children.

"Don't forget Oz!" Marisol reminded her brother.

The Tasmanian tiger did a small spin as the repellent washed over him. The velociraptors hissed even louder. But when it was Victor's turn, and Marisol tried spraying her brother, nothing came out.

Marisol shook the repellent can.

It was empty.

"Maybe we can huddle together?" Jake suggested. "The way bison do to protect their babies."

"I am not a baby bison!" Victor huffed.

"No," answered Marisol, "you're a tasty, tasty snack."

"That might be the first nice thing you've ever said to me," Victor replied, and after a moment, she realized he was teasing. "Come on then," he said, sidling closer to her as the T-rex rumbled.

Marisol, Jake, and Oz formed a minty circle around him—and they began to shuffle forward. The dinosaurs responded by drawing back into a formation of their own, a scaly outer wall around the cousins.

They were completely surrounded.

And every time they moved, the circle of dinosaurs matched each step precisely.

"What are they doing?" Victor craned his neck to look.

"Waiting for the smell to wear off?" Marisol swallowed. How long did T-rex repellent last, anyway? The largest of the dinosaurs had stopped sneezing and was glaring down at the children with eyes yellow enough to electrify a city. Its teeth were yellow too.

"Maybe we can backtrack to that whirlpool?" Jake suggested. "None of the dinosaurs are wearing bubblers—"

"The whirlpool with the tentacles in it?" Marisol clarified.

"The water would wash off the repellent," Victor pointed out. "We'd really just be hastening our demise. Not to mention throwing a sea monster into the mix."

Jake's face was pale enough to turn his freckles polka-dotted. "Do you have a better idea?"

Victor nodded. "Dinosaurs are cold blooded. If we retreated to that patch of snow we walked through, the temperatures would put them to sleep."

"That's all the way back toward the basalt wall!" Marisol couldn't help but wail with frustration. They'd spent hours out here already, and their friends only had so much time left.

"It might not even be there anymore," Jake said. "This place is so out of order—"

Dinosaurs started screeching.

The sounds were like ice down Marisol's spine, and then it felt like her veins froze completely.

Oh no. Something above was calling back!

But a moment later the clouds parted to reveal a hang-glider. No—she realized. That was a *pterodactyl.* A pterodactyl with a . . . with a woman holding on to its legs! Her feather charm floated along with her headscarf, tickling the air just under the creature's leathery wings.

"Yusra!" Even without the small trail of dinosaurs, Marisol recognized her. "Yusra! We're down here!"

At the sight of the children, Yusra released her ride with a shout of thanks. The pterodactyl swirled back up into the fog while the woman drifted down—her face as calm as a mountain morning.

The velociraptors had broken rank to begin jumping. Jake was right, they could leap incredibly high! Yusra didn't seem scared by how close their jaws got. She smiled instead, landing among them and scratching each eager dinosaur beneath the chin. The T-rex nuzzled in like a cart horse in search of an apple.

"Hello!" She pushed her way through them to greet the children. Her dress smoothed down while her nose wrinkled. "I smell that you've used the repellent Amelia

Earhart gave you. I told her that was unnecessary."

"Unnecessary?" Victor snorted, then sneezed.

The T-rex growled.

"The dinosaurs were about to eat us," Marisol said.

"Are you sure?" asked Yusra.

"Um, yeah?" Jake frowned, as if maybe this wasn't the correct answer after all. "Why else would they hiss and snap their teeth?"

"Well . . ." Yusra turned to the creatures, who'd formed a chorus of coos and clicks and grunts. Almost like the tail end of a music box song. "It sounds to me as if they're guarding something."

"You can speak dinosaur?" Marisol wasn't sure why *that* surprised her, after watching this woman use a pterodactyl as a parachute.

"I spent many years in the old world training as an archaeologist. I never went to university, but I learned a great deal from bones and stones back in Palestine, and if I say so myself, I made some important discoveries," Yusra said. "After I found myself in the World Between Blinks, I decided to find out what *living* fossils could tell me."

"Huh," murmured Jake.

"It's really not that hard to understand dinosaurs," Yusra continued, "but most people are too afraid to listen. They spray that nasty peppermint stuff and then get even more scared when the dinosaur tries to defend itself!"

"Oh . . ." Now that Marisol thought about it, most of the hissing *had* happened after the cousins had emptied the can of repellent.

"First impressions can be misleading. Usually all they want is a good scratch under the chin," Yusra explained. "Especially T-rexes, since their arms are too short to reach. The poor things."

"Well, can you tell them that we're sorry for spraying?" Jake offered. "And that we'd like to get past, please? We have to reach the Administrator's old cottage before it's too late."

Beautiful patterns swirled on Yusra's garments as she turned. She started to growl, and all of the dinosaurs— horned and plated—cocked their heads to listen. They seemed to take turns speaking when she finished. Chirping and grunting and crooning.

"The cottage is what they're guarding," she interpreted for the children. "The Administrator put them here many years ago, asking them to guard it in return for a place of their own, where nobody would scream or spray them with peppermint."

"We're really sorry about that," Marisol offered again guiltily.

"The dinosaurs think he's forgotten about this place," Yusra continued. "And lately, things have started changing.

Apparently there's a huge mountain of pens now?"

"We saw that," Jake confirmed. "Pretty much skied down it."

"That's harder for a T-rex," Yusra said. "I'm sure it's a result of the rezoning out in the rest of the World. Anyway, I've explained our situation, and they have agreed that they'll let you pass as long as you apologize."

"We really *are* sorry," Marisol told them.

"They'd also like wider roaming rights under the new leadership," Yusra explained. "They're tired of the chaos here in the Wildlands. They'd like to find somewhere they prefer to settle down. It's why they're even willing to broker a deal."

"We can't let dinosaurs roam around residential areas!" Jake whispered frantically.

"No," Marisol agreed. "But there must be some happy middle ground. Maybe they can move to the Amazon rainforest once it's been fixed. Tell them that once we defeat the Administrator, we'll find a more stable home for them."

The T-rex threw back its head when Yusra delivered the deal, and the velociraptors hopped aside.

"They accept your terms," the archaeologist told the children. "You may pass, but I'd suggest we hurry. There was quite the hubbub at the wall when I flew over. The Curators must have seen you cross."

Marisol took a deep breath and started walking toward the dinosaurs. She chose a gap by the stegosaurus, which, despite its massive plates, looked the least threatening. The creature stepped back as she passed. But the T-rex's tail landed in its place.

"They would like to remind you to keep your promise," Yusra translated its growl. "Or else."

When Marisol nodded, the tail slithered away and the path cleared. There was only more fog ahead, but she knew the house was close. Her hands felt like emergency flares. Brighter and brighter, until the mist finally peeled back to reveal a house.

"This is it!" she said excitedly. The feeling in her fingers snuffed out like a candle. "The Administrator's old cottage."

The building had been painted a robin's-egg blue, and it looked small, though this was tough to tell because of the surrounding sand.

It was as if they'd stepped back into the ever-stretching desert. Dunes rolled ahead of them like waves, and one was trying to wash across the house. Sand choked the chimney, pressing against the windowpanes like an eager cat. The front door would have been impossible to open if Oz hadn't been there to help dig it out.

The humans stood back, watching the Tasmanian tiger fling showers of sand skyward.

"Wow!" Victor clucked his tongue. "You really *did* find this place by following your fingers, didn't you, hermana?"

Jake shot their cousin a look. "I told you so!"

"You did." He swallowed, his Adam's apple slicing down his throat. "Look. I—I'm sorry I doubted you both before. It's my fault the Curator patrol saw us, and I know they'll probably report it to the big baddie. . . ."

Marisol blinked.

Victor? Was saying . . . lo siento?

He didn't stop there. "I'm sorry I called you a robot too, back at Nefertiti's palace. You're right. I'm scared, and . . . it's amazing that you aren't. Jake's right. You're kind of like a superhero."

Marisol blinked again, to make sure this wasn't some sort of weird Unknown side effect. But no. Victor—the brother who never passed up the chance to give her a noogie or make a joke at Marisol's expense—had paid her a compliment.

She had no idea what to say back.

Before she could think of an answer, Oz trotted over and tugged Jake's shirt.

"Door's open!" Her cousin grinned. "Let's go and see what the Administrator has been hiding!"

10

JAKE

THERE WAS NO ROCKET IN THE LIVING ROOM.

There wasn't even much furniture when Jake stepped inside the cottage. The place was mostly bare, though it was obvious there had once been papers pasted to the walls. Sun traced their absence. Red strings were still tacked up—connecting nothing. Sand covered the floors and dusted the lone table. There was a vase on top, but when Jake opened the lid, all he found was more sand.

It had wormed its way into everything. So much so that most of the other rooms were sealed off, completely full up to their ceilings. There was barely any room for the five of them as they searched, bouncing from corner to corner in a frantic sweep that had them bumping into each other and ricocheting off walls like Ping-Pong balls.

Jake tried each room in turn, knowing he was retracing

everyone else's steps, but somehow having to see for himself that there was nothing to find.

Oz scrambled past, nearly tripping Jake, and pushed through into the bathroom to start digging sand out of the base of the shower. But it was the sixteenth hole he'd started so far—clearly their furry friend didn't have any more idea where to look than the children or Yusra.

The cottage was a dead end.

The humans assembled in the living room, and Jake pressed his fingers to his temples, trying to slow the pulse he could feel beating there like an urgent drum. They *couldn't* have wasted all this time getting here for nothing. There had to be more than just sand in this house. But as Jake looked around at the floor—hope trickling through his throat, going, going, gone—he tried not to think of his friends' hourglasses.

"We're just running around everywhere," Victor said helplessly. "We need to *think*."

"In Australia, they'd say we're running around like headless chooks," Jake agreed. "Let's try each section one at a time, make sure we don't miss even a single grain of sand."

Marisol stood in the center of the room, staring at her empty palms, but she nodded. "I guess we should start at the door," she said. "Any clues in the doorframe?"

She felt her way around the threshold while Yusra

reached up to check the top and Victor crouched down to peer inside the keyhole.

"Nothing," the archaeologist said eventually, and Marisol and Victor nodded their agreement.

"Okay, the walls next," Jake suggested, and they each spread out to take one as he kept talking. "All this red string, and you can see where the paper was pinned up . . . he was trying to figure something out. This must have been how he tracked his progress as he looked for the Rocket."

"The question is," said Victor, "did he find it?"

"Or did he leave a clue we could use to search with?" Marisol added. "If I could just find out a little more about it, my magnet fingers might work."

Jake looked back at the sun-etched squares on the wall, trying to imagine what sort of papers had filled them. Maps? Photographs? Newspaper clippings? He searched in vain for a useful silhouette, but whatever the Administrator had pieced together with this yarn was long unraveled, and the more Jake stared at the loose strings, the more his own insides knotted.

"There's nothing on this wall," he said.

"Or this one." Marisol stared at her corner with damp, dark eyes.

It was the same with the other two walls: Victor and Yusra shook their heads at the peeling paint, the faded yarn.

But still they kept searching. Oz dug up most of cottage floor and then buried it again. Jake and Victor even carried the table out into the light to see if there were any indentations on it, any word the Administrator had ever written on a piece of paper that had left some secret message in the wood.

Yusra cradled the vase in her arms as she followed the cousins outside, and she leaned down to scratch at Oz's ears as Marisol crawled under the table to see if anything had been pinned to the bottom.

No luck.

"Is there anything inside the vase?" Jake asked.

"Just sand!" Some scuffed beneath Marisol's boots as she scooted free from the table. "I looked already."

Jake kept studying the vase. It was beautiful, with glossy yellow enamels and flowers sprouting across the porcelain, but something about the sight wasn't quite right. . . .

"It's weird that sand would get under the lid," he said.

"Is it?" Victor wondered. "Sand gets *everywhere*. Socks. Sinuses. Sealed jars."

When Yusra lifted the lid and peered inside she went very, very still. "I think Jake is on to something."

Jake's heart gave a kick in his chest. "What do you mean?"

"I'm not sure why," Yusra said slowly, "but the sand in this vase is unlike any of the sand around us. It has a different texture, a slightly different color. I'm an archaeologist, I should have noticed this already."

The three children hurried over, each peering inside. It hadn't been as obvious inside the house, but here, they could see Yusra was right. The sun was slowly setting, burning off the overhead fog and setting the reddish sand around them aflame. The sand inside the vase was coarser, and just a little yellower.

"Is that . . ." Marisol trailed off, as if she barely dared speak it aloud.

"Is it what?" Victor demanded. "Is this special sand? Some kind of lost sand?"

"Not lost sand," Jake breathed. "Those are lost *memories*. Those are from someone's hourglass."

Victor's mouth fell open. "The Administrator's?"

"There's only one way to find out!" Jake fumbled in his pocket, pulling out the Illuminator. "Thank you, Great-Uncle Christopher. This is his Illuminator, Victor. You shine it through a grain of memory sand, and you can see the memory."

Yusra's eyes lit up when she saw the small flashlight. "I cannot imagine the adventures that brought your great-uncle such a powerful treasure," she murmured.

The cottage's bright-blue wall made a good projection screen—last time, in the Amazon, they had used a white jacket hanging from a washing line. With great care, Jake fished a single grain of sand from the vase, holding it up to the Illuminator.

He switched on its light.

Immediately, a memory leaped to life.

It was tinged blue by the wall but perfectly clear. A man was trudging along the side of a road in the rain, the collar of his coat turned up against the relentless pitter-patter. Even from here, outside the picture, Jake could tell it was the sort of rain that found ways to sneak drops down the back of your neck, like little lines of ice keeping score of your misery.

With a flare of headlights and the rev of an engine, a car sped past him—it was an old-timey car, but Jake didn't know when from. He didn't have time to wonder, either: just as it drew level with the man, its tires found a puddle of muddy water, sending up a sheet of muck that coated him head to toe.

The man cried out, stumbling away from the assault, his arms windmilling wildly as he found the edge of a ditch, then tumbled down in a tangle of arms and legs.

It was his memory, so Jake's view of it followed him as he landed on his back in the mud with a deep, final *squelch*. And there he lay, staring up at the sky with resignation as the rain fell onto his face.

"Happy New Year to me," he said quietly, and closed his eyes tight, as if he were trying not to cry.

"This is a terrible memory," Victor muttered. "I'd try to forget this one too."

Jake didn't blame the Administrator for getting rid of such an awful day either. Loneliness practically radiated from the memory in waves—and Jake knew a thing or two about that himself. Hadn't he just come to the World from a long, lonely stay in Australia, wishing he had someone to talk to, someone to listen?

He was about to change over to a new grain of sand, one that might relate to the Rocket, when something happened.

A soft sound began somewhere near the man's feet, as if someone was opening and closing a rusty gate.

Squeak-SQUEAK.

Squeak-SQUEAK.

Squeak-SQUEAK.

Oz danced in place, trembling, nose twitching, and all the humans leaned forward as the man sat up. There was barely any light, but he felt around with his hands, and after a few moments they closed on something. He lifted it up to examine it.

It was a tiny, wriggling puppy—impossible to tell what shape or color under all the mud.

"What are you doing here?" the man asked, tucking it in against his chest. "What's your name, little friend?"

Just as he spoke, the sky lit up in a thousand colors—red

bursts overlapped with frantically turning green wheels, pink and blue sizzling down from above. The rainbow reflected off the raindrops, seeming to paint the entire sky above them.

The man and the puppy watched together from the muddy ditch, snuggled together.

"Huh," the man said, looking down at his companion. "Your name's Rocket, is it? Happy New Year, Rocket."

"What?!" said Victor.

"*What?!*" said Yusra.

"*WHAT?!*" said Marisol.

"Rocket is a DOG?" said Jake as the memory faded.

"Ahhhh-whuff!" said Oz.

"Find another memory!" Marisol urged as the image vanished from the wall.

Jake scrambled for more sand, shining the Illuminator through grain after grain. Together they all watched as Rocket turned his wobbly steps into a run, then grew into a dog before their eyes. He was golden brown, lithe and strong, his tail constantly wagging.

They watched as man and dog hiked together in beautiful mountains. As they curled up together in front of warm fires, as they wrestled for their share of the quilt as they curled up in bed.

"Hold still," said the man in one memory, crouching beside Rocket and wrapping one arm around him as the dog tried to wriggle free, his nose twitching and questing after interesting smells. "You've got burrs stuck in your tail, I'll just . . ."

The dog wriggled again and gave a bark.

The man—the Administrator, though Jake could hardly believe it—laughed, and dug in his pocket with his free hand. "You're the only dog I ever heard of who likes peppermint," he said, holding out some green leaves in the palm of his hand. "Now, remember, *only* the plant. Peppermint candy is dangerous for dogs. Stick to the vegetative version, Rocket, and only eat one or two leaves. Any more might upset your stomach!"

The dog gobbled them up, then held still as the man picked the burrs out of his tail, one at a time.

"Why would you want to forget any of this?" Jake asked as the two set out to run across a meadow together. "This looks amazing. He looks happy—Rocket's his friend. And he's Rocket's companion, look what good care he takes of him."

"But he lost Rocket," Marisol said, soft and sad. "Remember, everybody said he was looking for him."

As though her words had summoned it, the memory arrived.

The man and the dog were walking through a city, part of a long, snaking line of people. They were shrouded by mist, but Jake could see that all the people were carrying

186

bundles in their arms, or holding hands with their children to keep them close.

Their heads were down, their shoulders rounded. They were afraid. And as Jake watched, he realized something was wrong with the city. The buildings were half collapsed, and rubble lay strewn across the road.

"I can't see," Marisol said softly, squinting at the mist. "Should we go inside the memory?"

"You can go *inside*?" Victor whispered, his brows lifting. It felt right, somehow, that they were whispering.

"Christopher took us into one last time," Jake said. "But . . . I don't think we should now."

Something about this memory sent a shiver down his spine. He kept his hand steady on the Illuminator, when it wanted to shake.

"I think," he whispered, "this is a memory from a war."

"It is," Yusra murmured. "The Great War. Some people called it the war to end all wars, but—"

BOOM!

An explosion blossomed to one side of the line of people, and with screams they scattered, dropping their belongings, snatching up their children, running for safety. The whole memory shook as Jake involuntarily started forward, and Yusra grabbed him by the arm.

"We must see how the story ends," she said softly.

They could only get snatches of it, though—the fog swirled. Smoke and dust rushed through the air to form concealing clouds.

"There he is!" cried Marisol, pointing as the Administrator appeared, carrying an injured woman out of the debris to safety.

"Rocket?" he cried as another man came forward to help the dazed woman down the road. "Rocket! Where are you, boy?" The Administrator's glasses slipped down his nose as he searched through the smoke. "Rocket, it's all right, come back! *Rocket!*"

"Help!" someone called out. "Someone help me lift this beam!"

The Administrator looked around desperately, helplessly.

"Help!" came the voice again.

With an anguished cry, he turned and plunged back into the bomb's destruction.

For a moment, there was only smoke and splinters and the cruel swirl of ashes as the buildings stood skeletal against the gray sky. The house the Administrator had plunged into was only half standing. It seemed as though a stray breeze might topple the rest of the stones over.

Jake held his breath until the Administrator reappeared, this time leading two little girls—he pointed out their mother, and as they ran for her, he turned into the wreckage again.

"He's rescuing people." Victor almost sounded annoyed. "Doesn't look very evil to me."

"Perhaps the Administrator has something in common with the dinosaurs," Yusra murmured. "And first impressions are deceiving."

"The dinosaurs listen when we're polite," Marisol pointed out. "The Administrator is *not* the same! He's had plenty of chances to prove himself, but he still wants to steal everyone's memories, make them forget who they are."

"I dunno," Victor chimed in. "Maybe Yusra has a point. Sometimes you can live with people for years and not really know them." He tilted his head toward his sister as he said this, and Jake knew it was a nod to Marisol's magnet fingers, to Nana's magic before that.

The Administrator, though . . .

Jake looked back at the man who dug so desperately through the ruins, covered in dust and dirt. He'd pause every so often, lifting his voice in a desolate cry. "Rocket! Rocket, where are you?"

But no matter how long they watched, Rocket didn't return.

The dog was gone, and the memory was over.

They all stood in silence as the image against the wall

faded. Back to sorrowful shades of dusk and blue.

"Try one more," said Marisol, her eyes bright with tears.

They tried two more, then three, then four. They saw the Administrator at a desk, making long lists. There was a line of people in front of him, slowly shuffling up for their turn to speak. Sad, timid people, curled in on themselves like question marks, hugging their belongings to their chest.

"What's that list?" Jake murmured. "It doesn't look like a Curator's ledger."

"I don't think he's in the World yet," Yusra replied quietly. "But I think he might be helping find lost things."

Just then a woman at the front of the line straightened, her voice rising. "She's alive?" she cried. "Here in the city?"

"Here's the address she left," the Administrator replied, scribbling something on a tatty piece of paper with the stub of a pencil. "In case anyone came looking for her."

The woman grabbed at the paper, turning to run for the entrance. Everyone in the line looked after her in hope, and the Administrator sat a little straighter.

"That's one lost family found," he said, with quiet satisfaction. "My lists are working." But then he seemed to remember something, and his smile faded. He leaned forward to check on the piece of paper taped to the front of his desk.

LOST DOG, it read in large letters. *LOVES PEPPER-MINT LEAVES (BUT ONLY ONE OR TWO A DAY). ANSWERS TO ROCKET.* There was a black-and-white photograph of the man's best friend stuck to it.

The man who would become the Administrator was learning the power of cataloging the lost, of making sure everything was where it could be found. But he couldn't find the one thing that mattered most.

Jake clicked off the Illuminator and slowly put it back into his pocket.

Eventually Marisol spoke. "That was so sad," she whispered. "I know he's doing a terrible thing to all our friends, but . . . I feel sorry for him. For *that* version of him, anyway."

"Me too," said Jake. "But . . . I don't understand. Why would the Administrator go from helping families find each other to stealing memories and destroying lives? It's like he's a completely different person!"

"I don't know," Marisol bit her lip and stared at the empty wall, as if she might find an answer somewhere in its knotted wood. "And it doesn't change the fact that he emptied Nefertiti's hourglass. The Administrator is still going to hurt our friends, and we still have to stop him."

She was right, of course. Jake thought of the fierce

queen's blank face and shook his head. They *couldn't* let it happen again. But there was only one problem: their secret weapon wasn't here. Well, two problems, if you counted the fact that the Rocket wasn't even a real weapon. . . .

How in the worlds were they going to stop the Administrator?

"Look," said Victor, scratching his jaw thoughtfully. "Do you remember a couple of summers ago, when I was messing around with my basketball inside, and I broke Nana's fancy shepherdess ornament? The little one made of china?"

"Oh, Mom was soooo mad," Marisol breathed, her eyes half closing at the strength of that memory.

Jake's curiosity was piqued—he and the other cousins had been sent outside, and he had never discovered what happened after the door to the living room closed with Victor, Aunt Cara, and Nana inside.

"Well, Nana said it was okay," Victor told them.

His sister's eyes snapped open in surprise. "What?"

Victor nodded. "She said that she knew I was mad because I didn't make the basketball team at school, and that I wasn't being my best self that week."

Jake's mouth fell open. "Victor, that was really nice of Nana, but you're not saying we're supposed to forgive the Administrator for what he's doing, just because some bad things happened to him, right? And just, what, let him do it?"

"No," Victor replied, with a wave of one hand. "Nana still made me donate some of my pocket money, by the way, I didn't just get away with it. But . . ." He scowled, scuffing the ground with one sneaker. "I'm just saying, you can do something bad, and it's not who you are. It might still not be who the Administrator is. It's complicated."

Everyone was silent. *Huh.* Jake hadn't expected that from Victor, of all people, who was always so quick to tell him and Marisol what they were doing wrong.

Then again, he hadn't been doing that as much since they'd arrived in the World, had he?

It was Oz who eventually moved, giving a soft *whuff* and gazing up at Victor with an expression that Jake had a feeling might be agreement.

"All right," Yusra said thoughtfully, "so the Administrator is obsessed with sorting everything, with cataloging and confining, so nothing around him will ever be lost again. A bad action, but judging by those memories, perhaps not who he *is*."

"He just really, really wants to find his dog," Marisol said.

"Wait a minute . . ." A new idea was dawning on Jake now, and it made the back of his neck prickle. "Do you think these are *all* his memories of Rocket? Is it possible he doesn't even know what he's lost anymore?"

"Perhaps his memories were too painful," Marisol murmured.

Jake thought back to his first—and last—encounter with the Administrator. He'd been caught red-handed, sneaking hourglasses out of the Library of Alexandria. All of the World's lost memories sat on the surrounding shelves, but the Curators' leader only seemed to care about the ones Jake held on to. *Life is full of loss*, he'd said, *and sometimes it's too much to carry around with you.*

"I think you're right," Jake told his cousin. "The Administrator wasn't wearing an hourglass when we met. . . ."

Suddenly, the vase in Yusra's hands looked a lot more like a funeral urn. Its memories, ashy. Had the Administrator buried them here on purpose? Was Rocket so lost that his owner couldn't bear to remember him?

Maybe Rocket didn't need to be a weapon after all . . . maybe the dog was meant to be a reminder. To show the Administrator that he wasn't always this way. That he could change again . . .

Jake's heart leaped at the thought.

Had Rocket died in the explosion?

Or could Marisol's magnet fingers find the dog again?

Everything came down to that.

"If we bring Rocket back to the Administrator, maybe he'll realize that he doesn't have to sort this World apart," Jake said. "Maybe he'll see he's"—he nodded to Victor—"not being his best self. Mari, anything in your fingers? Is Rocket here in the World Between Blinks?"

His prima closed her eyes, slowing her breath and lifting her hands so she could hold them out, turning slowly in a circle. Yusra watched with some interest, her head tilted to one side, but remained silent.

Marisol's lips curved slowly to a smile, and her lashes lifted, still glittering with tears. "It's very faint," she said triumphantly, "but there's definitely something that way." She pointed back past sneezing dinosaurs and mountains of miscellaneous objects, toward the basalt wall and the zoned sections of the World beyond.

One by one, they all began to smile.

"We'd better bring big baddie's memories with us, so he knows *why* Rocket is important, when we reunite them," Victor said.

"Good idea," Jake agreed. "Is anyone else kind of relieved Rocket is something we can give *to* the Administrator, instead of something we can use *against* him?"

Marisol raised her hand, and after a moment, so too did Victor and Yusra. Oz whuffed heartily.

"All right," Jake said, grinning. "Now let's go get our hands on this dog, and de-grumpify the Administrator."

Marisol grinned back. "One family reunion, coming right up!"

By the time they reached the mountain of lost pens, the sun had long since set. The lava behind them lit the scene with a soft red glow, and when they pulled flashlights out of their backpacks, the beams of light bounced off the shiny plastic. They were all tired, and they'd stopped talking some time ago, but everybody agreed they needed to get out of the Wildlands before they risked a rest.

Jake was near the peak of the pen mountain, Marisol and Oz in front of him, catching their breath at the top.

Yusra was scrambling behind him with Victor bringing up the rear, muttering something about how he'd never complain about losing his pen ever again. Both of them were heavier than Jake and Marisol, and as they tried to climb the hill, their feet kept sinking into the piles of pens. Sharpies sucked at their ankles like quicksand, so they couldn't even jump-start their floating charms.

"Here, I'll take the vase," Jake offered, and Yusra gratefully handed him her bag, inside of which sat the vase of sand, wrapped in their spare clothes and propped upright so it couldn't spill. He slung it carefully over his shoulder.

"I will rest easier when we find a safer container for the sand," she said. "I—"

But she got no further, her words cut off with a shriek as a hand suddenly burst from a pile of highlighters and grabbed her by the ankle.

Down the mountain, Victor bellowed in surprise and alarm. "¿Qué está pasando?"

Suddenly the pen mountain was alive! Figures

emerged from beneath the plastic piles, sending cascades of ballpoints and markers slithering down toward the waiting lava at the base of the hill.

Figures clad in *white*.

It was an ambush!

The light from the children's flashlights bounced everywhere as a dozen Curators rose from their hiding places, shouts echoing through the night.

"Stop in the name of the library!"

"Prepare to be zoned!"

"Ow, stop kicking me, you horrible boy!"

"AUGH! MY UNIFORM!"

Two of them had Yusra in their grip already, and another three were wrestling with Victor, who'd uncapped a red Sharpie and was *scribbling* all over his attackers' stark white outfits. The rest of the Curators scrambled up the mountain toward Jake, Marisol, and Oz, arguing loudly.

"We should have pounced earlier!"

"I thought you were going to tell us when!"

And down below, Victor was shouting: "¡Corre, hermana! Go, Jake, go!"

Jake was frozen in place as the Curators closed in, Marisol and Oz a step behind him. The thylacine scrambled down past Jake to stand between him and the Curators, a low warning growl in his throat. There were so many—how could they possibly fight?

"*RUN!*" Victor screamed. "Go get Rocket!"

"Go!" Yusra shouted as the Curators wrestled her to the ground. "You must finish your mission!"

Jake looked back at Marisol, and their eyes met.

They couldn't leave Victor and Yusra.

And if they didn't, they'd lose their last chance at saving *all* their friends.

"Just stay right where you are," said the nearest Curator, scrambling over a pile of four-color pens. "We'll have you back where you belong in no time."

They only had one choice.

"We'll be back for you," Jake yelled.

"¡Te amo, Victor!" Marisol shouted, tears streaming down her cheeks as she began to run.

Victor's voice floated up from behind them. "Oh, you're gonna take me to Karen? Let's get moving, then. Time I told her she *sucks* at Candy Crush!"

~ 11 ~

MARISOL

THE BASALT WALL BLENDED PERFECTLY INTO the night.

So did Marisol, Jake, and Oz as they drifted over it. Flashlights off. Feathers floating. She couldn't see any Curators stationed below—probably because they were all back in the Wildlands, trying in vain to get red Sharpie stains out of their shirts.

Another smart move on Victor's part.

Wind blasted across Marisol's face, forcing more tears from her eyes. Her brother would be okay. *Wouldn't he?*

She glanced back over her shoulder, but the lava river was just a string and the rest of the restricted area was cloaked in darkness. She'd hated that Victor had followed her here, to this World that he didn't understand, and she'd spent most of their time together wishing they were apart, but now that it was actually happening . . .

She missed him.

The brother she'd found here in this magical place hadn't seemed like the same one she'd had back home—or maybe he was, but she was seeing a new side of him. He wasn't nearly as annoying. He seemed to listen to her. He thought about what she said.

Perhaps he was seeing her a little differently too.

Her stomach lurched as she landed on the Curators' side of the wall. There was an abandoned village called Polphail not far from here, which Amelia had pointed out on their flight in. *A good rendezvous.* According to Marisol's monocle, the Scottish town had never been inhabited in the old world, and it didn't look like it had been occupied much in this one either.

Empty windows watched the cousins walk past the buildings. Eyes did too—though these had been painted on. Graffitied faces splashed across walls, their bright colors washed out by lost starlight.

Jake paused beneath a picture of a hand holding some flames. With one hand he gripped the walkie-talkie, and the other held the strap of Yusra's bag, the vase of memories tucked safely inside. He watched Marisol with an expression that reminded her she was still crying.

"I know—" she sniffed, before he could say anything. "We have to keep going. For Nefertiti. For Yusra. For—for Victor."

Jake's lips slanted. Almost frowning. "Let's rest here while we call Amelia. We're going to have to wait for her to pick us up anyway."

Marisol slouched against the painted wall, and Oz curled up next to her as the walkie-talkie's static crackled around them.

Jake clicked the button and held the transceiver to his mouth. "Come in, Amelia! This is Jake and Marisol! Do you read?"

The air fuzzed with radio silence, and Marisol looked down at her fingers. They were prickling too—pulling her toward wherever Rocket was. Somewhere past Polphail's gutted buildings. Somewhere . . . up? Qué raro. What would a dog be doing in the sky?

"Jake! Marisol! It's good to hear your voices!" But it wasn't Amelia's bell-chime voice that answered. "We were beginning to fear the worst!"

"Who's we?" Jake asked.

"Oh, er, this is Percy. Fawcett. Apologies. I'm not used to talking without faces. It's most disorienting! Where are you two? Did you find the Rocket?"

"Almost." Jake shifted under the weight of his backpack as he explained what he was carrying. How they'd discovered the vase and the Administrator's memories inside it. And inside of those . . .

"A *dog*?" Percy repeated incredulously. "The Rocket is a dog? As in D-O-G? As in woof-woof?"

"Yes," answered Jake. "And we think that if we find Rocket and return him to the Administrator, we can show him that he doesn't have to tear the World apart. Marisol has a lead, so we need Amelia to come extract us."

"A lead! Indeed?" Percy exclaimed. "Where to?"

"Up. But not *straight* up." Marisol tried her best to describe what she was feeling. Pinpointing a direction was hard without a map, but she did her best to explain the sensation.

"Hmm . . . that sounds like . . ." Percy's voice flickered out and Jake tapped the walkie-talkie, but it wasn't the transceiver's fault. The explorer on the other end of the signal was simply thinking. "I wonder if . . . hold on . . ." This was followed by a scuffle and more static. Several minutes passed with this sound scratching the air, and Marisol huddled in closer to Oz.

"Sorry about that, friends! I had to double-check with Naomi. He used sled dogs during his old expeditions to the North Pole, and he still gathers teams here from time to time. He says that lost dogs in the World Between Blinks tend to gather together in packs and, oh, here, I'll let him tell you—"

More static.

Then Naomi's voice softened the receiver. "Based on what Marisol is describing, I'd say your destination is the Floating Mountains. One of the largest lost packs lives there."

"The Floating Mountains?" That explained the strange skyward tug on her magnet fingers.

"They're about thirty kilometers from where you're hiding. You can't miss them. I've been meaning to summit them one day, so I will look forward to hearing your adventures."

Marisol looked past Polphail's empty buildings into more emptiness. Stars were tossed like salt against the black. Were there mountains somewhere between them? She hadn't recalled seeing any rising from the horizon when they flew here with Amelia. Then again, they'd been more focused on Christopher's map of the Wildlands. . . .

"We won't miss them," Jake promised. "Can you ask Amelia to come pick us up from Polphail?"

The walkie-talkie crackled a few seconds too long.

The hairs on the back of Marisol's neck started to rise.

She knew what Percy would say before he said it.

"Amelia . . . Amelia's gone."

Marisol let out a cry. Oz whimpered and buried himself into her chest. Jake's face went ghastly, blending in with the surrounding graffiti.

Gone.

It was almost impossible to imagine Amelia Earhart without her memories. . . . Would the famous pilot smile wide enough to show the gap in her front teeth? Would she smile at all? Would she even remember what an airplane was?

This wasn't just the Administrator not being his best self. This was the Administrator being . . . awful. Heartless.

They had to stop him.

Percy cleared his throat. "The Administrator overturned her hourglass. It happened about an hour ago. She was sitting in the dining hall telling us all about the eelmails when . . . well, you saw Nefertiti."

Marisol would never forget watching the personality drain out of the Egyptian queen's face.

And she had a feeling that this was her fault again. That same gnawing dread that had snacked on Marisol's stomach while she stared out the window over Amarna— where the desert gave way to a gleaming row of planes. The *Flying Laboratory* was so bright. A Curator must have seen it flying where it wasn't supposed to.

"Can you send one of the other pilots?" she asked.

Another crackling silence.

"I wish. But we don't have any to send," Percy explained. "They've all left to fly people back to their assigned zones before the deadline. Perhaps we could send Johann's ship— ah, what's that? Never mind. Naomi just told me that won't work. There's no sand where you're headed."

"Thirty kilometers from here?" Jake's brow furrowed, bending numbers in his head. "That's . . . almost twenty miles!"

And they would have to walk it.

Alone.

Marisol, Jake, and Oz were on their own. There were no adults coming to help them. No daring explorers or ancient queens or archaeologists who spoke dinosaur or even a bossy older brother. All of those people were now counting on the Beruna cousins to reach the Floating Mountains and find the Administrator's dog.

"Twenty miles?" Marisol flexed her fingers and stood. "We'd better get going!"

But it turned out they weren't completely alone.

The cousins discovered this not five minutes after they left Polphail. A constellation of flashlights swept toward them, strung together with fraught voices. The cousins and Oz listened from a cluster of bushes. Hearts hammering.

"Please, you must see that this is a mistake!" A woman dressed in long, flouncing skirts that swept out to each side of her begged the Curator at the head of the group. "Shouldn't my husband be assigned the same zone as me? We appeared in the World together, and we've lived side by side all this time—"

"That's not my department, ma'am," the official replied sterilely.

"Can't you make an exception?"

"I have been ordered to escort you to your allotted zone. I'm simply doing my duty."

"You're tearing my life apart!" She sobbed. "You're tearing all of our lives apart!"

Marisol could see the rest of the group as they passed. Bobbing lights revealed gaunt faces. A man holding a chicken. A woman clutching a baby. More children who looked as if they'd just been yanked out of bed, their eyes rubbed raw. The Curator who herded them had a matching number of hourglasses on his necklace. . . .

"Then I advise you fill out a complaint card in the future." He picked out one of the timepieces and rattled it at the crying woman. A threat. "For now, you must keep moving!"

They did.

Marisol watched the group's lights fade into the distance, grateful for Oz's steadying presence at her side. For Jake's outraged murmur.

"What a . . . they can't do that! That's *evil*!"

"Evil things happen when people just follow orders like that, without ever asking if they're right," Marisol said softly.

"We have to do something! We have to make him see!"

"We will," Marisol said. "We'll find Rocket."

The cousins couldn't use their own flashlights, for fear

of being spotted, and the old world's burnt-out stars cast just enough light to see the next step and no more. Oz quickly took the lead, guiding the cousins through giant boulders and underbrush with his stiff striped tail. Thylacines, it seemed, had excellent night vision.

"Do you think there's ever a moon here in the World?" Jake asked wistfully, after running into a branch too tall to bother Oz.

"Maybe during new moons back home?" Marisol suggested. "Or whenever there's a lunar eclipse?"

Jake snapped through more branches. "So where does the sun come from?"

Leap years? That didn't make sense. "Maybe it's not *our* sun. It could be any star, couldn't it?"

They spent several miles like this—picking through brambles and talking about anything but their mission. Trying desperately not to wonder about Victor and Yusra, and what was happening to them right now.

She knew Jake was thinking about it, though, because during one of their silent periods, his lips suddenly slipped into a smile. "I can't believe Victor scribbled on those Curators with a red Sharpie!"

"I can." Marisol smiled too, but the expression felt wobbly. "Did I ever tell you about the time he drew moustaches on the fingers of every single glove in our house? He tried to blame me when Mom found out, but some of the ink had smudged off on his upper lip when he was playing around, so he got in trouble anyway."

Jake snorted. "Victor being annoying is great when it happens to other people. I'm glad he's finally using his powers for good."

"I hope Victor's okay."

Her cousin snorted again. "Honestly, I'm more worried about the Curators who have to keep track of him."

But Marisol couldn't stop thinking about her brother's expression back when they boarded that first hot-air balloon—when he was so afraid but trying to be brave for his sister. What would the Curators do with him this time? Would he get locked back in the Lost Dutchman gold mine? Were there even worse prisons out there?

Jake paused as if sensing her thoughts, then reached out to take her hand. "He'll be okay, Mari. Victor's tough. And smart."

"It's just . . ." She could feel a sob in her throat, and she swallowed hard, taking a big breath in and letting it out slowly, until she could speak properly. "He's been a lot less annoying lately. I—I can't believe I'm saying this, but he's being his best self! And look where it landed him! If something happens to Victor because he followed me here, I'm not sure I could stand it."

"Nothing will happen to Victor," Jake said confidently.

"How do you know?" She remembered with a start

that her brother had asked the same thing up in the hot-air balloon. *Tranquilo con la ruta*, she'd told him. *Be calm with the route.*

But Jake didn't say that. Her primo simply squeezed her hand. "Because he's Victor! Why, right now he's probably reciting the alphabet backward and counting out of order to distract the Curators while he plots his daring escape!"

The thought of Victor sling-shotting vowels and odd numbers at his captors made Marisol giggle. Oz trotted back from where he was walking out in front to run in a quick, cheery loop around them, and they managed to turn the conversation to other things.

Eventually, though, their words petered out once more. Jake glanced up at the sky, and Marisol could tell he was thinking about Amelia's missing smile. His shoulder slouched as he pushed forward, as if his backpack were getting heavier and heavier. The vase inside *was* so full of sand. . . .

"Let's take a break for a snack," she suggested.

Oz rounded back again eagerly.

The night stretched on. The cousins followed Oz until their feet felt too sore to hold their knees, much less anything else. Every few hours they stopped—sometimes to hide from more relocating groups, but mostly to rest and eat Ansault pears. Golden juice dripped like nectar down

Marisol's chin, almost sweet enough to forget her growing blisters.

The air around them was getting sweeter too—pine needles and snow crisp enough to catch your footprints and wind that seemed threaded with silver. Mountain smells. Scents that reminded Marisol of the Andes, in all their jagged glory. It was still too dark to see anything ahead, but she and Jake and Oz had to be close. . . .

They kept walking.

Slowly, surely, their trail became easier to navigate. Blue crept into the sky, washing back night with navy, and the stars started to wink out. *Good morning!* Sunlight ribboned the horizon with ruddy pink, brighter and brighter until they could finally see their destination.

Jake halted. His jaw dropped. "What in the worlds?"

Marisol stopped too.

Her toes throbbed.

Her fingers thrummed.

Straight *up*.

Mountains loomed overhead. The tallest of them reminded her of the view outside her bedroom window, back home in La Paz, where Huayna Potosí peeked over the city. Sharp edges veiled in snow. This summit was covered with white too, only it didn't dip down to bare stone, like the peaks in Bolivia did.

Instead, it just . . . ended.

There were no slopes connecting *any* of these mountains to the ground below.

They were actually *floating*.

"Well," Marisol managed. "The name makes sense now."

Jake's neck craned almost all the way back, staring at the where the hills slipped into thin air. "But . . . how? How can mountains *float*?"

"This *is* a world with underwater cities," Marisol pointed out. But she was curious too.

A quick glance through their monocles revealed the answer.

"They're mountain*tops*!" Marisol read on. The largest one was Mount Saint Helens, which—according to the Curator's entry—had appeared here on May 18, 1980, following a gigantic volcanic eruption. Vesuvius hovered next to it, along with several slopes from the Appalachians, which had appeared in the World thanks to coal mining. "Their bases must still be back in our world, which means they look like they're floating here! Remember the missing bricks at the Morris Island Light?"

"Yeah, but there was something left at the bottom of the lighthouse to climb," Jake said. "How are we going to get up there?"

The Floating Mountains were much too high to reach by jumping, even with the extra boost from their feather charms, and there wasn't much else around the cousins that looked useful. The ground beneath the hovering hills was flat. Devoid of trees and even grass, because of how much sunlight was blocked. Marisol looked farther down the range, her heart falling.

They'd come so far . . .

And now there was no way up.

"I don't know—" Her despair was cut short by one of the more distant hills. "Uh, Jake, is . . . is that mountain moving?"

Jake frowned and looked to where she was pointing. Darkness smudged the morning sky, bleeding out past the other hills, changing shape too fast. With each jerky move, a thunderous crack echoed. "Maybe it's a cloud?"

"Tal vez . . ." But Marisol had never seen a cloud shift like that, especially one so massive, so she consulted her monocle again. "Oh, Jake! They're birds!"

"No way!" His frown grew, but then he looked through his own charm and began reading the same entry.

Name: Passenger pigeons

Entry into WBB: September 1, 1914

Notes: Passenger pigeons were once the most numerous birds on Earth, with populations reaching an estimated 3 to 5 billion. Because they make such tasty pies, people hunted passenger pigeons until they appeared in the World Between Blinks. Here their population has rebounded heartily. (Beware: Flocks are so massive they can block the sun for days at a time. If caught in such an event do NOT look up. Forecast: showers of poop.)

"POOP SHOWERS?" Jake groaned, glancing down at his crusty shirt. "My T-rex snot has *just* dried."

Still, the flock was headed their way. Marisol couldn't help but be awed as the birds flew closer. Feathers: gray and iridescent bronze. There had to be thousands of them—tens of thousands—and the rush of so many wings caused the air to vibrate, like the last long note of a gong. *Buzzzzzzzzz*. Every so often, the birds changed course quickly. *CRACK!*

"The way they fly all together looks like silk!" She had to shout for Jake to hear her over the pigeon hurricane.

"Or an oil spill!"

"Or a flag caught in a storm!"

"Or a flying carpet . . ." A grin spread across her cousin's face as he reached out and grabbed her hand. "Mari! I have an idea! You know how Yusra used her floating charm to fly with that pterodactyl? Maybe we can do the same thing! We can surf them like a wave!"

Marisol's eyes went wide as she looked back at the birds. They did remind her of the swells at Folly Beach, gray gathering itself and rolling forward with a crash. Could she and Jake *surf* on that? Could they reach the Floating Mountains with a few million extra feathers?

There was only one way to find out.

"Let's do it!" she agreed.

Oz woofed his approval, sitting on his haunches like a kangaroo ready to spring.

Jake's hand tightened in hers. The flock flew closer and closer as he counted down. "Three, two, one . . . JUMP!"

Marisol sprang into the air, trying not to watch the sharp-arrow beaks soaring toward them. The feather on her necklace lifted her just as high as last time. Higher even, so most of the leading pigeons passed below the cousins' feet. Oz began barking. The birds bunched together in response, so when the trio started drifting down, they landed on a solid stretch of feathers.

"See!" Jake laughed with delight. "A flying carpet! If only Richard were here!"

Marisol giggled too. She had no idea what her cousin was talking about, but the birds beneath her *tickled*. It was like riding a very soft, whispery wave.

Jake and Oz dipped in and out of sight as the flock swirled higher, closer to the ice-crusted edges of Mount Saint Helens. All she could hear were their whoops of delight, muffled by the featherstorm all around them.

The pigeons' wings stirred up the snow, and it billowed like a bag of dropped flour, so when the birds finally parted to let their passengers land, the cousins sank into blinding white.

"That was awesome!" Marisol was thankful for her boots as they landed in the wintry landscape. Too bad she no longer had Amelia's jacket. . . .

Poor Amelia.

This thought of her friend grounded her.

The birds' excitement whisked off with them, rolling down the mountain range. The snowflakes whirling in the air around Marisol parted, and the view below became clearer, revealing the miles Oz had just led the cousins across. From here she could see that the boulders and bushes were strangely arranged, as if someone had taken a ruler and shoved them into lines.

Someone *had* . . . Marisol reminded herself.

She could see more groups being relocated too, strung along by callous Curators. The sight made her sick, so sick, and she shoved all of this anger into her fingers.

They burned bright. Rocket the dog was close, maybe even somewhere on this very mountain!

Snow crunched behind her.

"My magnet fingers are on fire, Jake!" Marisol said. "We've got to be cl—"

Her voice died when she turned.

It wasn't her cousin she was addressing.

It wasn't Oz either.

Marisol Contreras Beruna found herself standing face-to-face with a yeti.

∼ 12 ∼

JAKE

SO THE ABOMINABLE SNOWMAN WAS REAL.

Or . . . snow*woman*? Jake studied the muscular creature that towered above his cousin. It was nearly twice Marisol's height and swathed in shaggy white fur, staring down at her with razor-blue eyes. Jake himself was some distance away, lying in the snow beside Oz, but he saw the moment his cousin wanted to scream.

She didn't, and he felt pride swelling beneath his initial panic. They'd learned a lot about first impressions here in the World. . . . Perhaps yetis weren't all that different from T-rexes?

Marisol drew herself up, trembling, cleared her throat, and spoke in a voice that sounded like thin ice. Only one step from cracking.

"Hola, amiga. Nice to meet you. My name's Marisol."

The yeti made a soft, rumbling noise, leaning down until the pair of them were nose to nose, and blinked slowly. She—for Jake was now positive the creature was an abominable snow*woman*—wore a brown leather bandolier strapped across her chest, like a belt covered in pockets. It was the kind of thing soldiers wore to war. Were there weapons inside?

Jake's breath was frozen in his throat as he snuck through the snow. Silent, silent. What was he going to do when he reached them? Attack this giant creature from behind? Distract her, maybe, so both of them could run?

Then the yeti straightened up to her full height, stuck out her hand and held it in front of Marisol, speaking words that rumbled like some far-off avalanche.

"Welllcommme to the floating mmmountains, tiny hummman!" She stopped, cleared her throat, and continued in a voice easier for human ears—more a cascade of pebbles skittering over rock. "What brrrings you to our slopes?"

Then Jake realized what was happening. The yeti . . . was offering to shake hands.

Marisol must have realized too—she squeaked out a reply as she tentatively let the yeti enfold her tiny hand in a huge, white furry one. "Um, a flock of passenger pigeons and a feather charm."

"Whattt?" rumbled the yeti.

"That's what brought us here," Marisol clarified.

The yeti blinked pale, ice-blue eyes slowly. "You . . . came from belowww?"

Marisol drew out her reply, the way Jake always did at school when the teacher asked him a question he knew he was supposed to know the answer to. "Yee-eee-eess?"

Jake had crept as close as he dared and then crouched behind a snowdrift. If he needed to cause a distraction, the best he could think of was to fling some snowballs, and hope the cousins and Oz were faster than the giant yeti when it came to running. Not a sentence he'd ever expected himself to think . . .

The yeti inspected Marisol for a long moment. "You are nottt a Curator?"

Marisol planted her hands on her hips. "Of course not!"

"Then what brrrings you to our mmmountains?" the yeti rumbled.

"We're looking for a dog," Marisol replied.

The yeti drew herself up to her full height, roaring a reply that set the snow around them trembling. "YOUUU WILL NOT REZZZONE THE DOGS! WE ARE THE PROTECTORS OF THE DDDOGGGS!"

The snow shivered and quivered, some of it snaking off the ledge and falling to the barren plains below. When Jake glanced farther up the mountain, he saw that the white slopes were shimmying with movement. Was an avalanche coming? What were you supposed to do for an avalanche? Run away? No, run *across* the flow of snow. He'd had a lesson one time in Switzerland. He'd have to grab Marisol first, and—

Oz leaped over the bank of snow—a bold blur—and head-butted the yeti in the leg. Immediately she twisted around, then crouched down to inspect the Tasmanian tiger.

"Oh, hhhello, Oz!"

"Seriously, Oz?" Marisol laughed with relief. "Do you know *everyone*? How did you even get up here last time? And why didn't you show us that way when we were confused?"

"The wwway Oz knew is no longer therrre," the yeti replied, scratching Oz behind the ears with one hand and reaching into her bandolier with another, drawing a snack from one of the many pockets and feeding it to the thylacine. The mountain's shimmering snow stopped moving. Avalanche averted!

It didn't really seem worth hiding anymore, so Jake straightened up and waded out from behind his snowbank.

"Therrre are two of youuu." the yeti observed.

"I'm Jake," he said, coming to stand beside his cousin.

"Annnddd I am Annapurna." The yeti offered him

her hand. The skin there was a gray that bordered on silver and when he shook it, it was cool as metal, her palm leathery, her fur tickly. "Nameddd after my faaavorite mmmountain," she added. "Nowww, whattt do you wwwant with our dogggs?"

Jake and Marisol exchanged a long look.

I don't really want to be caught in an avalanche, his eyes said.

Me neither! said hers. *But we need Rocket!*

Annapurna observed their hesitation. "Smmmalll humans, if you are frrriends of Oz, I will not throwww you off our mmmountain. But if you thinkkk we are handing over our canine frrriends . . ."

"We want to help one of your dogs!" Marisol clarified.

Annapurna relaxed, the icy blue of her eyes melting a few degrees. "Ohhh?"

Jake nodded. "We think one of your dogs—he's called Rocket—might be the answer to getting the Administrator to stop rezoning everything. We think Rocket's an old friend . . . and he might be what the Administrator's looking for."

Annapurna considered this and looked down at Oz, who whuffed softly, puffing out a foggy breath. "Youuu had bettter come to the Frostmoot," she rumbled.

The snow was powder white beneath their feet as Annapurna led them up the slope, and Jake couldn't stop shivering. When he looked across at Marisol, her teeth were chattering too, but she shot him a rattly grin.

Just as Jake was starting to wonder where they were going, the big yeti led them around a huge boulder, and before them loomed a dark cave entrance. This time, Marisol's smile was a lot less sure, but Oz trotted happily after Annapurna, so the cousins joined hands and followed.

Almost as soon as they were inside the tunnel, they turned a corner and Jake could see the light at the other end. When they emerged inside the mountain itself, his feet stopped moving, and he simply stared, openmouthed.

The inside of the mountain was completely hollow, and sun streamed in at the top. Jake had thought it would be dark here, but the snow-capped peaks that had blown apart back in his own world had been reassembled like jigsaw puzzles with pieces missing, leaving plenty of gaps to light the place up.

All around the interior of the hollow mountain were cave mouths, and zigzagging across the empty space in the middle were hundreds of slides made of clear blue ice, twirling and looping around each other like a giant knot of roller coasters.

"Wow," breathed Marisol, her eyes lighting up. "Annapurna, can we try those out?"

"They are the onnnly way to reach the Frrrostmoot," Annapurna rumbled.

Jake got a twitchy feeling between his shoulder blades—it was a *long* way down from those slides—but he didn't have much time to think about it.

Annapurna turned and took down a mallet from where it hung on the stone wall beside an enormous gong. She raised the rod high, then swung it down to strike the gong, which sang its own name in a rich, bass, metallic voice that set every part of the mountain trembling, growing and growing as it reverberated around the inside of the peak.

GGGOOOOOONNNNNNNGGGG!

Yetis came lumbering out from every cave mouth, looking up and around, then climbing onto their slides to set off on a whistling, loop-the-loop journey through the giant tangle of ice, all converging on one cave mouth on the far side of the mountain. Jake could see now that every slide led to the same place, and he held his breath as the yetis shot out the other end and into the darkness one after another, somehow never arriving at quite the same second.

"Offff we go," said Annapurna, gesturing to the chute of ice that led from their own ledge. "I willll go firrrst, so nobody is surprised when you arrrive."

She climbed onto the slide and gripped both sides to

propel herself forward—then she was slipping down and away with a gleeful shout. With a skittering of claws Oz launched after her, and then it was just Jake and Marisol left.

"We're about to take a giant ice slide," Jake said. "To a meeting of yetis, in the middle of a floating mountain, to see if they can help us find a dog that got lost a hundred years ago."

Marisol shrugged. "We've done weirder stuff," she pointed out. "It's the World Between Blinks, Jake. Let's go convince some yetis!"

She climbed on to the slide, and like Annapurna, grabbed both sides with her hands and pulled herself forward, keeping her legs bent so her bare skin didn't touch the ice. With a squeal of joy she was away, plunging down the slide and leaning into the first turn.

Jake looked after her and swallowed hard. "Eyes ahead," he murmured. "Don't look back."

He lowered himself onto the slide, and before his courage ran out, he pushed and was away!

It felt as if his stomach snagged at the top—unraveling behind him as he plummeted down the slide, picking up speed, then hurtling around a corner so quickly that he was grateful the high sides stopped him from spilling out. He heard a yeti whoop cheerfully as their slides curled around each other like a strand of DNA, and only the speed at which they were traveling stopped them from falling to the ground thousands of feet below.

He squeezed his eyes shut, decided that was worse, then opened them in time to see rock and ice and sky fly by, and suddenly he was out the other end, landing in a huge pile of pillows, and big hands were reaching out to pull him clear of the landing pad before a yeti popped out right behind him.

The hall where the Frostmoot met was . . . pretty awesome, actually. At least a couple of hundred yetis were gathered in tiered seating that rose up on either side of the hall, taking their places and talking among themselves in voices like rocks falling. But these weren't hard benches like the bleachers at school. Instead, the yetis reclined on couches of every size, color, and fabric, arranging the cushions just as they liked.

Marisol appeared beside Jake, nudging him with her elbow until he followed her gaze to the center of the floor, where a yeti at least twice the size of Annapurna was sitting in a huge recliner, reaching over the edge to pull the lever that would bring up the footrest.

"Huuumannns," the recliner yeti rumbled, then cleared her throat and tried again in a slightly less bouldery voice. "Come forwarddd to the Paisley Couch of Judddgment."

"Which couch is that?" Jake whispered to Marisol.

"The other one in the middle?"

They both hesitated—there was an intricately pat-terned couch sitting in front of the large yeti's . . . well, throne, really. The sofa's upholstery was bright and splashy—in a way that reminded Jake of Nana's favor-ite wallpaper, only it boasted teardrop shapes instead of flowers. That was probably paisley, he reasoned. But if it wasn't, then it would hardly make a good impression, plonking themselves down in the middle of everything like that.

Oz solved the problem by trotting forward and jump-ing up onto the couch.

"Oh, hello, Ozzz," the head yeti—for that must be what she was—said, sounding much more cheerful. There was a general murmuring up in the stands as the other yetis echoed the greeting. Annapurna waved from where she was sitting.

Together Jake and Marisol walked forward, and perched on the edge of the paisley couch. *Of judgment . . .* Jake tried not to shiver. An impossible feat, here where his breath spun out into cotton candy wisps and more than one hundred abominable snowpeople watched with glowing blue eyes.

Marisol squeezed his hand, then cleared her throat. "We've come to ask for your help," she said.

"But what we're doing might help you too," Jake added.

"You haddd betttter tell us what is happpppening," the large yeti said. "I am Manaslu, leaddder of the Frost-moooot. Speak nowww."

Jake and Marisol exchanged a long glance. Where to begin?

And then, Jake knew.

He pulled the Illuminator from his pocket, and Marisol, understanding, pulled the vase full of the Administrator's memories from her backpack.

"Once upon a time," Jake said, "there was a man who was having a really, really terrible New Year's Eve. . . ."

By the time he and Marisol had finished their story, Manaslu was sniffling, and she fished down the back of her recliner to find a handkerchief to blow her nose.

"That poooorrr mannn," she said. "And his poooorrr doggg. Also, that was verrry enjoyyyable to watch. Someone please puttt the questionnn of a cinnnema on the agennnddda for the nexxxt Frostmooot. It mighttt fit nexxxt to the ice hockeyyy rinkkk."

Her voice was drawing out, becoming rockier and rockier, but with a deep breath, she steadied herself.

"If Rockettt is here, who is to sayyy he will be happierrr with the man the Administrator has becommme?"

"He might be a different man, if he had Rocket back," Jake pointed out. "He's not just the person who's doing all this rezoning. He's also the man we just saw helping people in need. With Rocket and this vase of memories, we could help the Administrator remember that!"

"Also," said Marisol, "he really loved Rocket, and it looked like Rocket loved him back. Don't you think that dog deserves to be with his person?"

"Perhappps," Manaslu allowed. "But that is only a mayyybe. Rocket willll be safe herrre."

"Will he really?" Jake pressed. "For how long?"

"His Curatttors came here in their balloooons," Manaslu said, drawing laughter from the crowd of yetis to either side. "They wished to rezzzone us."

"Did they fail because you're huge and look really scary?" Marisol asked, tilting her head to one side.

"You are smallll but cleverrr," Manaslu told her. "They have takennn our glacier, though. It was once the larrrgest of our slidddes. It was the wayyy to and from the grounddd."

"They'll take more than that soon," Jake said. "They'll take your memories, turn your hourglasses, if you defy them." His heart ached as he spoke, and he knew desperation was in his voice, as he tried not to think of the smile fading from Amelia's face. "They've already done it to some of our friends."

"Please," Marisol added, wrapping her arms around herself with a shiver. "We don't have much time."

Manaslu regarded her in silence, and then looked up

at the rows of couches, from which yeti after yeti regarded them. Then she looked back down.

"Ozzz," she said gravely. "Do you vouch forrr the humansss?"

Oz sat up straighter. "Ah-ah-ah," he replied, just as solemn.

"Then we willll vote," Manaslu said. "Allll those forrr a favorable judgmenttt?"

Annapurna's hand shot up, and Jake held his breath as he turned to study the rest of the yetis.

They took their time, whispering to one another, scratching their chins as they studied the children.

Slowly at first, and then faster and faster, the yetis began to raise their hands.

Yes.

Yes.

Yes.

Jake felt tears of relief prickling behind his eyes.

Marisol squeezed his hand so very, very hard.

"You are frrriends of the yettti," Manaslu said, breaking into a smile. "We willll help you finddd your Rockettt. Kangchenjunga, brrring them coattts, they are turrrning an unnaturalll shade of blue. My smallll friends, we musttt go to the Hallll of Fammme."

~ 13 ~

MARISOL

MARISOL WASN'T SURE WHAT YETIS WERE famous for.

She also wasn't sure why she and Jake needed to visit this Hall of Fame, but that didn't stop her from accepting the coat that Kangchenjunga offered. Well, it seemed to be more of a heavy sweater—knitted with the coarse white fur their hosts no longer needed. It was much too large, draping all the way down to Marisol's ankles. Jake's sweater was no better. From a distance, the cousins might be mistaken for yetis themselves.

Just . . . tiny yetis.

Whose skin was no longer turning blue.

Manaslu noticed the resemblance too. The head yeti laughed so loudly that the icicles clinging to the cavern's ceiling started to *riiing*. "Youuu look likkke chillldren!"

"We *are* children," Jake pointed out.

"Ohhh?" Manaslu raised her eyebrows. White fur disappeared into white. "It is harrrd to tellll with humm-mans. You are allll so smallll!"

"Are you sure we have to go to this Hall of Fame place?" Marisol asked. She couldn't see cracks in the mountain dome from here—all of the light was cast by colorful paper lanterns—but she knew the sun hadn't stopped rising. Of course it hadn't. Hours were ticking away. They only had so many left before the Adminis-trator made good on his threats, and one by one, their friends' faces went blank forever.

"The Floattting Mounnntains go on and on and onnn. . . ." Manaslu's voice echoed as she turned and waved for the cousins to follow. "So dooo the dogggs. Rockettt could be anyyywhere."

"He's . . ." Marisol had to rub her frozen fingers, thaw-ing them just enough to point toward a frost-covered wall. ". . . that way!"

"Maybe nowww. Mayyybe not when we get therrre. We must callll him," the head yeti explained.

They walked out of the Frostmoot, waving farewell to Annapurna as they passed. The yeti smiled, and even though her teeth still looked ferocious and oh-so-sharp, Marisol grinned back. Who knew yetis could be so cheer-ful? Or that they spent their days knitting sweaters and

231

taking care of stray dogs? Or that they used ice slides? She would've missed out on so much if she'd given in to fear and screamed at the first sight of Annapurna.

Most people are too afraid to listen.

Yusra had been talking about dinosaurs when she'd said this, but Marisol was beginning to see that the idea stretched much further than that.

It might even apply to . . . well, to the Administrator! Already he'd turned out to be someone different than who they'd imagined, now that they'd seen his memories.

Would he be brave enough to hear out the cousins' case if they brought back Rocket? Would he stop tearing apart the World because he feared losing things? Would he want to become his best self?

There was only one way to find out.

By finding his dog.

The Hall of Fame was a long corridor of ice that clung to the bottom rim of Mount Saint Helens—it was inside the last remains of the glacier the Curators had confiscated. It felt almost as if they were underwater again, only the waves were frozen. Thankfully, the floors were sturdy, too thick to see through to the drastic drop below. Shelves had been carved into the walls, creating a stained-glass effect: clear, blue, hazy white.

"What is this place?" Marisol asked as they stepped inside.

"The Hall of Fame. I belllieve the Curatttors would call it an archivvve."

Jake glanced around. "Are there memories here?"

Marisol studied the icy shelves. It didn't look like they held any sand, but there were plenty of other cool objects. Film from an old-fashioned camera. Giant footprints preserved by plaster casts. Framed newspaper clippings. When she went up on her toes to look at them, she saw most of them were older, from the 1950s, and had been hung on the frozen walls the way a proud mother might display their child's fingerpainting.

"Memmmories." Manaslu nodded. "Yes. Secrrrets that the other worllld forgggot. Secrrrets we keep. We must stay myths if we want to stay here. The World Between Blinkkks is the only plllace big ennnough for us. Or . . . it used to be."

The shelves held more than just lost evidence. There was memorabilia too: stamps featuring yetis, and mugs and silly Halloween costumes and plushies, and even an action figure Marisol recognized from a recent animated film.

Jake paused in front of a fuzzy photograph. Even though it was in black and white, you could tell the creature strolling through the trees had dark-brown fur. "Is that Bigfoot?"

Manaslu stopped to see what he was looking at. "Our

233

cousssins prefffer Sasquatch," she corrected. "Bigfoot hurrrts their feelllings. It is like beinggg called abommminable."

"Oh," Jake's cheeks turned pinker. "Good to know! Is that Sasquatch?"

"His nammme isss Vernon. He livvves with the rest of our cousssins in the Vanissshed Forrrests, but mayyybe not anyyymore." Manaslu frowned. "Mayyybe the Curators came for themmm too."

"They're reorganizing *everybody*," Marisol said. It was hard to forget the scene she and Jake had seen last night—with the woman who'd been torn apart from her husband and the Curator who did not care. Even though her new sweater was toasty thick, she shivered. "I don't think they'll stop unless we find Rocket."

"If he isss here, weee will finnnd him."

They rounded a bend as Manaslu said this, and the stalactites on the ceiling gave way to . . .

Collars. There were hundreds of collars. No. *Thousands*! Big, little. Short, long. Leather, vinyl, reflective material. Black, blue, green, pink, camouflage, gold. All of these and more hung from the overhead ice. Name tags shimmered from their ends, winking at the cousins as they passed below.

"What is all this?" Marisol glanced at the walls, which were now covered in LOST: DOG posters. Thousands of doggy faces gazed out from them, as many and varied as their collars. Most of the tattered posters looked like something you'd staple to a telephone pole.

"Dogggs like to runnn free. Runnn, runnn, runnn. It is no use chasssing their packs around the mmmountains. We ussse the whistles to callll them instead." Manaslu gestured up at the name tags, and Marisol saw that a whistle hung beside each one. "If we find Rocket's collar, we find Rocket's whistle."

Jake was standing on tiptoes, trying to read the names. "Are they alphabetized?"

"Alphabetized?" Manaslu laughed—a great booming sound that made the name tags sway and chime throughout the icy hall. "We are not Currrators. We do not *collllect* dogggs. They are our friendsss."

"You have a lot of friends," Marisol pointed out.

It would take hours and hours to read these name tags, maybe *days*, and she wasn't even sure that Rocket *had* a collar in the first place. She hadn't noticed one in the Administrator's memories, and when she tried redirecting her magnet fingers to the task, they sputtered. Numb. She was colder than she'd thought . . . her nailbeds had turned a dusky purple.

"Anything?" Jake had been watching.

She tucked her fingers back into her sleeves and shook her head. "Thank you for showing us this place,

Manaslu, but we don't have time to sort through all of these collars."

"It is the fastttest way!" The head yeti's teeth snapped when she drew out the *t*. Insistent.

Was it? Marisol wanted to argue, but she had no idea how long it would take to reach Rocket otherwise. Normal mountains took hours to hike on foot, and if the Administrator's dog was two, or even three Floating Mountains away, that distance added up. Hours into days. But it didn't seem like there was any other way. . . .

"You twwwo still looook like icicles!" A new gravelly voice. It belonged to Kangchenjunga—the yeti who'd given them the sweaters. This time he'd come bearing a different offering. "I havvve brrrought tea!"

Giant ceramic containers—more bowls than mugs— steamed from the tray in his hands.

"Oh good." Jake sighed. "To quote our friend Percy: everything's better with tea!"

Oz whuffed his approval.

"Gracias." Marisol accepted her cup carefully. It was too hot to taste, but the ceramic warmed her palms and the mist that tickled her nostrils had a sweet, clear smell. It reached all the way to the back of her mind, stirring some memories. "What kind of tea is this?"

"It isss steeped *Monardella leucocephala* leavvves." Kangchenjunga's explanation was met by two blank stares, so he cleared his throat and tried again. "A type of minnnt tea."

Oh. An idea crystallized inside Marisol's head.

Her eyes went wide.

Oh!

"Manaslu?" She turned to the head yeti so suddenly that some tea slopped from her mug, landing on the icy floor with a *hiss*. "Is there a way to call all of the dogs to us at once?"

"Yesss." Manaslu frowned. "We havvve a lituus." She paused at the confused looks on the cousin's faces. "It is a verrry long horrrn," she explained. "But there are mannny packs. Many, many." A furry white hand gestured to thousands of collars. "These are but a few of the collection. How would you find Rocket?"

Marisol's hands tightened around the mug. Of course, her magnet fingers would help, but among a horde of tightly packed lost dogs, it would be hard to pick out just one. Still, if all went according to her new plan, she wouldn't have to use them at all. "We don't need to find Rocket. We need to let Rocket find us." She looked at Jake meaningfully. "We need peppermint."

They needed a whole lot more than peppermint, it turned out.

Calling the Floating Mountain's dog packs all at once

required more strategy than Marisol had first thought—for when they were called, the dogs quite rightfully expected to receive a treat.

Manaslu had to rally every yeti in Mount Saint Helens, asking them to pack their bandoliers full of biscuits to distribute after she played the summoning lituus horn. Hundreds of them came lumbering in to collect their allocation, carefully stowing them away in preparation for the onslaught.

"Arrre we surrre this is wwwise?" asked one, as she grabbed the last of her treats. "We mayyy be overwwwhhhelmed, covereddd in cannnines!"

"Wwwe can do it," Manaslu said stoutly. "We willll not bite offff more thannn theyyy cccan chewww."

Once everyone was equipped, they all had to ski down the mountain to the much less snowy summit of Mount Vesuvius, where they then hiked onto tree-covered slopes that were only dabbed here and there with hints of white. *To avoid avvvalanches and rrrockfalls.*

It was midday by the time they were finally ready.

"Myyy, but it's hottt here," Manaslu said, fanning herself.

"I'll keep my coat on, thanks," Jake said, still snuggled inside it. "I'm beginning to get used to yeti hair."

Marisol, Jake, and Oz stood side by side, clutching handfuls of extinct mint leaves and covered in the last of the T-rex repellent. There had hardly been any left when Manaslu had helped the children smash the can open with a rock, but a few drops went a long way. Besides, didn't dogs have super-powered noses?

It wasn't *quite* the peppermint plant they'd seen the younger Administrator sharing with Rocket—back before he was the Administrator and either of them was in the World Between Blinks. But surely it smelled pretty close, and hopefully what mattered was that it was leaves. She remembered the Administrator's words as well, as Rocket gobbled his snack: *Only the plant. Peppermint candy is dangerous for dogs.*

This mint *had* to do the trick. After all, Marisol told herself, she'd follow something that smelled sort of like chocolate, so Rocket would follow something that smelled sort of like peppermint, right?

Right? They certainly smelled strongly enough, that was for sure.

"I feel like a Starbucks Holiday Drink again." Marisol tried to make herself laugh, but the joke had been Victor's, and it only made her miss her brother more.

"I'd give a lot for a peppermint hot chocolate right now." Her primo rubbed his belly with gusto. "With extra whipped cream and sprinkles. When this is all over we'll go back to the Frost Fair and get some cocoa with Amelia."

Oz responded with a whining sound that matched exactly how Marisol felt inside. Hope and worry all twisting together tighter and tighter and tighter until she thought she might snap. *This had to work* because if it didn't . . .

She looked past some trees to the far horizon, where the World lay waiting.

"That would be nice," she made herself say. "We'll take Victor, he'll love the jugglers."

"He *will*," Jake agreed.

Manaslu took her place beside Oz and the children and was unpacking the lituus horn from its case. The instrument was almost eight feet long, its brass curved like a J at the end, but the yeti's massive silver gray hands made it look manageable. "Posssitions, everyone!"

The rest of the yetis had placed themselves in large concentric circles, facing outward, with their bandolier pockets unbuttoned. The biscuits inside were within easy reach, and Oz had already succeeded in begging two or three or four or probably more from the innermost defense.

"Arrre you ready?" Manaslu asked the children.

Marisol nodded eagerly. "Sí."

"Let's do this!" exclaimed Jake.

The head yeti filled her lungs with a breath that seemed to last forever, set the lituus's mouthpiece to her lips, and blew. The note was piercing.

Marisol could feel the sound buzzing through her bones and then down into the ground, all the way to where the mountains' roots tapped into the sky.

It stretched up as well—to the snow and the clouds and that strange star of a sun. It folded into Vesuvius's stones and echoed into itself again and again. It became so ingrained in Marisol's ears that she wasn't entirely sure when Manaslu stopped playing.

The Floating Mountains' dogs heard too.

One by one, howls rose to answer. They sprang up all along the mountain range—a throaty chorus.

"Braccce yourselvvves!" Manaslu shouted to the farthest ring of yetis.

Not ten seconds later, the first dog arrived. It looked very much like a wolf, except for the cute little white marks that stood in for eyebrows. There was a pink stripe down the middle of its nose too—twitching eagerly at the sight of a biscuit.

"Sit!" The yeti holding the treat commanded. "Gooood dog!"

A tawny dog followed soon after, lithe and springy, rich caramel fur lightening to a sunnier shade on his belly, velvet ears flopping as he stopped in front of a yeti and sat up on his back legs to beg for a treat.

Marisol's heart gave a little leap at the sight of that

fur—an exact match to Rocket's—but the snout was too narrow. A dark-brown mutt burst through the bushes. And another. And then there were too many canines to get a long look at. Huskies and Great Danes and dachshunds and golden retrievers and pound puppies poured into the clearing.

"Sit! Gooood dog! Sit! Gooood dog! Sit! Gooood dog!"

The first round of yetis was soon overwhelmed, and the wagging tails poured into the next ring. Eager to sit and get their treats. Even though most of the dogs left afterward, the wave of wriggling fur only grew.

"Here, Rocket! Here, boy!" Jake had started shouting, waving like a person directing airplanes on the runway. "Come and get your tasty, tasty leaves!"

The mint in Marisol's hands was crushed almost to a pulp, she'd clenched them so hard. Picking the Administrator's dog out of this stampede seemed impossible.

It would have been for anyone else.

But the flare in her fingers told her Rocket *was* out there. And getting closer.

"ROCKET!" she screamed. Her hands were burning. There were so many brown dogs around. . . . "He's close, Jake! I feel it!"

Her cousin responded by tossing handfuls of mint into the air. They drifted to the rocky ground like sad confetti, and watching them fall, Marisol was suddenly scared that this plan had been a waste. What dog would choose dried leaves over a biscuit? Even Oz wasn't interested, and Oz ate pretty much everything. . . .

"Mari!" Jake grabbed her arm. "Look!"

He was nodding toward Annapurna, who stood in the innermost ring with her treats at the ready. There, between her shaggy white legs, peered a golden-brown dog.

Rocket!

He looked just as he had in the Administrator's memories. There were even a few burrs stuck to his tail. Annapurna was trying to get him to sit, he clearly wasn't listening.

His dark eyes were on the children, and his head was cocked to the side, as if to say: *What have we here? A mint that is not quite pepper? Hmm* . . .

Marisol wanted to dash over, but if Rocket ran away it would take forever to find him, so she knelt down instead.

The dog did not move.

"Here, Rocket!" She waited and waited and finally opened her burning hands. "I know it's not exactly peppermint, but we have an even better treat! We've come to take you home!"

Rocket took a step forward. His tail wagged.

Oz gave an encouraging whuff.

"That's right!" Jake had lowered himself to the ground too, and was collecting some of the leaves he'd thrown, brushing them into a sorry pile in his palm. "I'm sorry there's dirt on them, but you aren't supposed to eat this many at once anyway!"

And then Rocket trotted into the middle of the circle.

He ate the mint leaf she was offering him in one happy bite, snuffling breath tickling her palm. Next he started licking T-rex repellent off Marisol's cheeks with a gritty tongue.

"Eres tierno." A sweet feeling of victory bubbled up her throat, turning into a giggle. "I can see why the Administrator couldn't stand losing you!"

"It's time to reunite them!" Jake gave Rocket a good scratch between the ears. He glanced up at the sun, which was balancing over the top of Mount Saint Helens, ready to roll off into afternoon and evening. "Past time. We only have a few hours left before the deadline hits! Let's get Rocket and the rest of the Administrator's memories back to him before it's too late."

Half an hour later, the cousins stood at the edge of Mount Saint Helens, loading their backpacks into a hot-air balloon. It looked almost identical to the one that had arrived to arrest Marisol back in the Phantom Islands Sector— yellow like a summer evening, littered with jars of wind for steering and marked-up maps for navigating. Several long white yeti hairs lay on the basket floor as well.

"We tooook this from the Curators who cammme to tttake us," Manaslu explained. "Now the ballooon is our onnnly way onnn and offff the Floating Mountains."

"But—" Marisol swallowed. "We can't take that!"

"We have to," Jake whispered as he helped Rocket jump into the basket.

"The Frostmoot wiiishes to helppp you," the head yeti assured them. "We would raaather have our glllacier back. Gooo and help the Administrator finnnd a better way!"

"Okay!" Marisol turned toward the balloon, pausing when she saw the wind directions written on the mason jar lids. There were so many possibilities! She didn't know where to start, or even where she wanted to end up. "Um, Manaslu, do you happen to know where the Administrator is? Does he live in, like, a castle or something?"

The head yeti shook her head.

"Someone at Queen Nefertiti's court might know!" Jake suggested. "Try calling Percy! We need to tell them about Rocket anyhow."

"¡Buena idea!" Marisol jumped over a pile of maps to dig the walkie-talkie from his bag. After a few button clicks the device fuzzed with static. "Colonel Percy Fawcett! Come in, Percy!"

Silence crackled through the speaker.

Marisol strained her ears to listen—hoping for an

answer—but all she heard were the howls of dogs still receiving treats two whole mountaintops away. "Come in, Percy!" She tried again. "Come in, anyone! ¡Por favor!"

Jake frowned. "Maybe the reception is bad up here. . . ."

Or maybe there was no one left to answer them.

Had the Administrator wiped Percy's and Naomi's memories too? Marisol's stomach flipped as she imagined Queen Nefertiti's great columned dining hall, filled with hundreds of vacant stares. Harold Holt, Bessie Hyde and her husband, Glen, Alexander Helios, the son of Cleopatra, Richard Halliburton, Min-jun, the garum vendor . . . In her mind's eye she could see all of their friends turned into stoneless statues. Sitting in front of platters of stale donuts.

The walkie-talkie suddenly felt heavy in her hand. "Please come in!" She tried again, trying not to cry. "Jake and Oz and I found Rocket! We just need to know where to take him!"

But it was no use.

Jake bit his lip as he watched Marisol switch off the walkie-talkie. "We could try visiting the Great Library of Alexandria?" he suggested. "That's where I ran into the Administrator last time. And it's where he keeps the hourglasses. . . ."

"I don't know, Jake," she answered with a shaky

breath. "He's rearranged so much of the rest of the World. What if he changed that too?"

"We have to go somewhere," he said. "Do you have any better ideas?"

Marisol looked around the balloon. Rocket was sitting like a *very good boy*, his tail thumping dangerously against the mason jar glasses. Oz was busy nudging aside papers to make a resting place of his own.

But wait! The Tasmanian tiger wasn't just scratching. He actually seemed to be unrolling the maps with his claws. Reading them . . .

"I don't have any better ideas," she told Jake. "But I think Oz does!"

The thylacine made a *yes! look here!* sound, and stamped his paw over the map's bold title. Marisol's stomach did a loop the loop when she read what it said:

THE HEADQUARTERS SECTOR
(all reports may be filed at the Administrator's office on the 34th floor of the Singer Building)

She scanned the cartography with a harshly beating heart. The Singer Building wasn't hard to find. One of the map's previous users had marked it with a bright-red marker.

Marisol grinned when she saw it. "*X* marks the spot!"

14

JAKE

"WE SHOULD'VE ASKED OZ IN THE FIRST PLACE!"

Jake glanced back at the map. The red X was due north, so the cousins started scrambling through the jars of wind, hunting for a southerly breeze that would blow them in that direction. They were just like the ones Marisol had seen when she'd been escorted to the gold mine jail when she'd arrived in the World—they must be standard issue for the Curators, stocked in all their balloons.

They both agreed that the thylacine's advice was the way to go—who knew the World Between Blinks better than Oz? Everyone else in this land trusted the Tasmanian tiger. Even the Curators! Of course he would know where their leader was. . . .

"If Oz is sure," said Marisol, "then we can be sure too. And you're sure, aren't you, Oz?"

Their friend gave a decisive yip. Rocket joined in with a throaty bark. Jake didn't think the dog really understood what was going on, but as long as someone scratched Rocket behind the ears every so often, he seemed happy to have made new friends.

Still, the *thump-thump-thump* of Rocket's happy tail echoed the *thump-thump-thump* of Jake's racing heart, as Marisol held up a jar labeled SOUTHERLY BUSTER in neat handwriting.

"What do you suppose a buster is?" she asked.

"I don't know," Jake replied. "But it sounds friendly, like 'hey, Buster, how are you?', and it's blowing in the right direction."

"Good point," she said. She angled the large container away from them and unscrewed its lid.

For a moment, nothing happened.

Then a breeze began to snake around the cousins, cool air tickling their noses and ruffling their hair.

Oz made an uncertain sound and crouched lower in the basket.

"Uh, you don't think a buster busts things up, do you?" asked Marisol, gazing down at the jar she'd just opened. Jake couldn't tell how much of the wind had spilled out. It looked just as empty as before. "Maybe we should hold on, just in—"

Her words were erased with a scream as a wall of

freezing cold wind hit them, sweeping the balloon up and away! The basket rocked violently as it launched, all four of them thrown to the bottom in a tangle of limbs.

Jake scrambled upright to look out over the rim, and spotted Manaslu, Annapurna, Kangchenjunga, and a host of other yetis pausing in their dog duties, waving farewell, and shouting something—probably *good luck!* It was impossible to hear, though.

They had unleashed a storm, and now they had to ride it.

At first he worried that the wind was so strong it would tip the basket, or blow out the flame heating the air that lifted the balloon, but the Curators' transport was made of sturdy stuff—it held together, though it felt like the SOUTHERLY BUSTER was trying to tear them apart!

The cousins huddled together inside their yeti coats, taking turns to pop their heads up over the rim and check their progress. The sun was climbing across the sky, and it was past the halfway mark, now.

At sunset, their thirty-six hours would be up.

The balloon raced along, faster, faster, ever faster, but was it fast enough?

Every so often, Jake caught glimpses of the land below, everything laid out in neat lines and careful divisions. The Curators must be down there continuing their sorting and zoning—by nightfall everyone would be in their place, and anyone who protested would have forgotten why they cared.

He shivered and ducked back down into the shelter of the basket. Rocket was there to greet him, licking the side of his face, then snuffling behind his ears to see if any treats were hiding there.

Jake wrapped his arms around the pup, burying his face in the caramel-colored coat. So warm. So alive. So happy. There was something comforting about dogs— they felt like home no matter where you were—and Jake had always wanted one, though his mother always said no. *We travel too much*, she reasoned. *It wouldn't be fair to the puppy.*

He knew his mom was right, but this hadn't stopped Jake from imagining what it would be like to have a wagging tail greet him every time he came back to his apartment. To have a friend no matter where he moved next . . .

Rocket's tail *thump-thumped* against the backpack and its sand-filled vase. Jake swallowed when he remembered the memories inside. The Administrator must have lost everything during World War I. His house, his friends, his livelihood. How much worse was it then, to lose Rocket? His four-legged friend. His home away from home.

Jake's chest ached just thinking about it.

A hollow hurt.

He hugged Rocket harder as their balloon flew over zone after zone. The broken pieces of a world that would never be right enough . . . not for the Administrator. Could one dog fix all of that? Jake wondered. Was the Administrator's best self so long gone that even his memories couldn't uncover it? He worried that too much been lost already.

Bleak wind kept roaring.

He shivered again.

Their balloon soared on.

It was about an hour later when Marisol spotted the other balloons. She squeaked and ducked down into the basket, pinning down a map that wanted to fly away.

"There are Curators out there!" she told Jake.

His heart leaped into his throat. He peeked out at the sky through the gaps in the wicker basket. Sure enough, the clouds were dashed with color. Tiger's-fur orange. Mermaid teal. Neon green. White uniforms weighed down the baskets beneath, and even though they were too far away to tell, Jake bet the passengers were holding clipboards too.

"Well, we *are* flying toward their headquarters," he reasoned. "Did they see you?"

"I don't know," Marisol admitted. "Maybe they'll think the yeti sweater is a uniform? It's white? Hopefully they won't try looking at us through their monocles. . . ."

Jake's throat tightened at the thought. "They're too busy dealing with the Administrator's deadline." He tried to sound calm. Sure. But his windpipe kept getting smaller and smaller.

Two yeti sweaters and a lost dog: that was it.

That was their plan.

How could he and Marisol possibly pull this off?

Jake used his own eyepiece to scan the closest balloon, and that was when he finally choked, reading the information inside the glass:

Curator (Karen), arr. 1985.

Assignment: Prisoner transport, rezoning.

Rating: 9.99/10

"Mari, it's, it's . . ." He couldn't finish, only point, and she pushed him aside to press her own monocle up to the wicker gap.

"¡Ay, no! It's Karen! Do you think she has Victor? There's nobody else in the basket with her, my monocle says so. But if he still hasn't been processed, then maybe he wouldn't show up? Oh, Jake!"

"Should we try to rescue him?" He was torn in two, one part of his heart pulling him toward the end of their quest, the other tugging back toward his cousin.

Marisol hesitated, her mouth tug-of-war tight, and he sensed the same struggle in her. She finally shook her head in a sharp movement.

"No," she said. "He would say the same thing he did when they caught him. We have to keep going. Everyone's depending on us."

Her eyes were leaking, though, and Jake knew it wasn't just from the cold wind howling around them. He pulled her into his arms, hugging her tight. "If you'd asked me what Victor would say before all this," he said, "I'd have guessed something like 'This sucks! Where can I recharge my phone? You'd better rescue me straightaway, forget everyone else!'"

Marisol laughed, and though it was shaky, the sound was real. "And then he'd probably insult the Curators' fashion sense," she added. "'Why wear white unless you're a polar bear?' Or a yeti . . ."

Wind kept roaring around them, whittling her laughter into nothing.

"He'd probably still say some of those things," Jake said, considering. "But I don't think I'd mind as much. There's more to your brother than I thought."

"Me too," she murmured, burying her face in his yeti coat, just as he'd buried his in Rocket's fur a few hours before.

"We'll tell him ourselves, in person," he promised, hoping against hope he was right.

By the time they spotted the skyscrapers on the horizon, the sky was turning orange—ripe as the fruit and fire bright.

Buildings rose up from the ground like a cluster of fingers pointing accusingly at the heavens. Jake's jaw dropped as their balloon swept closer to the Headquarters Sector. Based on the map Oz had shown them, he'd expected one or two office buildings, but this place . . . it was huge. Sprawling. Like, New York City–sized. There had to be over two hundred towers, and there was even a section in the middle that reminded Jake of Central Park. Trees surrounded a glass structure that looked both instantly familiar and out of place.

Marisol spotted this too. "Is that the Crystal Palace?"

It was. Through his monocle Jake could make out the gleaming form of the vast repository where the Curators kept almost all of their records in giant tomes. It was swarming with officials now, no doubt making corrections to the books at a furious pace, recording where everything was now to be kept.

"The Administrator must have rezoned it," he said, reading on. "Look! There's the Irish Public Records Office where Great-Uncle Christopher wrote our names in the ledger! And, and right behind that is the Great Library of Alexandria!"

Where everyone's hourglasses were kept . . . The

ancient structure wasn't see-through, so there was no way to tell if it was as busy as the Crystal Palace. Jake's stomach turned at the thought of so many timepieces being turned, all of the world's memories falling away. . . .

"Good thing we didn't head to the library's old location!" Marisol shouted back. "But which one of these is the Administrator's office?"

"The Singer Building!" Jake reminded her.

"Lo sé," she answered. "Which one is that?"

Jake began scanning the taller buildings around the park. *CPF Building (Singapore, 2017), City Investing Building (NYC, 1968), CAGA House (Sydney, 1992),* and on and on. There were so many, and the cousins' balloon was traveling too fast to keep track. Names began to blur together while windows grew larger, close enough to reflect Jake's own panicked face.

"Um, Mari . . ." He could hear his voice quavering. "How do we stop?"

"I'm on it!" She crouched by his feet, bottles and jars clinking as she hunted frantically through them, reading label after label. "You just figure out which one of those skyscrapers is the Singer Building!"

"Uh, Oz?" Jake looked down at his friend, who gazed back up at him with big coffee-colored eyes. "Any hints, buddy?"

Oz ducked down as a jar went flying by. He made

256

himself as small as he could in the bottom of the basket, his tail sticking straight up, like one of the skyscrapers ahead of them. But *which* skyscraper? The basket swung wildly as Jake tried using his monocle again. Names kept blending together—fast, fast, in your face—and it was no use. Everything was chaos! Rocket had joined in on Marisol's efforts. It seemed like the Administrator's dog thought they were digging for treasure—his two paws sent maps and bottles flying everywhere, his tail whipping back and forth.

Oz's tail, though, remained straight as a post, sticking up in the air.

Jake looked back toward the buildings ringing the record repositories, and in that moment he wasn't sure whether it was the cold wind bringing tears to his eyes, or his own tiredness and the growing hopelessness enveloping them.

In less than a minute, they would smash straight into a skyscraper, and *it probably wouldn't even be the right one!*

"Marisol," he shouted, and she tossed another jar away.

"I'm looking, I'm looking," she yelled. "There has to be something here that can stop us!"

Then his gaze fell on a building different from the others. It was square and squat, rising more than a dozen stories into the air, its dark-red brick decorated with wrought iron and intricately scrolled stone around the windows and balconies.

But sitting atop the building, rising from it as surely as Oz's tail rose from the huddled form of his body, was a taller, thinner tower, culminating in a spire hundreds of meters above the ground.

Could it be?

Was Oz trying to tell him . . . ?

He steadied himself against the wild rocking of the balloon's basket, pressing his monocle to his eye.

The Singer Building (NYC, 1968)

"I see it!" he yelped, dropping his monocle to watch as they hurtled toward the skyscraper.

In those last seconds, it was as if time was slowing almost to a crawl.

Jake looked up and saw the balloon shivering above them as the SOUTHERLY BUSTER threatened to tear its yellow fabric to shreds.

He looked straight ahead at the brick—red as rust and oh so solid—while the setting sun to their left cast shadows across the face of the building.

And he looked down, a small part of him realizing with detached interest that the crowds gathered around the base of the skyscrapers weren't white-clad Curators at all.

They were rebels.

They knew they were out of time, and they were making one last, desperate effort to save themselves—and their memories—by attacking the Administrator's headquarters.

He saw the glinting shields of the Lost Army of Cambyses, the jostling helmets of the Ninth Roman Legion. He saw redcoats and Vikings and so many others swirling like eddies in a fast river, pouring past little white islands of Curators, and all converging on the Singer Building. There was even a woolly mammoth in the mix! And . . . was that Sir Percy Fawcett on its back? Leading the charge?

"I've got it!" Marisol screamed, pushing up to her feet and ripping the top off a small jar that read BECALMED on its label.

For a heart-stopping instant the furious wind intensified, roaring past Jake's face like a fast-moving train, stealing his very breath. And then it spiraled, twisted, and funneled itself straight into Marisol's jar!

The writing on the label slowly erased itself, and then it rewrote a new label in the same neat hand: SOUTHERLY BUSTER.

Everything around them was perfectly still, and perfectly silent, save for the soft whoosh of the flame that was heating the balloon's hot air and the rush of the rebels down on the ground. Far below, the mammoth let out a bellowing battle cry.

"Told you I'd get it," Marisol panted, grinning, but she dropped the jar and threw her arms around Jake, squeezing him until she stole his breath as surely as the magical jar had. "And look," she said cheerfully, releasing him and starting to pull off her yeti coat, the cold wind suddenly gone. "Counting from the ground up, we're pretty much level with the thirty-fourth floor."

Jake glanced down, trying to ignore the flashing armor as he counted windows. A few of them had opened; Curators poking out their heads to see what all the fuss below was about. One had grabbed a bowl of paper clips and was tossing them at the Romans' helmets.

"I'm glad we don't have to climb," Jake said, as their balloon drifted toward the building, the last of their momentum slowly dying. "We'd get stuck fighting that battle instead of stopping it! And we'd probably lose Rocket too."

The dog had stopped digging up maps, though his ears had perked up and his snout swiveled straight around to the Singer Building. They were almost to the window, closer, closer. Jake caught a glimpse of warm, wooden furniture and a richly patterned rug. And then . . .

. . . and then they were looking straight at the Administrator himself!

He sneered through the glass, face pale and puffy. His

chin was still pointed and his eyebrows had not stopped growing—they were even more jungle-y than Jake remembered. More like angry ferrets than the caterpillars he'd imagined them as last time. They made the man beneath look wild.

Looking at that glare, it was very, very hard to believe that somewhere deep inside, the Administrator might have a best self.

Rocket started to bark by Marisol's feet, but it wasn't a vicious sound.

No, despite the scowl, the *glare* the Administrator was directing at them, Rocket's bark was . . . happy.

The dog's tail wagged so hard that the maps started to flutter again. He whined and did an *it's-you-it's-you-it's-YOU* dance with his front paws. Rocket recognized his old owner, even after all this time, even when Jake couldn't. Again he tried searching for even a hint of the kindness the Administrator had shown Rocket in the memories, but none of it was there.

In fact, his scowl only grew when he saw the dog.

The Administrator started to shout, but his words got caught on glass. His eyebrows zigzagged. He shoved the window open. "YOU TWO! I should've known you'd come to mess things up! As if it wasn't enough, that ragtag army down on the ground is trying to breach the building and overturn hourglasses! That's it, I'm having all your fellow rebels' memories erased this minute, I'm going to write a memo the second I've—OH!"

Rocket simply could not contain himself.

It didn't matter that he did not have a feather charm, or that they were thirty-four stories high. One second the dog was in the balloon basket, and the next he was a *rocket*. Golden fur blurred through a golden sky into the open window. Onto the Administrator's chest.

The two of them went tumbling across the rug.

"Rocket!" Marisol screamed. "Oz!"

The Tasmanian tiger launched for the window too, his feather charm floating along with his paws. He drifted lazily through the bluestone sill, paddling as if he were underwater.

"Here goes nothing!" Jake grabbed the backpack, double- and triple-checked to make sure that the feather was still attached to his charm necklace. The balloon had come as close as it could to the Singer Building, but the basket dangling underneath it was still some distance away.

"Eyes ahead, Jake." His cousin didn't even glance down as she climbed to the edge of the basket. "That's what you always told me. Don't . . . look . . . back!"

On the last word she drifted across the gap, grabbing hold of the window ledge and slithering inside, pulling herself along as easily as if she were rock climbing with

Uncle Mache back in Bolivia.

Jake swallowed and gripped the straps of his backpack. Armies swirled below at the base of the building, tiny figures crashing against it like waves on a rock. If he fell—well, if he *floated* down—he'd get caught in the battle to storm the building. The vase might even get smashed, the Administrator's memories scattered, and then—

"Jake!" Marisol waved from the window. "¡Ya pues! JUMP!"

He did.

The feather hadn't lost any of its Unknown magic. As soon as Jake's feet left the wicker, the air around him turned pillowy. He bounced straight into the Administrator's office. The place smelled like shoe polish and wet dog.

"GET THIS DIRTY MUTT OFF ME!" The Administrator was still on the rug, stiff arms trying to hold Rocket at bay. There were pawprints all over his white three-piece suit, and it made Jake think of that very first forgotten memory, when the man discovered the puppy in the mud-filled ditch, when the dirt didn't matter at all. "IT'S RUINING MY UNIFORM!"

"His name is Rocket," Jake said, studying the Administrator's expression carefully.

It didn't change.

"I don't care if his name is Kalamazoo! Call him back!" The Administrator shoved his old friend away, looking thoroughly disgusted, and straightened his suit in a series of quick, sharp, and furious movements.

Rocket began to whimper, and Oz trotted protectively between the dog and his former master.

"Oz!" the Administrator snapped. "Don't think you're off the hook, just because you're you. I *still* haven't forgiven you for tripping me up in the hourglass repositories. Speaking of . . ." His gaze went sharp, cutting to the cousins' charm necklaces. "I might not know where your large hourglasses are—though mark my words, we *will* find them—but I can make sure you don't receive any more help plunging this world into chaos! I'm blaming the rebels for all of this, and judging by your outerwear, the abominable snowpeople as well! I'm writing a memo this very minute."

He turned to storm toward his desk without a backward glance, and after a moment frozen in place, the children went flying after him.

"Stop!"

"Wait!"

"I'll do no such thing," the Administrator snapped, riffling through his drawers and producing a notepad. "This memo will be replicated in the repositories the moment it's written, and my instructions will be followed posthaste. That is, immediately. Hourglasses can and *will* be turned, and order will be restored."

"Just listen to us for one minute," Marisol pleaded as Jake dug frantically in his backpack for the Administrator's memories. Without them, he clearly had no interest in Rocket, who'd started wandering around the office sniffing everything in a way that Jake suspected meant he might pee on something soon, though he really hoped not.

"And why in the name of A to Z would I listen to you?" the Administrator asked, picking up his pen.

"Because . . ." Jake searched frantically for a reason— any reason—that the man might listen to them.

They *couldn't* repay Manaslu and all the others by getting their memories wiped. They couldn't fail the citizens of the World Between Blinks, who only wanted a chance to grow, and think, and learn, and change, and live where they wanted, befriend who they wanted.

And then it came to him.

They had to gamble *everything*.

"You should listen to us," he said, voice shaking, "because if you try what we want you to try, and you still don't agree we're right, then we'll tell you where to find our memories. And you can wipe them yourself."

Marisol's fingers found his shoulder and squeezed tightly.

And the Administrator put down his pen.

"That would be more efficient," he said slowly. "So go on. What is it you want? Besides complete and utter anarchy?"

Jake pulled the glazed yellow urn of memories out of his backpack and took off the lid. The Administrator sucked in a quick breath.

"These are your memories," Jake said. "We'd like you to take one back."

"If I discarded them, I clearly had no use for them," the Administrator replied, white brows lifting high. "Why would I take them back now?"

"Do you remember our last conversation in the Great Library of Alexandria?" asked Jake.

"Vividly," the Administrator scowled.

"You said I *wanted* to be lost. And part of that was true." Jake swallowed. "It's hard, moving around the world so much, always saying goodbye to friends. It's hard waking up in a new city and knowing that everyone you love is miles away. It's . . . lonely." He stumbled through the word. "And sometimes it's easy to let that loneliness grow. And I think . . . I think *that's* why you gave up these memories."

"Because I was lonely?" the Administrator asked, his eyes narrowing. "I'm not alone! I have hundreds of employees!"

"That's not what I meant—" Jake bit his lip in frustration. The Administrator hadn't understood last time either. *Life is full of loss,* he'd said during their previous meeting, *and sometimes it's too much to carry around with you.*

"Then what *do* you mean?" The Curators' boss sounded impatient.

"You wanted me to surrender all of my sand, so nothing would ever hurt me again. I almost did," Jake admitted. "But that would have been a mistake, because giving up the pain of the bad memories would also mean losing the joy from the good ones. If you choose to forget the things you've lost, how will you ever be able to find them again?"

A frown crept over the Administrator's face, shrinking his eyebrows.

"You helped me realize that life is messy, and that's okay." Jake nodded at the man's blemished suit. "Sometimes it's worth getting a little dirty."

"Is it?" The Administrator gazed at him for a long moment, as if he could see straight through Jake and into his thoughts and hopes and wishes and fears. And . . . and his loneliness.

"You'll see for yourself," Jake promised in a whisper. "Just as soon as you put a grain of sand back in your hourglass."

The Administrator said nothing. Jake held his gaze, and held his breath, and waited.

Then, slowly, without taking his eyes off the cousins, the Administrator leaned down to open the bottom drawer of his desk.

"One grain," the Administrator said. "But not because you're convincing me. It's just the easiest way to get my hands on your hourglasses."

Thump-thump-thump went Jake's heart.

This was it.

"Rocket, come here," Marisol called softly, dropping to a crouch. The dog immediately came trotting over to her, leaning in so they could snuggle, and sniffing her hopefully in case she had any treats, or mint leaves.

The Administrator lifted an almost-empty hourglass out of the drawer, set it down on the desk, and then carefully removed the top.

Thump-thump-thump.

Thump-thump-thump.

Jake offered him the urn, and with a roll of his eyes, the Administrator leaned forward and picked out a grain of sand.

"This won't change anything," he said. "As soon as I've added it to my glass, you're going to tell me where your hourglasses are, and this will be over. And everyone—including you—will be happier. That's all I've ever wanted, you know."

Thump-thump-thump.

"Just one memory," Jake agreed, hoping against hope it was good.

The Administrator dropped it into his hourglass. The grain of sand landed atop the others that sat in the top half, nestling in as if it had always been there.

The silence drew out.

Thump-thump-thump.

And then the Administrator blinked slowly.

And blinked again.

And then he shot up out of his seat like he was powered by a southerly buster, eyes wide as he stared down at the dog beside Marisol.

"ROCKET!"

～ 15 ～

MARISOL

THE ADMINISTRATOR CHANGED IN AN INSTANT.
It's amazing what love can do to a soul, thought Marisol.
One grain of sand—one memory—and the man standing
at the mahogany desk was transformed. His eyes widened. His face lit up. His wrinkles shifted from a scowl to
a smile and finally, *finally*, Marisol could see the person
from those blue-wall memories. Right there on his face,
she could see the Administrator's best self.

"ROCKET!"

At the sound of his name, the honey-colored dog shot
into his owner's arms, smudging more dirt on his vest.
The Administrator laughed as they tumbled back onto
the rug. Marisol's heart fluttered. She looked back at
Jake, who wore a triumphant grin.

"Do you understand now?" her cousin asked the

Administrator. "Or should we tell you where our hour-glasses are?"

"I—oof—" The man could hardly answer, with Rocket eagerly licking his face. Minutes before, he would've shoved the dog away. Now the Administrator hugged his pet tighter, nuzzling his head under his jaw. "I think you should pour the rest of the sand in. Please," he added.

Marisol let out a heavy breath. She really *hadn't* wanted to give up all of her memories, and even though she knew Jake knew what he was doing—knew he was right to do it—his offer to surrender their hourglasses had scared her.

"All of them?" Jake asked, as he picked up the vase.

The Administrator hesitated, and Marisol felt a fresh spike of fear. Maybe she was wrong. Maybe the man hadn't really changed. He was looking down at his dirt-smeared suit, frowning again.

"Yes," he said finally. "*All* of them."

Her primo carefully began to sift the rest of the Administrator's memories back where they belonged. Into the hourglass. Into his mind. There were thousands of grains, and as they settled the Administrator's expressions began to shift. He grimaced. He smiled. He hugged Rocket tightly.

"I can't believe I lost you, boy." Even though he was

whispering into the dog's ear, it was loud enough for the rest of the room to hear. "I can't believe I forgot. . . ."

Rocket licked the old man's cheeks.

Clearly, all was forgiven.

"You two!" The Administrator looked up at the cousins. "You did this!"

Marisol puffed up her chest. "That's right."

"Oz helped too," Jake added.

"I searched this world for years . . . but it was impossible. It was chaos. Everything was everywhere. Oceans flowed into the sky and ships got stranded on mountains. Dinosaurs laid eggs in cars and one time it even rained diamonds . . . which isn't nearly as nice as it sounds! How could anyone find a single dog in that?"

"We saw the Wildlands," Marisol agreed. "Was it all like that?"

The Administrator shook his head. "Worse, often. I began to draw up maps. I discovered that there were certain places in the World where the ground was thin, where new lost things appeared. I started digging and then I discovered what we now call the Unknown—magic.

"I found ways to manipulate it into charms, such as those feathers around your necks. I started recording items that appeared, and slowly, slowly I organized everything. The World began to look like a world . . . with cities and separate climates. My language charm meant that people who'd lived apart for centuries could suddenly understand each other. Everyone began working together to make the World a better place.

"But despite all of these new systems, I still couldn't find Rocket. I scoured deserts and jungles and seas. I called for him until I lost my voice. I lost hope too. And then I began losing my memories. . . . There was no one left in the old world to hold on to me. No one anywhere, but Rocket."

The Administrator scratched his dog behind the ears and looked up at his full hourglass.

"I invented the hourglass system to capture the memories this place might try to take. But when I saved all of mine, it was too much. Every grain of sand that held Rocket reminded me that I hadn't found him. . . ."

"So you chose to forget," Jake said. "You buried your memories in that blue cottage."

"The blue cottage?" The Administrator blinked. "Yes . . . my house. I'd forgotten about that too."

"But you didn't stop searching," Marisol pointed out. "Yusra said that's why you're so obsessed with sorting things, because you didn't want anything else around you to get lost ever again."

The Administrator blinked again. He looked a little dazed. "Maybe? I don't know who Yusra is, but she sounds smart."

"She is," Marisol replied. "You had her arrested."

Two pale eyebrows crumpled, and there was a twisting silence, fraught enough to hear yells through the open window. It sounded as if the rebels had reached the Singer Building's doors. While the Administrator considered what had happened, below a desperate battle was being fought—their friends were in danger.

"I only wanted to make this World better," the Curators' boss repeated, sounding almost bewildered. "There was so much chaos. So much that could go wrong. I just didn't want anyone else to suffer the way I did."

Somewhere outside, glass shattered. The mammoth bellowed again.

"Can't you see that you're making things worse?" Marisol grit her jaw, remembering the crying woman from the night before. "Your new rezoning rules are tearing families apart—they're losing each other just like you lost Rocket. The people outside, they're fighting because they want the World to be better too."

The Administrator sat still for a moment, considering.

"You're right, Marisol Contreras Beruna," he said slowly. "I went too far. I lost my way."

"You lost your best self," Jake said. "Someone smart told us recently that can happen sometimes. But we can help you find it again! That's why we brought Rocket back."

The Administrator stood. "For that, I'm in your debt."

"You can repay us by restoring the rebels' memories," Marisol said. "And making every zone free for everyone. And making the Amazon a rainforest again! And giving the yetis their glacier back!"

"There's also a bit of a complicated promise we made to some T-rexes," Jake added. "We can talk about that later. But most of all . . ." He looked across at Marisol, and she nodded.

"My brother, Victor, is out there somewhere. Karen captured him. We need to find him."

"We will," promised the Administrator. "But first we have to stop the fight. I'd write a memo, but my Curators would think I'd somehow been hijacked. I don't think they'd follow it. I'll have to do this in person. . . ." The Administrator began walking to the office door. Rocket trotted after him. "It would also be better if you two were with me."

Jake looked at Marisol.

Marisol looked at Jake.

They nodded together.

"We're in," Jake said.

Marisol grinned. "Let's go save the World. Again."

"Are you sure this is an elevator?" Marisol asked when the Administrator unfolded a set of ornate doors. The inside looked a lot like a cage, but a fancy cage. With wrought-iron grillwork and small roses cast out of bright, bright brass. There was an old-timey phone attached to the wall and somewhere, somehow a soft song was playing.

"It's perfectly safe," the Administrator assured them.

He even stepped inside first and jumped a few times before waving to Rocket, Oz, and the cousins.

"Why does all elevator music sound the same?" Jake wondered as he entered the elevator.

The Administrator's eyes lit up. "Fun fact, it's called Muzak. It was invented to make people less nervous when they were riding elevators for the first time. I—" He caught himself midsentence. "Sorry. I have a habit of sounding like a glossary entry. I had to occupy my mind with *something* after I buried those memories of Rocket."

"Apart from cataloging things," Jake replied. "At least now we know why you did it."

"Before, we thought it was just because you were an evil villain. . . ." Marisol meant this as a joke, but the words came out a little too true.

Rocket whimpered.

His owner looked crestfallen.

"Evil?" he repeated.

"We know you're not," Jake said quickly. "Now, I mean! Evil villains usually don't admit their mistakes. And they certainly don't offer to fix them!"

"That's right!" Marisol chimed in. "You and your scary eyebrows are just misunderstood, like a T-rex! Or a yeti!"

"You're full of compliments this evening, aren't you, Miss Contreras Beruna?" the Administrator sounded wry.

"No—I only meant that you're frightening on the outside, but not on the inside!"

The eyebrows in question rose even higher, and Marisol stumbled over her tongue to keep explaining. "We had to pass a T-rex to reach your old house, and gosh was it terrifying. I almost peed my pants. I sprayed it in the face with repellent instead, but then Yusra explained that the T-rex only wanted its chin scratched and . . . well, then I remembered that when I first met Annapurna, the yeti, and I didn't scream even though I really wanted to, and she didn't try to eat me either. Even *Victor* turned out to be different than I thought. I guess what I'm trying to say, is that it's good to give people a second chance."

"So I should pretend you did not just suggest that my eyebrows are monstrous?" The Administrator asked.

Oops.

"Exactamente," Marisol said.

"Very well, then."

The elevator rumbled downward. Rocket leaned into the Administrator's leg. The cousins' feather charms began floating to their noses, their shoes lifting off the rubber floor tiles. Oz made an annoyed sound as his striped rump drifted to the ceiling. Marisol grabbed one of the bars to hold herself steady and Jake did the same. Muzak played—some forgettable song that must have been forgotten in the old world too—but it didn't do anything for Marisol's nerves.

What would they find when they reached the bottom?

A fight, for sure. And a big one at that. She could hear shouts through the doors, growing louder and louder with each new floor, until the Muzak was completely drowned out. Rocket's ears pinned back, and his tail slunk between his legs. The Administrator gave his dog a reassuring pat as the elevator settled.

Marisol, Jake, and Oz landed back on the ground.

The doors opened. . . .

The Singer Building's main corridor had turned into a battlefield.

Clipboards clashed against shields. Screams echoed up arches and their rib-like columns. Curators ran back and forth across the white marble floors, trying their best to block the rebels marching through the front entrance.

It was a huge entryway, but most of it had been covered in decorative brass, again like a cage, so only a few soldiers could walk through at a time. Marisol could see the outline of a mammoth beyond the bars, silhouetted by the light of gas lanterns, too massive to burst into the corridor itself.

The rest of the lobby was lit with skylights—or rather, lamps that looked like skylights. These reflected off the rebels' helmets as they wrestled farther and farther into the white suits. Charm necklaces were ripped off by both sides and more than a few noses were bloody.

Marisol had been afraid in the World before—she'd fled from T-rexes and run a heist on the Crystal Palace—but this was something new, and something awful. The Curators were simply fighting for order, but from the residents of the World Between Blinks . . . this was desperation. This was a fight for their lives.

The cousins hurried out of the elevator, keeping close to a bronze-studded marble column, which provided protection from at least one flying shield.

A nearby Curator with fraying french braids scowled when she saw the cousins, aiming her Swingline 747 Classic stapler straight at them. "Halt, agents of chaos! You children just can't help yourselves, can you?"

Marisol swallowed. She didn't *think* the staples would actually hurt, but she didn't want to test the theory.

"No." The Administrator exited the elevator doors and lowered the Curator's weapon with his hand. Rocket stayed close to his leg. "They've helped me instead."

"Sir?" The woman did a double take. "Oh, sir! Thank

goodness you're here! We've received some . . ." She hesitated, looking around the corridor as if she might find the right word amid broken glass and flying punches. "Complaints."

"So I see," he replied.

"We told them to fill out forms, but it's no use! They insist our system is broken! What do you want us to do? Should we arrest them all? Should we overturn everyone's hourglasses? That would make everything peaceful again—"

The Administrator cut her off with the shake of his head. "Tell the rest of the Curators to stand down."

"What?" The woman lowered her stapler, frowning. "Stand down? But, sir, if we do that they'll *destroy* everything."

"If you fight, it will only get worse," Marisol said. "Let us talk to the rebels!"

"Talk?" She laughed. "Good luck."

As if to prove her point, a fully loaded clipboard hit the column above Marisol's head, exploding into a cloud of documents. A Viking came roaring through, tackling the Curator with the french braids. She started smacking his helmet between the horns with her stapler.

"Stop it this instant!" The Administrator commanded, using his most *I-am-in-charge-here* voice. "Everyone stop fighting! We must have order!"

Marisol and Jake joined in the yelling, but it was no use. Their voices got lost in the cacophony of the main corridor.

No one was listening.

No one would stop.

Marisol watched more rebels spill through the doors, and more Curators rushing down the opposite staircase to meet them. The two sides crashed together, just like the helpless feeling in her chest.

It made her think of the T-rex and the peppermint repellent—hurt someone and they'd hurt you back, and the fight would go on and on and on and on. How could you end something like that?

"I wish we had that lituus horn!" she shouted over to Jake.

"What about a megaphone?" Her primo's blue eyes brightened as he pointed into the crowd. "Look! There's one!"

Marisol's heart lurched as she spotted the device. A fair-haired Curator was using it—not to shout through— but to beat back a Roman legionnaire. Every time the megaphone landed on his armor, it let out a high-pitched shriek. "Jake! We have to grab that! It's the only thing that can get everyone's attention!"

The only problem?

The Curator holding the megaphone was at the

opposite end of the main corridor, pushing his foes back through the broken doors. The cousins would have to do some pushing of their own to reach it.

Jake began to roll up the sleeves of his sweater. "I guess we'll have to get a little messy!" he said. He braced himself like he was about to jump into cold water at the beach near Nana's house, then rushed into the fight.

Messy was one word for it. . . . Marisol took a deep breath as she dove into the fray, trying to make herself as small as possible. Someone grabbed at her necklace, and snagged her yeti sweater instead. She squirmed out of their grasp, trying not to hit back. No one here was her enemy. Not really. And Marisol didn't want to make the hurt worse. She just wanted to get to that megaphone!

She dodged and twisted and slid across the marble floor. From the corner of her eye she could see that Jake was doing the same. And Oz. The thylacine had a clear path, though . . . everyone paused their fighting to nod *hello* as he trotted past. Everyone loved the Tasmanian tiger.

Everyone trusted him. . . .

The megaphone was lying on the ground when the cousins reached it. Thankfully, the device was still working. When Jake pressed the trigger switch, an earsplitting sound rattled the already shattered glass at their feet. He brought the megaphone to his mouth, his chest puffing up for a yell.

"Wait!" Marisol put her arm out before he could speak. "The Curators won't listen to us without the Administrator." And *he* was still back by the elevator, half hiding behind the column. "We should let Oz do the talking!"

Oz seemed to agree.

He sat at Jake's feet expectantly. It was the first time Marisol had seen him so eager for something that wasn't a snack.

"Okay, boy." Jake pointed the mouthpiece down and the amplifier up. "Tell them what they need to hear!"

Oz let out a noise that reminded Marisol of an ambulance siren. The ceiling's decorated domes caught this sound and folded it up, over and over, until it dripped back down the columns and washed through the corridor, back out the broken doors, and into the crowded streets.

Hair prickled on the back of Marisol's neck and goose bumps covered the rest of her as she watched the room react. Vikings, legionnaires, redcoats, a Neanderthal, pirates, sailors, vendors from various markets, Curators . . . *everyone* paused. Stiff enough to be statues. Silent enough to listen.

It stayed that way until the echoes faded.

"Oz?" A cry came from the other side of the entryway. "Is that you, old chap?"

"Is that you, Percy?" Jake called back.

"Is that *you*, Jake?"

The silhouette of the woolly mammoth began moving—it had an extra head, wearing a hat—and Marisol realized their friend was riding the creature, craning his neck for a look through the brass latticework. "And Marisol? You're there too?"

"¡Sí!" she reassured him, all too aware that the room was starting to get restless. "We're here, and we have something to say! Well, our new friend does." Marisol waved over at the Administrator. "Will you tell them what you told us?" she asked.

Every head in the room turned toward the Administrator, who cleared his throat and drew himself up a little taller.

"I've changed my mind," the Administrator said.

"What?" gasped Jake.

Marisol's mouth suddenly felt full of cotton balls, like she couldn't talk at all. How could he say such a thing with Rocket at his side?

The Administrator stepped away from the column and began walking toward them. His dog followed, sniffing at leg armor and polished shoes.

The soldiers stiffened.

The Curators looked confused.

Everyone was listening, and Marisol felt frozen in place, dreading what they were about to hear. Had they just fought their way through all of this for nothing?

Or . . . did he mean *they'd* changed his mind?

Just as she thought her heart might explode, the Administrator turned his head and offered Jake and Marisol a solemn, respectful nod. She heard Jake let out a slow breath beside her as the man began to speak.

"When I first found this World, I was a broken man," said the Administrator, raising his voice to be heard through the shuffling silence. "I'd lost everything dear to me—my family, my friends, my job, my home, and after all of that, my dog. My life had been torn apart by the Great War, and nothing felt safe or secure.

"I was scared. This was not unwarranted. The World Between Blinks was a scary place then. It was wild. Untamed. There—well—" he nodded at a legionnaire as he passed, "many of you remember what this place was like before."

"No thanks to you!" the Roman soldier replied. "If it was up to you, we wouldn't remember anything!"

Others in the Ninth Roman Legion shouted their agreement, and Marisol was scared that the fight would start all over again, but the Administrator simply kept walking, over the door's glass remains and out into the open night.

His Curators began to follow him. Marisol and Jake joined in, stepping outside to find an entire street filled with rebels.

285

Percy *was* riding the woolly mammoth, his signature hat askew.

Below him was a host of familiar faces: Raleigh, Jack, Naomi, Min-jun, the garam vendor. Marisol's heart ached for the ones who weren't there—Richard, Amelia, Nefertiti. Would they ever stand with the gang again? Everything hung on these next few minutes.

It turned out that the explorers' memories hadn't been wiped after all. Judging by the torn-up state of their clothes, Marisol suspected they must have misplaced their walkie-talkie in some kind of scuffle, but that wasn't important now. Not while the Administrator kept walking down the street, shouting his story.

"I wanted this World to be different from the one I left. A place where everything had a place. But I got so carried away with organizing things that I forgot what was important. . . ."

The Administrator paused and looked down at Rocket.

Then he stared around at the rebels.

"I forgot about you," he said. "I don't want to tear families apart or destroy your houses." A pause. A swallow. "I'm sorry for the pain I have caused, and I am going to do my best to make things right. Starting with all of the memories I've confiscated. So let us now go to the Great Library of Alexandria to start the work of restoring lost minds. Then, *together*, we will decide how to tame this World and make ourselves a home here."

A few cheers went up from the crowd.

The Curators following the Administrator began whispering among themselves. The woman with the french braids—which were now mostly unraveled—raised her voice.

"But, sir, are you sure? Queen Nefertiti will NOT be happy!"

"I am sure," he said. "We're also going to make every zone free for everyone. And restore some of our more extreme rearrangements. Okjökull glacier will be returned to the yetis, and we must let the Amazon rainforest grow as wild as it wishes." The Administrator paused and looked back at Marisol and Jake. "Is there anything I'm missing?"

"I don't think so," Jake said.

"We can talk about the dinosaurs later," Marisol added.

"By Jove!" Percy crowed happily from the mammoth's back. "You did it, Jake and Mari! You know, I had my doubts, when you told me that Rocket was a dog and not a weapon of mass destruction, but this is a much better solution!" He waved at the Administrator. "I was in the Great War too, you know, in the Royal Artillery. So many people said it would be heroic, but every single shell I shot chipped away at my soul . . . When all was said and done I threw myself back into the Amazon to forget that horrid war, and the wilderness swallowed me. It brought me here, to this wild, beautiful World, where men hadn't shot all the trees to pieces."

Marisol listened, rapt. She hadn't known Percy was a soldier, although, now that she thought about it, he was a *colonel*, so that made sense.

"I don't think any of us want that sort of destruction," the explorer went on. "I also think this World is big enough for forests *and* formal gardens. We can work together to find that balance and make it beautiful."

The Administrator smiled, and the Curators copied his expression.

Rocket's tail wagged.

Marisol felt a surge of triumph as staplers started to lower and shields were stowed.

She and Jake had stopped the fight.

More than that, they'd started something new. A partnership between the World's Curators and its citizens.

A peace.

But then . . .

"YOU HAVE GOT TO BE KIDDING ME!"

"Uh-oh!" Jake grabbed Marisol's hand and squeezed. Oz growled next to them. "Someone's not happy. . . ."

That someone was . . . oh no.

Karen.

Her balloon—which matched the fiery orange of her hair—was descending to hover a few meters over the crowd. She was still in the basket, and the fire that kept it aloft flickered just above her head. An evil halo. It made her look even more angry than she already was.

"Curators!" she shouted down to her fellow white suits. "You are being deceived! Our Administrator is clearly not himself! His hourglass has been tampered with, and he needs our help! ATTACK!"

16

JAKE

A RIPPLE WENT THROUGH THE CURATORS' ranks. With a flurry they lifted their pens aloft, ready to take notes, ready to write memos, and . . . and to do what, actually?

Jake wasn't sure. The Curators didn't seem too sure either. One by one their clipboards lowered, and the white-clad army and all their free opponents turned their gazes from Karen to the Administrator, like some great, many-headed beast.

The Administrator was standing with his mouth open, simply staring up at his second-in-command, and there he remained until Rocket whined softly, and leaned against his leg. That seemed to bring him back to his senses.

"Karen!" he shouted, craning his head to look up at the balloon. "What are you doing?"

Karen's nostrils flared. "I'm following *your* orders!"

"But I've changed my orders," he called. "Not through trickery or skullduggery, but through conversation! I've found what I lost, which means I can stop searching!"

Karen snorted. "You? It's not all about you, Administrator! It's about what's best for *everyone*. You never would have lost anything if this place had been properly ordered. All this could have been avoided. You told us yourself: 'A place for everything, and everything in its place, that's what keeps us safe!'"

"That does sound like something I'd say," the Administrator muttered, pinching the bridge of his nose.

"Somebody has to choose where things belong!" Karen's voice rang out over the crowd. "For the good of all! You wouldn't tell a child they never need to clean their room again! You wouldn't let people go to the beach every day, instead of work or school! Sometimes there must be rules we don't enjoy, to keep the World safe for everyone!"

"Safe?"

A laugh erupted from the bottom half of the balloon. It was hoarse and familiar. It was scuffed-up sandcastles and sandy sneakers worn past Nana's porch door and the sound of all the benne wafers being eaten before Jake could reach the kitchen. He didn't understand how something could be so annoying and so wonderful at the exact same time. . . .

Karen was forced to shuffle to the side in the basket,

setting it swinging gently as someone else rose to his feet, stretching his arms and arching his back. His black hair was wind-whipped and his expression . . . well, Jake would recognize his older cousin's smirk anywhere. It was, in fact, contagious. Marisol broke out into a mischievous grin, and Jake felt his own lips curling into a smile.

Victor was back.

And from the look of things he'd been hard at work using his irksome powers against Karen. She was getting that twitch that people often got after they spent a long time around Victor. Her lips pressed together hard. Her hairline looked ready to snap. The bun above it, already windswept, seemed to grow even more frazzled when she glanced at the teenager.

"You wanna talk about *safe*, Karen?" Victor said loudly. "You almost popped our balloon on the spire of that skyscraper over there because you wouldn't let me fly!"

"That's quite enough out of you, Victor!" she snapped.

He snickered. "You're just mad because I'm a better pilot than you."

"Shut up," the Curator muttered.

The whole crowd below the balloon was frozen in place, fascinated. The only sounds now were Karen and Victor's voices, and the soft hiss of the gas powering the hot-air balloon. It hovered over the street like an orange harvest moon—round and full.

"I'll admit that I had an unfair advantage," Victor ventured. "All of those hours I've spent playing Air Balloon Buddies on my phone is basically flight training."

At this, Karen raked her fingers through her hair. Exasperated. "Playing games doesn't make you a pilot! You have to take special classes and get a permit!"

"Well *actually*, things have changed a lot since 1985. There's this thing called a flight simulator that aviation schools use to help pilots get their license now. So video games *can* count toward—"

"AGHHH!" Karen screamed and tugged her bun so hard that it fell out completely.

"You were right, Jake." Marisol looked as if she might burst out laughing. "This is even better than a backward alphabet!"

Jake felt relieved. Victor was okay—only, he didn't seem to be trying to escape. There were no enchanted ropes anchoring him to the balloon, and he still had a feather charm looped around his neck, but the older boy remained next to Karen. When he saw Jake and Marisol in the street below, he gave the kids a wave.

"Hey, Mari, hey, Jake," Victor called. "Glad to see you're both in one piece! Are we friends with the big baddie now?" He nodded at the Administrator.

"Yep!" Jake yelled back.

"Turns out the Administrator isn't so bad!" Marisol

added. "He's a mini baddie. At most."

Karen clutched the sides of the basket, her hair falling down her shoulders in waves. She looked like a completely different person now that it was down—several years younger. But this didn't change the fact that she was still mad. Her nostrils flared. Her knuckles were getting whiter by the second.

"You . . . you . . . children!" She spat down at them, failing to think of a better insult. "The Administrator isn't some ultimate level boss! This isn't an amusement arcade! It's real life! You can't just walk around bending the rules until you break the World! If you had any idea about what this place looked like before the Administrator brought some order to it you would be *thanking* him."

"Oh, we know," Victor butted in. "There were tangled strings and stuff!"

"The Great String Entanglement wasn't just some stray ball of yarn," protested Karen. "It was *dangerous*."

A murmur went up from the crowd—mostly from those who looked old enough to remember the capital-letter event from five hundred years ago. Jake even saw one of the Roman legionnaires nodding, which made him think that maybe both sides could still find a way to work together.

"Listen," Jake said. "We get what you're saying about keeping people safe, but who says you get to make up all the rules?"

"¡Sí!" Marisol chimed in, planting her hands on her hips. The hot-air balloon reflected like a fire in her dark eyes as she stared up. Her voice was heated too. "Even the Administrator didn't want to be king when everyone asked him to be! You can't just make yourself the queen of everything!"

Karen took a sharp breath and looked down at the crowded street. "Well," she huffed. "I don't see anyone else stepping up."

"That's because *they don't feel safe!*" Jake shouted. "They're too busy running and fighting and hoping that their hourglasses don't get flipped! Your rules have taken away the chance for people to live their lives!"

These words seemed to hit home. One of Karen's hands went to her necklace, where her own miniature hourglass dangled. She pressed the glass protectively to her chest and stared back at the Administrator with pleading eyes. "Sir, you can't seriously consider undoing all of our hard work—"

"That's absolutely what I'm considering," the Administrator replied. He pushed his glasses back up the bridge of his nose and scratched Rocket between the ears. "We've had our fun, Karen. Perhaps it's time to pack away the monocles and put up the pens."

The look on Karen's face was like a *HAPPY BIRTH-DAY* balloon several days after the party—low and shriveled and past popping. "FUN?" Her voice fell too, scraping the bottom of her throat. "I don't do this for fun, you know. Do you think I *enjoy* it when everybody rolls their eyes when they see me coming?" Her gaze raked over the crowd, who were all suddenly looking down and shuffling their feet. The mammoth's movement made the whole street shake. "I see it, you know," she continued, sounding . . . almost hurt.

It was a new side of Red Bun, and one Jake had never known was there. *Huh.*

He tilted his head. "If you don't like it, then why do you do it?"

"Because someone has to make sure that while you're all exploring lost jungles and searching for legendary treasure, you don't get any nasty surprises. Getting hugged by a Titanoboa is not all it's cracked up to be!" she snapped. "Someone has to be responsible around here!"

"But there can be good surprises, too, don't you think?" Jake countered, making his voice gentle. "When you find out unexpected stuff? When you give people room to grow and change, and see what they become? You might find there's more to them than you thought."

Karen's eyes narrowed.

Her grip on the basket loosened.

Her hourglass swung forward with her fiery hair as she leaned down to study Jake, and he didn't dare move, waiting, just waiting to see if she'd tip in the right direction.

Would she understand what he was saying? Would she agree to let some of the rules slide so the World Between Blinks could breathe again?

He held his own breath, hopeful. . . .

Then Karen snapped upright. Her hair flared as she shook her head.

"Sure," she replied. "But those aren't the surprises I'm worried about. It's all very well to say, 'Oh, look how much fun this place is, let's have afternoon tea with a yeti, then go on vacation to Atlantis!' *I'd* like to go on vacation to Atlantis, you know! But how do you think we keep the megalodons out of the underwater cities? Who do you think makes sure the ships you sail there are seaworthy?"

The Administrator raised a hand in protest. "I don't think we should abandon *every* single rule."

"You're not thinking at all," she growled at him. "You can't just take all the years we've spent working ourselves to the bone to keep everyone safe, and say they meant nothing!"

"Now see here," the Administrator protested. "I'm not—"

A sea of urgent whispers rose up all around him, passing back and forth among the crowd.

"She's right—take up your clipboards once more, be ready!"

"You see, we can't trust them!"

One of the Vikings below let out a war-like roar, stopping only when a nearby centurion elbowed him in the ribs. The rest of the rebels eyed the balloon restlessly, as did the Curators. Jake understood their uneasiness. How were the two sides supposed to work together with something like this hanging over their heads?

Victor had his elbows propped on the edge of the basket, chin cradled in his hands. And . . . *why* was his cousin smiling? Did Victor understand how awful this situation was? Did he even care? Apparently not. The older boy's smirk was so wide it made Jake want to climb into the balloon and shake him.

"You knowww," Victor drew out the word slowly as he addressed Karen.

"No!" The Curator whipped around to face the teenager, her hands thrown toward the sky. "I do not want to know! I do not want to hear anything else from you, Victor Contreras Beruna!"

"Oh, well, that's a shame," Jake's older cousin drawled. "I was going to say that you made a good point."

"I did?" Karen paused, hands still raised so high it looked almost like a soldier trying to surrender.

"Yeah." The strings on Victor's red hoodie twitched when he shrugged. "But you don't want to know, so—"

"Gah! *Victor!*" the Curator said, through gritted teeth.

"I have never been so tempted to tip someone out over the edge of my balloon."

Jake winced, but Victor just laughed his carefree laugh. "Yeah, I'm being pretty annoying," he agreed.

Karen's eyes narrowed, as if sensing some sort of trap. Jake couldn't blame her—for Victor to admit he was annoying seemed like a giant change from the teenager who'd first stumbled into the World Between Blinks. "You are," she agreed. "Very annoying."

"Seems like I should probably change that," Victor said.

"I'd appreciate it," she said, uncertain now, and clearly wondering if this was just a new trick.

"Okay," he said simply.

"Okay?" she asked.

"I'm sorry," he offered.

Karen gaped at him, and Jake's mouth dropped open too. Marisol's lips stayed shut, but they curled into a small smile. Her brown eyes shone with that same *close up* look her brother had worn, the first time he realized the truth about her magnet fingers.

Up in the balloon, Victor kept talking. "I've been realizing the last few days that sometimes people aren't what you first thought," he said. "I learned it about this whole World, I learned it about dinosaurs, I even learned it about my little sister. She can do this thing with her fingers that—anyway, I'll tell you about it another time. It's the coolest."

"Do you have a point?" Karen asked, still cautious. "What was *my* good point?"

"I'm getting to that," Victor assured her. "So, now that I've listened to everyone's speeches, it sounds like the Administrator isn't what I first thought either. Not a big baddie after all. And you know what, Karen?"

"What?" she wondered quietly.

"Neither are you," said Victor. "My first impression was wrong. I thought you were like the worst kind of teacher, making everyone stick to the rules just because the rules are there, and that's a good enough reason. But you just said so yourself, a minute ago. You said, *I don't do this for fun, you know.* So you must be doing it because it's important."

"It is." Her voice rose an urgent notch. Almost cracking.

"And you want people to be safe."

"I *do*."

"But aren't you, like, super tired?" he asked. "You made a very good point when you said you'd like to take a vacation, and if you haven't gone on one since you arrived in 1985, well, I'd say that you're long overdue! You *have* worked hard and you *have* kept people safe, but if you don't bother taking care of yourself too, you're going to break."

Karen simply stared at him. And so did everyone else. All eyes in the crowd were fixed on Victor, and the only sound was the slow thump of Oz's tail against the ground.

"I—but—what will happen when I'm gone?" the Curator wondered. "What if everything falls apart?"

"It won't," Victor said, all confidence. "I've only been in this World for a few days, but I can tell it's too big for one person to keep it together all by themselves. Even you, Karen. I think your boss and that explorer guy are right—"

"Percy," Marisol called up helpfully.

The man in question tipped his hat at the balloon.

Victor nodded back. "Right, Percy. Percy is right! There's room in the World Between Blinks for forests *and* formal gardens. If everyone works together, you can transform this World into a place that every citizen enjoys. *Plus*, you'd have that much extra help! You can take all of the vacation days in Atlantis that you want!"

"But only after she helps flip back the hourglasses!" Jake added. Nefertiti and Amelia and the others shouldn't suffer any longer than they already had.

"Right," Victor agreed. "You have to right some wrongs first, but I'll bet there's a whole lot of people who'd help, if you're willing to trust them with some responsibilities. What do you say, Karen? Will you change people's first impression of you? Will you prove

301

that you're not uptight and take a break?"

The red-haired Curator clutched her hourglass charm again. It looked close to cracking in her fist, but then, slowly her jaw relaxed and her shoulders slumped. "But . . . but . . ." she faltered. "What would I even *do* on vacation?"

"Anything you'd like!" said Victor. "Crosswords! Sudoku! Flying lessons!"

"I don't know. . . ."

"Tell you what," Victor whispered. "I'll sweeten the deal. I'll be grounded for the rest of my life, but when I get home and I get a new phone . . . I'll load it up with Candy Crush and then lose it all over again, along with a bunch of power packs. You can spend your vacation defeating those jelly levels. I believe in you."

It felt like the whole crowd was holding its breath, gaze fixed on the pair in the basket. The balloon hovered. Karen hesitated. She was standing locked in place, her jaw squared but moving a little—she was grinding her teeth in indecision. Jake was biting down hard on his lower lip.

Would she accept Victor's terms?

She straightened. "All right!" she called down, turning her gaze to the Administrator. "All right, we'll try it your way. We can reverse some of the stricter rules. But we're leaving the butterfly collection exactly where it is, it took us *forever* to gather them all in one place."

"That's fair," the Administrator allowed.

"Victor," called Marisol. "Can you climb down now? I can't believe I'm saying this, but I want to give you a hug."

The party that night was *epic*. The banquet tables at Nefertiti's palace were crowded with friends both old and new, and the main celebration was taking place in the grand Amber Room. Its panels gleamed in the candlelight—honeycomb gold, brassy orange, and maybe just a *hint* of magic.

The whole room felt enchanted. Amelia and Richard were back in fine form, arm-wrestling Percy and Naomi, and in the corner Glenn Miller was filling up the dance floor with a performance on his trombone and a backing band. Alexander Helios and Bessie Hyde were conducting, urging the musicians to play faster and faster. Harold Holt was dancing with Nefertiti, whose blue wig was a little askew. The queen was smiling, though, her dark eyes shining with restored memories.

All around Jake and Marisol, people were toasting their reunions with Black Cherry Vanilla Coke. The cousins sat side by side, keeping one eye on Victor, who was telling Yusra a story that involves a *lot* of wild gestures.

"You know," said Marisol, popping a handful of

Reese's Bites into her mouth and speaking through the peanut butter, "that worked out pretty well."

"The Administrator seems happy," Jake agreed, craning his neck to check the dance floor, where Oz and Rocket were chasing each other in circles under the man's watchful eye. Nearby, a group of white-clad Curators were all dancing in unison. It was like attending a very weird wedding reception.

"You think Karen will go along with all of the new changes?" Marisol asked, thoughtful.

"You know, I think so," Jake said. "I think maybe Victor had a point, and our first impression of her wasn't the right one. And maybe she'll see her first impression of the way to keep this World safe wasn't right either. I hope we'll be able to exchange some letters with our friends here and find out."

"I still can't believe he offered her his phone. Again," Marisol murmured. "He's going to be grounded until he's an old man. Or a futuristic robot."

Before Jake could find something comforting to say, Min-jun took the seat opposite them, raising his usually quiet voice to be heard over the celebrations.

"Whether they know you or not, everyone in the World owes you a debt of gratitude, my friends."

Jake felt his cheeks heat up a little. "Anyone would have done it."

"Perhaps," said Min-jun. "Perhaps not. What we know is that *you* did it. On ships and planes, past dinosaurs and yetis, into the heart of the Administrator's lair, not knowing what would become of you. Of all the things that have been lost here, your courage was never among them. I wish there were a way we could repay you."

"*This* is repayment," Marisol answered firmly. "Getting to see this party, getting to see everyone happy together. But speaking of the dinosaurs, you'll take care of our promise to them, won't you?"

"Without fail," Min-jun said. "Yusra has agreed to join the team that will make arrangements for them—we'll find them some more interesting places to roam, without causing general carnage."

"Then everything really is done," Marisol said, sharing a satisfied smile with Jake. "Can we stay one more night, and say goodbye to everyone in the morning?"

"I think—" Min-jun paused, frowning at something behind them. "Did you see that?"

"See what?" Jake twisted around, but all he could see was Jack Fawcett and Raleigh Rimell in animated conversation with Annapurna the yeti.

Min-jun shook his head. "It seemed as if the walls flickered for a moment. Perhaps it's simply an after-effect of the cracks that were left behind when your great-uncle Christopher, uh . . ."

"Sent the whole Amber Room back to our world, causing chaos and nearly breaking everything," Marisol supplied.

"I was going to say 'experimented,'" Min-jun said. "But your version works too. I'll make a note that someone should look into it. For now, what do you say we dance?"

"Let's do it," said Jake.

And they did.

17

MARISOL

EVERY PARTY MUST COME TO AN END.

Marisol didn't want to stop dancing. She didn't want the sun to rise or the music to fade or for goodbyes to be said, but the band had long ago stopped playing, and many of the candles in the Amber Room had burned down to the stubs, and the cans of Black Cherry Vanilla Coke she had drunk made her teeth feel like they were made of sugar. She didn't think Queen Nefertiti had any lost toothbrushes lying around—and even if she did, Marisol absolutely did not want to borrow one.

It was time to go home, back to her parents and a toothbrush she *knew* no one else had used.

"And here we are once more!" Colonel Percy Fawcett, who still had mammoth fur stuck to his outfit, waved at the Beruna cousins, who stood side by side on the center of the dance floor. "A happy ending, if I say so myself. You kids really worked out how to turn a pickle back into a cucumber!"

"We . . . what?" Victor furrowed his brow and looked down at the necklace he was wearing over his hoodie. "Is my language charm broken?"

"You already speak English," Marisol pointed out.

"Yeah, but not British!"

Jack Fawcett laughed. "That's not British. It's just Dad. What he means is, we're glad we called you. You found a way through when no one else could. A happy ending indeed!"

Yet Marisol didn't feel happy when she looked around the ballroom. Everything around the edges of her vision was getting watery, and there was a lump in her throat the size of a golf ball.

Quite a crowd had stuck around to see them off. The explorers, of course, and Amelia Earhart, who'd worn her helmet and her goggles the entire evening to *make sure I always remember I'm made for the skies.*

Annapurna and the yetis had insisted that Marisol and Jake keep their knitted fur sweaters as thanks. The rest of the group made Marisol realize just how many friends she'd made during her time here: Bessie and Glen Hyde, the garum vendor, Yusra and her cat-sized pterosaur, Harold Holt, Alexander Helios, Johann,

Richard Halliburton, and Queen Nefertiti, who made sure to stay on the opposite side of the room from the Administrator, who was too busy nuzzling Rocket to notice the slight.

And then, of course, Oz.

The Tasmanian tiger sat on his haunches, watching the Beruna cousins with eyes so brown and sad that Marisol had to wipe her own. But the yeti sweater repelled water naturally—it helped when you lived in a place that was all snow all the time—so her sleeve was useless.

"Here!" Richard stepped forward to hand Marisol his pocket square. "Take this!"

"Gracias." She thanked the man and dabbed her eyes, until she could see that Oz was trotting over for one last hug. He buried his head deep into the folds of her yeti fur sweater, then moved down the line to say farewell to Jake.

"Can I borrow that handkerchief?" her cousin whispered.

He was also wearing a sweater, and also misty-eyed. Marisol had never seen him cry like this before. . . . She was more than happy to hand him the pocket square.

Even Victor kept clearing his throat again and again, when Oz pressed his nose into the teenager's palm, and then nuzzled even farther into his hoodie pocket to clean out some stray salteña crumbs.

"Are you three ready?"

It was Min-jun who asked the question no one else wanted to voice. The ex-Curator stood across from the Beruna cousins, holding the spare ledger page that had the cousins' names written and struck through, then written again. There was a pen in Min-jun's other hand. Ready to cross out *Marisol* and *Jake* and send them back home. Since Victor had stumbled into the World by accident, extra paperwork had had to be filed on his behalf—cataloging him so his name could be crossed out too.

"You sure this is going to work?" her brother asked.

Min-jun nodded toward the Amber Room floor. "This crack is still wide enough to let you slip back through, once I strike your names from the records."

Without a monocle, the parquet pattern beneath their feet seemed solid. Circles and crescents and squares and diamonds were all interlaid in an intricate dance, hopping from dark wood to cherry tones before swirling into more ashy hues. Marisol knew, though, that if she held up her vision charm, the wood would fall away to reveal a split in the fabric of the Unknown. Last time, she'd seen the other Amber Room in Russia's Catherine Palace on the other side.

Where would they land now? She and Jake had ended

up back on Folly Beach last time, standing in their grandmother's backyard. If that happened again, they'd have a
TON of explaining to do to Mom and Dad. . . .

"Will Victor and I show up together in the same
place?" she wondered aloud. "What about Jake?"

"The Unknown sorted all of that out for us last time,"
her cousin reminded her. "Remember how Hazel and
Christopher ended up in Europe? I bet I'll go back to
Australia and you two will be in Bolivia."

"Let's hope so!" Victor grunted.

Marisol took one last look at the group who'd gathered to see them off, her heart swelling with a mixture of
sweet and sad. She knew that she'd always leave a piece
of it here—in this World of wonders, with these wonderful people who called it home.

"You'll call us again if you need us?" Marisol asked.

"You betcha!" Amelia said. "In the meantime we can
be interdimensional pen pals!"

"Guess I should learn to read cursive," said Victor.

There was a final round of goodbyes and hugs and air-
blown kisses. Then it was time.

Min-jun crossed out Jake's name first, and Marisol watched as her cousin vanished. The Amber Room
seemed to tremble around them when it happened; a
shiver that rattled the sconces and made the amber look
almost liquid for a moment.

"Whoa!" Victor blinked at the space Jake had left behind. "That's wild!"

Marisol reached out for her brother's hand.

He took ahold of hers, squeezing tight.

Min-jun began counting down as he guided the pen to their names. "Three, two, one . . ."

Blink.

Blink, blink. Marisol and Victor found themselves standing at the edge of a dock. The air smelled like fish and damp wood, and the boat their family had taken to Isla del Sol was moored close by, but Marisol could see that they were no longer on that island. The Unknown had placed her and her brother back in Copacabana. It was dawn and the small lakeside town had yet to stir, the windows and doors of its colorful buildings were shuttered like sleeping eyelids.

Empty boats shaped like swans were beached on the rocky shore and beyond them sat tents where locals cooked freshly caught trout for hungry tourists. A stray dog paused by one of these, eagerly sniffing for scraps. The animal was about the same size as Oz, and the same color too. Marisol wondered if it would ever be lost enough to join the rest of the Floating Mountain dog pack.

"What a trip, huh?" Victor was still holding her hand. He nodded at the nearby boat, a wild smile on his face.

"I should leave an online review: *Great captain. Smooth sailing. Got a little lost, but it was worth it. Be sure to catch the side tour to the portal world where dinosaurs will sneeze on you and yetis will knit you sweaters and Amelia Earhart will ask you to jump out of her plane. Ten out of ten!*"

Marisol giggled. "It's the dinosaur snot that really sells it."

"I know. Right?" Her brother sighed. He stared up the rickety dock, past the trout tents, to the street that held their hotel. "How are we ever going to explain this to Mom and Dad?"

"Jake and I told the truth last time. I mean, we took out all of the exciting bits, the parts with pirates and cannibal rats and stuff—"

"I'm sorry, what?" Her brother interrupted. "You never told *me* about cannibal rats either! In fact, I don't really even remember what you guys said about getting lost last time. . . ."

"I think the Unknown's magic had something to do with that," Marisol explained. "Everyone was really worried at first, but then they sort of forgot that it happened. It's probably the only reason Mom let me back on a boat again."

"Probably." Victor glanced at his necklace, which sat over his hoodie, its charms winking. "I won't forget again this time, will I?"

"Nope," Marisol promised. "You're in on the secret now."

"Good." He smiled and looked back at the stirring city. "Shall we?"

"Sí."

They walked down the rickety wood dock, hand in hand.

~ EPILOGUE ~

THREE WEEKS LATER . . .

JAKE COULD HEAR CHRISTMAS CAROLS ON THE air.

It was a few weeks since they'd come back home from the World, and South Carolina felt almost as far from Australia as he did from the Floating Mountains right now. It was good to be back, though.

Dusk was falling, and the sky was crisp enough to make the palmettos stand out against the sunset. It looked as if someone had taken a cookie cutter shaped like a tree and cut out a colorful piece of sky, leaving sharp black behind. The night's first stars were beginning to shine over the darkening marsh.

If it had been summer, there would have been cicadas screaming, but as Jake and Marisol made their way up the driveway to what he would always think of as Nana's house, they heard "Silent Night" playing instead.

The song was wafting its way out to greet them through the open front door, warm, golden light pouring from the hall. The music had a slightly scratchy, old-timey quality—Hazel and Christopher loved using Nana's record player. Hazel said it wasn't old-fashioned, it was "vintage." Just now the music and light welcomed the cousins home.

They'd been to King Street in downtown Charleston with Uncle Todd and their cousins Veronica and Angeline for a little last-minute Christmas shopping, and the twins were still unloading their bags from the car, leaving Jake and Marisol to climb the steps to the front porch, where dozens of shark's teeth and shells lined the railings. These objects had sat there for so long, that if you moved one, you'd find its outline etched in the paint.

But Hazel and Christopher hadn't moved a thing.

They'd started to add souvenirs from their own adventures, but they'd kept Nana's furniture, her knickknacks, her pictures, her maps. For Jake, walking up these steps still felt like coming home.

"You think Victor will like it?" he asked, hefting the little wrapped bag in his hand.

"I think he'll get the joke," Marisol replied with a grin.

They'd found out that morning that Aunt Cara and

Uncle Mache were buying Victor a phone to replace the one he'd lost in the World Between Blinks—and then realized with a sinking feeling that if he was going to keep his promise to Karen, he'd have to have to load it up with Candy Crush, then lose his Christmas present. That was going to *suck*. So they'd pooled their money to buy him the biggest bag of candy they could afford.

"He might not have a phone for long," Marisol had said. "But at least he can crush some candy."

Jake toed off his sneakers and ducked inside past Uncle Matt and Aunt Jayla, who were draping tinsel along the tops of picture frames and ornaments.

Christmas this year was a mix of traditions from all around the world—mostly culinary. There would be picana and buñuelos from La Paz, and plenty of food from South Carolina, of course. Uncle Pierre was baking a bûche de Noël, a delicious chocolate Yule log cake, for tomorrow, and Jake and his mom were making a pavlova of meringue and cream and berries from a recipe they'd learned when she was posted to Sydney.

Jake could hear his great-aunt and great-uncle singing along to "Silent Night" in the kitchen as he and Marisol walked inside in their socks, and a delicious, cookie-related smell was wafting out into the living room. They tucked Victor's present under the tree, among the jumble of brightly wrapped presents.

317

Life with Victor had been different since they got back, though not always—he hadn't changed completely. But he and Marisol were a good team now.

The two of them had slipped back into Copacabana together, but just as it had done last time, the Unknown had deposited each of the returning adventurers just where they needed to be.

For Jake, that was a cove along the coast from Melbourne, a few days after he'd left. He'd wandered along the sand until he'd found Christopher and Hazel's camp tucked away in the trees, marked by a white wisp of smoke from their campfire.

"Are you all right?" Christopher asked, hurrying forward. "What an extraordinary sweater you're wearing."

"It's made of yeti fur, and I'm better than all right," Jake replied, grinning.

"Good. Then take a seat, and we'll make some billy tea," said Hazel, pointing to a tin of water hanging above the fire, "and you can tell us all about it."

"We had to tell your mother we'd taken a spur-of-the-moment camping trip," Christopher added, rolling up a log for Jake to sit on. "So we could come up here to pass messages with you. Lucky it wasn't too hard to find Lucy's old camping spot. Very well-built fireplace, I must say. You need to be careful of that around here—bushfires, you know. I read in an article that—"

"Sit down, Jake," said Hazel with a smile. "We want to hear how everyone is, and then we'll pack up for the drive home and you can tell us the rest on the way. Thankfully there's no mobile telephone reception here, but we should probably give your mother a call when we can."

That had been a few weeks ago. He'd told them the whole story, and they'd made their way back to the city together, still talking of dogs and dinosaurs.

When their trip came to a close, they'd all flown back to South Carolina together, arriving yawning and jet-lagged from their flight to meet up with the rest of the Beruna family.

Yesterday, Jake, Marisol, and Victor had taken a long, long walk along the beach with Christopher and Hazel, and they'd told the story again from the beginning—this time with his cousins adding in all the details he missed.

They'd come home feeling a little bit wistful, and a little bit sorry that they couldn't celebrate the holidays with all the friends they'd left behind . . . only to find that one of those friends had other ideas.

"He just let himself in," said Aunt Cara, looking flustered. "And went to sleep beside the heating vent."

"He took a cushion off the couch, and he's got his head on it," said Uncle Todd. "I think he's drooling."

Oz the Tasmanian tiger was right there in Hazel and Christopher's living room, taking a nap.

For a moment, Jake, Marisol, Victor, Christopher, and Hazel all just stared at him, and then they all started making excuses at once.

"Oh yes, didn't we mention that—"

"We adopted him just recently, and—"

"It's a pretty old cushion—"

"What a good, uh, dog—"

"Has anyone checked their snacks?"

Jake's mom squinted at Oz thoughtfully. "He's very unusual looking," she said eventually. "Did the shelter say what breed he was?"

"I don't think so," replied Hazel innocently.

"Something long-lost, perhaps," Christopher added.

Later, there had been a hurriedly convened conference on the stairs, conducted in whispers.

"What do you think Oz wants?" Jake asked.

"He seems to just be visiting," Marisol shrugged. "He's not acting like he has to pass on an urgent mission or anything."

"How did he get here?" Victor asked, eyes wide.

Hazel raised her hands helplessly. "I would have said it was impossible," she murmured. "But I've long since learned not to use that word."

"I have an inkling," Christopher admitted, his voice low. "The cracks I created, when I was practicing sending things back here, before we rescued Hazel . . ."

"Ohhhh," Jake breathed. "Min-jun said they were still there. Weak spots between the worlds."

"Looks like they haven't fixed the cracks yet, then," Marisol observed. "Does that mean we can get back there?"

"Who knows," Christopher replied. "I'd never say never, if I were you."

"I wonder if Oz will stay?" Hazel said.

Marisol had the answer to that: "Oz goes where he wants."

Oz was still snoozing by the tree today—so it seemed he planned to stay for a little while. He woke up, though, when Mom and Aunt Cara came out of the kitchen with trays of freshly baked sugar cookies. The buttercream icing on top was fresh too—sprinkled with extra sugar, just the way Nana would have liked.

"Snack time!" called Aunt Cara. "And hot chocolate on the way! Fill up! We won't be eating the picana soup until after midnight! I know that's late, but it's a Bolivian tradition!"

The whole family drifted in from all over the house, and Victor arrived to thump down on one side of Oz as Jake sat down on the other.

"You won't believe what I lost today," Victor said, giving Oz a scratch behind the ears. "I was helping Mom with the groceries, for the picana tonight and all the stuff we need to cook for tomorrow. But when I carried them in from the car . . . the mint was missing."

"Huh," said Marisol, squeezing in beside Oz, a cookie already in her hand. She giggled at his sniffing, questing nose and broke off a piece for him. "Now, who do we know who might want lost mint?"

"Only a leaf or two at a time," Jake replied with a chuckle. "He always said that."

"Maybe we'll get the chance to take him some ourselves again someday," Victor murmured.

Jake looked across at where Christopher and Hazel were clinking their mugs of hot chocolate together in a toast, and he grinned.

"Never say never," he replied.

CURATORS' FILES

CHAPTER ONE
Name: Chincana on Isla del Sol
Entry into WBB: Ongoing
Notes: This site was a holy complex for Incan priests on Isla del Sol, an island in the middle of Lake Titicaca in what is now Bolivia. Since it was built in the fifteenth-century, time has worn its labyrinth of stones into ruins, slowly bringing Chincana to the shores of the World Between Blinks.

Name: Phantom Islands
Entry into WBB: Ongoing
Notes: These islands are too fickle to stay in one place. Cartographers in the old world would draw them into their maps, only to find a few years later that there was only ocean in the spot instead. One famous example includes the Isle Phelipeaux on Lake Superior, which served as a landmark while drawing the border between

the United States and Canada. Even in the World Between Blinks these spots of land have a nasty habit of hopping around, which makes mapping them a nightmare. Pro tip: If assigned to such duties, use pencils. You *will* be using an eraser.

CHAPTER THREE
Name: Lost Dutchman gold mine
Entry into WBB: Nineteenth century. Give or take.
Notes: Quasi-mythical. Legends of this mine have inspired countless people to search the Superstition Mountains in Arizona for gold. How this treasure came to be there depends on the story you hear: Some say it is lost Apache treasure, others claim that the mine was discovered by two Dutchmen, and still others say that the place was staked by US soldiers. Whatever the case, no one found the Lost Dutchman gold mine long enough to make it stay in the old world. It always returns to the World Between Blinks, and every time we have to tidy up the mess inside all over again.

CHAPTER FOUR
Name: The *Lost Ship of the Desert*
Entry into WBB: Entrie*s*. Plural. Every so often this vessel likes to sneak back onto the horizon of the old world's Colorado Desert, so it can be spotted by treasure hunters. Cheeky, really.

Notes: *Quasi-mythical.* Another legend from the American West. There are many different versions of the story. In some, the *Lost Ship* is a Spanish galleon that got stranded by vanishing floodwaters. Others claim the vessel is a Viking longship. Still others say the boat is a ferry that was hauled into the Californian desert by oxen. More often than not, there's treasure woven into these tales, along with claims that the ship holds pirate gold or black pearls for anyone who manages to find it. As if a ship in the middle of the desert wasn't interesting enough!

Name: Leonardo da Vinci's notes

Entry into WBB: Extended (from sixteenth century onward)

Notes: Leonardo da Vinci was a man ahead of his time. Not only was he famous for painting the *Mona Lisa*, but he also was a gifted mathematician and a fantastic inventor. He designed an underwater breathing apparatus, an "aerial screw" (a helicopter), and a "mechanical knight" (a robot) all in the sixteenth century! His notebooks are overflowing with such designs, and most of them are right here in the World Between Blinks! According to scholars, only one-fifth of da Vinci's original notes remain in the old world. The rest are kept in the Great Library of Alexandria. WARNING: They're difficult to decipher due to da Vinci's habit of "mirror writing." .tfel ot thgir morf sdrow eht daer tsum uoY

CHAPTER FIVE
Name: Mayflower Donut

Entry into WBB: 1970s

Notes: Mayflower Coffee Shops were a popular restaurant chain in the United States from the 1930s to the 1970s. They served hamburgers, pancakes, waffles, and, of course, coffee, but they were most famous for their donuts! Plain, sugared, or cinnamon donuts cost five cents each, and the frosted ones were ten cents. Ever since these restaurants shut down in the old world, they've become a popular breakfast option in the World Between Blinks. Note: Be sure to try the Donuts à la Mode! A warm donut with ice cream on top is hard to beat. . . .

CHAPTER SIX
Name: Richard Halliburton

Entry into WBB: March 24, 1939

Notes: Richard Halliburton was one of the most daring travelers of the twentieth century. His more notable adventures include: swimming the length of the Panama Canal, flying around the world on a plane known as the *Flying Carpet,* and reenacting *Robinson Crusoe* by wearing a goat-skin costume and pretending to be shipwrecked on an island. Richard also tried to replicate Hannibal's trip across the Alps on an elephant by borrowing one such animal from the Paris zoo and naming it "Miss Dalrymple."

His final adventure in the old world was aboard the *Sea Dragon*, a Chinese junk ship that was set to sail across the Pacific Ocean from Hong Kong to San Francisco. The boat disappeared in a typhoon, arriving in the World Between Blinks, where Richard's adventures continue.

Name: Amarna (or Akhetaten in ancient Egyptian)

Entry into WBB: Ongoing (1332 BCE—Present)

Notes: This city was built by Pharaoh Akhenaten, the husband of Queen Nefertiti and predecessor to Tutankhamun, as an alternative capital to Thebes. The pharaoh dedicated its temples and palaces to the worship of Aten—a single god. This wasn't so popular with the ancient Egyptians, though, and they returned to the original capital of Thebes as soon as the pharaoh died. Amarna/Akhetaten became an abandoned ghost town, slowly swallowed by the sands of the Sahara desert. Archaeologists have "discovered" some parts that were left behind when it transferred to the World Between Blinks, though they might have found them considerably faster if they'd asked the locals.

CHAPTER SEVEN

Name: Silphium

Entry into WBB: Third or second century BCE

Notes: This herb was so valued by ancient Romans

that the emperor Julius Caesar kept stalks of it in his official treasury. The plant had many different medicinal properties, and was used often in cooking. In fact, the Romans loved silphium so much that the plants could not keep up. It was overfarmed. The last recorded stalk in history was given to Emperor Nero as a gift. Note: Having had some myself, I'm not quite sure what all of the fuss was about. It tastes like leeks.

Name: Taliaferro apples
Entry into WBB: After 1835. Exact date uncertain.
Notes: These were Thomas Jefferson's favorite apples. He grew them in his orchards at Monticello, his house in Virginia, but the fruit was lost to history several decades later. Note: They make an exceptional cider.

Name: Tybee Island bomb
Entry into WBB: February 5, 1958
Notes: During one of the US Air Force's simulated combat missions, an F-86 fighter plane accidentally flew into a B-47 bomber that was carrying a nuclear bomb. In order to protect the crew in case of a crash landing, the pilot ejected the bomb into the Atlantic Ocean. It landed near Tybee Island, Georgia, but despite many search efforts it was never found. That, of course, is because it's in the World Between Blinks.

Name: Hadrian's Wall

Entry into WBB: Ongoing (fifth century—present)

Notes: This defensive fortification was built by the Romans during the rule of Emperor Hadrian in 122 CE. The wall crossed Britannia (now known as Britain) from coast to coast, spanning 73 miles and boasting close to 160 turrets. After the Romans left the region in 410 CE, the wall began falling into ruin. Many of its stones were repurposed to construct other buildings and roads all the way up to the eighteenth century. Several of its turrets have appeared in the World Between Blinks, and strolling the distance between them is a lovely way to spend one's vacation.

Name: Woolly Mammoth

Entry into WBB: 1680 BCE. Give or Take.

Notes: These beasts are as large as elephants, and look like them too, with the exception of their thick fur coats. Males grow up to eleven feet tall and can weigh in at more than 13,000 pounds. They roamed the Earth during its last ice age and were well suited to handle the cold. Their blood even contains anti-freezing properties!

CHAPTER EIGHT
Name: Via Appia

Entry into WBB: Ongoing

Notes: The Via Appia, or "The Appian Way" was

one of the most important roads in ancient Rome. It was built in 312 BCE to help transport soldiers so Rome could expand its rule. Its stones stretched from the Roman Forum all the way to modern-day Brindisi—a total of 350 miles. Most of this distance has now been lost. Tourists can walk the first 39 miles outside of Rome, but the rest of the road leads here. . . .

Name: Yusra

Entry into WBB: Exact date unknown. Sometime after 1935.

Notes: This Palestinian archaeologist discovered one of the most important human fossils ever found—a Neanderthal skull known as Tabun 1—while she was excavating Mount Carmel. Though Yusra had no formal schooling, she was one of the most expert women employed by Dorothy Garrod, the British archaeologist who directed the digs there. Yusra worked with Garrod from 1929 to 1935, but not much else is known about her. She became untraceable after the Mount Carmel excavations ended. We Curators haven't even been able to discover her surname—her pet dinosaurs don't like us getting too close.

CHAPTER NINE

Name: Tyrannosaurus Rex

Entry into WBB: 66 million years ago. Give or take.

Notes: This "terrible lizard" is the poster child

of dinosaurs. They've been recorded to grow up to forty-three feet long and twenty feet tall. They have around fifty to sixty teeth the size of bananas, but much scarier—they can crush bones with one bite! It's not all bad news, though, as their arms are much less lethal. They can't even scratch their own chins! *KEEP OUT OF RESIDENTIAL ZONES AT ALL COSTS.*

Name: Giant Sloth
Entry into WBB: 8500 BCE. Give or take.
Notes: The *Megatherium Americanum* is one of the largest land mammals that's ever existed, growing up to 20 feet long from head to tail. Pretty impressive, for eating only plants! These herbivores roamed what is now South America during the Pleistocene epoch (also known as the Ice Age). *KEEP OUT OF ANY GARDENS YOU WANT TO KEEP INTACT, AS THEY WILL VERY SLOWLY DEVOUR THEM.*

Name: Great Auks
Entry into WBB: 1852
Notes: These birds look a lot like penguins, with their black-and-white feathers. They are also flightless, and excellent swimmers. When auks lived on Earth, they nested in the cold waters of the North Atlantic. Despite so many similarities, the great auk and penguins are not closely related.

Name: Velociraptor

Entry into WBB: 80 million years ago. Maybe 70 million. We haven't been able to get close enough to ask.

Notes: Forget what you've seen in *Jurassic Park*. These dinosaurs are actually the size of a turkey. They have feathers, too! Of course, anyone who's been chased by a turkey knows how terrifying the experience can be. Velociraptors also have twenty-eight very, very sharp teeth. And they can run 40 miles per hour. And they can jump up to 10 feet high. Moral of the story: Do NOT try to eat these terrifying murder turkeys for Thanksgiving Dinner. You might be the meal instead . . . *KEEP OUT OF RESIDENTIAL ZONES AT ALL COSTS.*

Name: Triceratops

Entry into WBB: 66 million years ago. Give or take.

Notes: This dinosaur has three horns protruding out of its very large skull, which helps with fending off the teeth of the Tyrannosaurus Rex. Their own teeth are far less sharp—Triceratops only eat plants.

Name: Stegosaurus

Entry into WBB: 150 million years ago. Give or take.

Notes: A stegosaurus is easy to recognize: They have spiny plates sticking out of their backs and four long spikes on their tails. Despite what you might see in movies, they did not use these to fight the Tyrannosaurus rex.

Stegosauruses went extinct almost 80 million years before T-rexes roamed the Earth. Here in the World Between Blinks they maintain an uneasy truce.

CHAPTER ELEVEN

Name: Polphail

Entry into WBB: December 2016

Notes: Polphail was a ghost town as soon as it was built! It was constructed in Scotland during the oil boom on the 1970s, to house workers who would operate an oil platform off the coast. But nearby tides turned out to be too treacherous, and the platform was never built. Polphail's houses stood empty, gathering graffiti and bat colonies, until the town was demolished in 2016.

Name: Ansault Pears

Entry into WBB: After 1917. Exact date uncertain.

Notes: When you think of dessert, you usually don't think of pears. At least, I don't. But the Ansault pear was often ordered for dessert by Americans in the nineteenth century. This fruit is said to be the best pear that ever existed. It has a buttery flesh and a rich, sweet flavor. But the trees are temperamental and hard to grow, which is why you can't find the pear in the old world's supermarkets. The Ansault pear is now a popular delicacy in the World Between Blinks instead.

Name: The top of Mount St. Helens
Entry into WBB: May 18, 1980
Notes: Mount St. Helens is an active volcano in Washington State in the United States. After its top blew off during a particularly violent eruption on May 18, 1980, the mountain was 1,314 feet shorter than before. That's tall enough to be another mountain! It is currently the tallest peak in the World Between Blinks's Floating Mountain range.

Name: The top of Vesuvius
Entry into WBB: Ongoing
Notes: Mount Vesuvius is most famous for burying the ancient city of Pompeii in ash in 79 CE, but it has erupted many, many times over the past few centuries. Each of these incidents changes the height of the main cone, usually adding more meters of Vesuvius to the Floating Mountain range.

Name: Passenger pigeons
Entry into WBB: September 1, 1914
Notes: Passenger pigeons were once the most numerous birds on Earth, with populations reaching an estimated 3 to 5 billion. Because they make such tasty pies, people hunted passenger pigeons until they appeared in the World Between Blinks. Here their population has

rebounded heartily. (Beware: Flocks are so massive they can block the sun for days at a time. If caught in such an event do NOT look up. Forecast: showers of poop.)

CHAPTER TWELVE

Name: Yeti/Abominable Snowman

Entry into WBB: They come and go as they please.

Notes: *Quasi-mythical.* Yetis are legends back in the old world—woven throughout Himalayan folklore and popularized in the Western mythos by twentieth-century mountain climbers. Many have claimed to see these creatures first hand, but evidence of such encounters is scarce. Footprints melt. Photographs are dismissed. The yetis seem to enjoy their quasi-mythical status, and have only sought to encourage it so that they can spend most of their time in the Floating Mountains, sliding down ice slides and guarding packs of lost dogs.

CHAPTER THIRTEEN

Name: Sasquatch/Bigfoot/Mount Vernon Monster

Entry into WBB: They come and go as they please.

Notes: *Quasi-mythical.* Like their Yeti cousins, Sasquatches are legendary back in the old world. Many people have claimed to see them in the woods of North America, yet none have been able to supply enough evidence to convince the scientific community. It's just as well. Sasquatches prefer to spend most of their time in the Vanished Forests of the World Between Blinks.

Name: *Monardella leucocephala*
Entry into WBB: After 1941
Notes: This mint plant was native to California. It grows in sandy soils, flowering from May to July. Its leaves make a most excellent herbal tea.

Name: Lituus Horn (Etrusco-Roman version)
Entry into WBB: Unknown
Notes: Many horns from antiquity have been called a *lituus*, but this version is the earliest. It is shaped like a J and makes a piercing sound that is perfect for funeral processions, which is often what the instrument was used for by the ancient Romans. *How* anyone could march with a such a long horn in their mouth is a mystery none of the Curators have been able to solve. . . .

Name: The Singer Building
Entry into WBB: 1968
Notes: This forty-seven-story skyscraper was the tallest building in the world when it was built in 1908. It rose 612 feet over New York City and remained one of the skyline's most notable landmarks before it was demolished sixty years later.

CHAPTER FIFTEEN

Name: Okjökull glacier

Entry into WBB: Extended (1850–2014)

Notes: Iceland's Okjökull glacier has been melting since the mid-nineteenth century. When its ice stopped moving in 2014, it was declared dead by glaciologist Oddur Sigurðsson. A funeral was held in Okjökull's honor on August 18, 2019, and its site in the old world was marked by a commemorative plaque. Here in the World Between Blinks, the yetis have been using it as a staircase for the Floating Mountains.

CHAPTER SIXTEEN

Name: Black Cherry Vanilla Coke

Entry into WBB: 2007

Notes: This fizzy variation of the classic Coca-Cola drink was delicious, but it simply could not compete with the even *more* delicious Coca-Cola with Lime. After only one year on supermarket shelves, it was phased out of production and into the World Between Blinks.

Name: Reese's Bites

Entry into WBB: 2003

Notes: Everyone knows that the combination of chocolate and peanut butter is delicious. Even Jake Beruna said so during his very first encounter with the Administrator!

Reese's Bites are not exempt from this rule. They are delicious, but they are also dangerous: in 2003 the Hershey Foods Corporation decided that the candy posed a choking hazard and discontinued it.

ACKNOWLEDGMENTS

Writing stories set in the World Between Blinks has been a truly joyful experience. From the moment the first hints of this idea appeared—a lighthouse guarding a lost land, a pair of cousins, and a world where *all* lost things ended up—it's been an adventure we'll never forget.

This book was written during a worldwide pandemic, and escaping into the World was a blessing for both of us. A whole virtual team of cheerleaders and helpers saw us through the experience, and we'd like to thank them here.

Once again, we are indebted to Marcelo Contreras and Cara Strauss Contreras for helping us with the colloquialisms of Bolivian Spanish and giving us glimpses into what Marisol's and Victor's lives in La Paz might look like. To them, and to the others who helped us so generously with their experiences and expertise, many, many thanks.

A mighty thank you to Karen Chaplin, who was a very good sport about lending us her name and stepped up to champion this series as our editor with insightful guidance and great enthusiasm. Thank you as well to Celina Sun, who bravely jumped into the World Between Blinks with us! Quill Tree has been such a wonderful home for Jake and Marisol, and we're grateful to Rosemary Brosnan for steering this series where it needed to go; to Jill Amack and Jon Howard for their thoughtful copyedits; to Lauren Levite and the publicity team; to Robby Imfeld, Emily Mannon, and the marketing team; to Laura Mock and Erin Fitzsimmons in design; to Andrea Pappenheimer and the sales teams, and to our wonderful team in managing ed. Additional thanks to Andrew Eliopulos and Bria Ragin, who were with us on book one. We're so grateful for everything the whole Harper US does to get books into readers' hands!

We love our team at Harper Oz just as much—to Chren Byng, Rachel Cramp, Yvonne Sewankambo, Michelle Weiss, Jemma Myors, and the whole crew in sales, marketing, and production, a thousand thank-yous. You're amazing.

To Julia Murray, for her absolutely ingenious cover illustrations—you brought this series perfectly to life. Thank you.

To Tracey and Josh Adams, Anna Munger and Stephen Moore, you're the best team we could ever ask for. We're grateful to be on this road with you.

From Ryan: a special shoutout to Samwise, my sourdough starter that got me through some very long lockdown days. An even bigger shoutout to David—this book literally would not exist without the time you spent with Sabriel. I love you both to the moon and back! Thanks to Corrie Wang, for long walks, to Roshani Chokshi, for phone calls and Zoom events, to Shannon Messenger, for your oodles of advice and support, to Laini Taylor and Clementine, for sharing your love of this series. And of course—to Amie. Penning these books with you was so fun, and so rewarding, and made me fall in love with writing all over again. Thanks to the Graudin family. Thanks to the Strauss family. Raiden, thank you for all the years you stood by my side. Run free with those yetis. *Soli Deo Gloria*.

From Amie: Brendan, you're my lighthouse when I sail off into fictional worlds—you show me the way home, because you are my home. Pip, there's no greater joy in life than the time we spend with you. I hope you grow up to love this fictional world Ryan and I built for you and Sabriel. And Jack—for the company and yet another cameo, thank you,

To the friends who have kept me afloat through the writing of this book, all my love: Meg, Marie, Leigh, Kiersten, Alex, Sooz, Shannon, Michelle, Kacey, Nic, Soraya, Kate, Cat, Jay, Sarah, the Council, my parents-group buddies, and the Roti Boti gang. All my love to the Kaufman and Cousins families, who are endlessly supportive. And Ryan—what an absolute joy this has been from start to finish. Thank you for saying yes, my friend.

To the booksellers, librarians, reviewers, teachers, and book nerds who helped readers find this series— we're grateful for your support every day, and we've never needed it more than the last couple of years. We see all that you do, and we thank you.

And finally, to all the readers who have picked up a copy of these books, and those who shared their love for Jake and Marisol and Oz with us—your letters and fan art mean the worlds to us! Thank you for joining us on such a special journey.